Here is the first appearance in America of Kenneth Giles and of his Inspector Harry James: young, imaginative, likable, juggling a dozen intricate cases—from shop-lifting to murder—with shrewd-ness, insight, humor and melan-choly; spending his few precious off-hours with mustard footbaths and Elizabeth, his down-to-earth Mod girl. He is the epitome of the New Look at Scotland Yard.

The pivotal puzzle here for James is the curious disappear-ances, first in one part of London, then in another, of a number of pavement artists—those down-at-the-heel purveyors of curbstone culture. His "inquiries" lead him to a covey of Flemish and Venetian paintings, stolen from Russia, to a

disconcerting number of murders and then, ever deeper, behind the Iron Curtain itself.

Mr. Giles's policemen—Inspector James, along with his superintendent, Hawker, and his sergeant, Honeybody—are believable, complex men; the crooks they pursue are splendidly larger than life, and so is their conspiracy.

A *Provenance of Death* is more than a story of police procedure. It is an urbane, witty novel, filled with the sounds and colors of London and its human oddities. Mr. Giles writes with enormous relish for baroque extravagances of plot and prose; and, above all, he is a storyteller.

By the same author

SOME BEATS NO MORE

THE BIG GREED

A Provenance of Death

AN INNER SANCTUM

MYSTERY

by Kenneth Giles

SIMON AND SCHUSTER · New York

First printing

Library of Congress Catalog Card Number: 67-22936
Manufactured in the United States of America
By Vail-Ballou Press, Inc., Binghamton, N.Y.

A Provenance of Death

Chapter 1

The Inspector finished his fried egg and trimmings with a certain trepidation.

Since Hildegard had been thought old enough, a matter of two summers, to journey abroad as the rear half of a scootered pair, her eggs had forsaken bacon for tomatoes, peppers and bits of pungent sausage.

Hildegard was now nineteen and intended to become a cookery writer. The main trouble was, thought Inspector James, that her budget limited her Continental experience to the more dubious places in southern Spain and Portugal. Not that he personally disliked garlic—Lord, he wasn't that square—but certain of his superiors did. Thank God for good old English marmalade! The Inspector spread it thickly and brought his attention back to his landlord.

"I miss him," said Hubert Stanisgate. The Inspector noted uneasily that he had avoided the marmalade and was smearing his toast with Hildegard's anchovy paste, domestically known as "Serpent's Tooth."

"I used to watch for him each morning. It set me up to face the Bleeders. He had a big thing done with household paint which I thought was a cow having a calf—never liked to ask."

"I should have thought, Hubert, that you could be certain if it were a cow or not," said the Inspector.

Stanisgate was an art director, he always stressed the *an*, with Blood, Cupping and Fulsome.

"All photography these days," he said. "Wouldn't recognize a bit of artwork if it got on my desk."

"Don't they have to be registered or something?" asked Dora.

Harry James was familiar with Mrs. Stanisgate's speech patterns and intervened,

"Not if you're a pavement artist and don't solicit alms or cause obstruction, which means that you keep sweet with the local constables. You're a self-employed person and outside the W.S."

"I should have thought they would be registered." The Inspector's landlady's long and normally rather charming face was at its stubborn setting.

Lor', thought James, I may have set her off! Dora had quite recently "gone into" politics and was a possible lady councilor.

"Nevertheless, I wish the fellow would come back," said Hubert.

Harry James became conscious that the whole Stanisgate family were looking at him.

"Dislike of change is a sign of incipient old age, discouraged at the Bleeders," said Hubert, starting to fold his serviette—"napkin" was a fighting word at the Stanisgates'. "However, I took some shots of him in September which turned out first class."

"Did he know you were taking them?"

"Lord, no, Harry! You know my cunning box of tricks. Anyway, I got a couple blown up. I was lookin' at 'em when the little Bleeder spotted 'em. Stared for seven minutes with his purple pointed tongue pokin' out. He then made the Napoleonic decision that he must have 'em for his cut-price paint gambit."

The sloe eyes, too prominent and wide-spaced, swiveled round at his wife. "It's rock salmon an' stout for the Margit holiday, old girl— But . . . I'll have to find the old gent, press a model's fee into his gnarled hands and get a model's release."

"You *have* got a release?" Harry James could scarcely resist a trifle of knowledge; further it slightly postponed what he uneasily recognized as an imminent Stanisgate request, which was as thorough in the long run as God's mills although a good sight more reasonable at first approach.

"At worst," said Stanisgate, "publishing your photo in

an ad without a release could be libel. In any case, you don't *get* 'em published unless the release part is taken care of."

"The old peon wouldn't see it. I'd take the chance. Ten thousand to one."

The voice was clipped and sounded nervous. Leicestershire Stanisgate—foreshortening was prohibited—was twenty but seemingly bogged down in the acne zone.

His father looked at him. "I've talked to you before on similar subjects, my boy." Hubert's voice never lost its baritone affability. A tough, though, thought the Inspector: close-clipped blond hair around a large oval skull, unlined white skin and full, mobile mouth.

Hubert stared at his son impassively. "Without success, apparently!" He turned to the Inspector. "If it's no bind, Harry, I'd appreciate it if the majesty of the law could get a rumble to the old chap that there's five nicker and an advertising man's blessing awaiting."

James felt relief. Mrs. Stanisgate's not infrequent requests were statistical and surprisingly trappy when you pursued them. This was simple—a word to Honeybody, the senior sergeant in the division where he was relieving, and being by lucky chance the district where he lived.

He considered the morning's work, while the others left table. At the Stanisgates' one was mercifully free of "excuse me's." He'd forgotten his toast again: one of the hazards of a Stanisgate meal was arriving at the end with some major portion forgotten and untouched. He bit into the cold toast and chewed automatically. He was conscious of Hildegard bending forward to peer at him and put the serviette down, managing to swallow.

"My God," he could not help saying.

"It's mermelada," said Hildegard, in her flat voice. "Spanish mermelada de los angeles. I made it in September when you were on hols."

This must be the first time they put it on, deduced the Inspector, pouring himself out the remainder of the coffeepot.

"I couldn't really get the stuff right," said Hildegard. She was still in the fat stage, thought Harry, and her eyes

9

were a kind of dull port wine color as she continued to peer at him. "It's a kind of melon that grows down walls, but I had to use marrow."

"It tastes kind of rancid," said Harry.

"Father says it tastes of goat manure."

"Your father has a curiously exact flair for words."

They shouldn't let her muck around in the kitchen without supervision, he thought bitterly.

"He wasn't there much, you know."

Harry swung round from the door.

"Who wasn't?"

The Inspector thought she regarded him with faint malevolence.

"The pavement artist. Mostly he wasn't there."

He spent a few minutes needlessly in his room. His way and Hubert's coincided and it was the thought of keeping up with Hubert's powerful lope which impelled James, who considered himself essentially an ambling type, generally to avoid these early morning encounters.

The Inspector peered out on to the street-lighting made ugly by wishy-washy dawn and blessed the fact that central heating was among the several conveniences of the Stanisgate home. He saw Hubert's plus six feet lope into the street, and put on his own overcoat. He checked his watch. Ten past eight, as always. Dora Stanisgate ran her home efficiently, but to a rigid timetable. Not that she lost her temper, but if you weren't there at the appointed time, you didn't get it. He supposed, when you thought of it, that Hildegard and Leicestershire were a good pair of kids to show at least no outward rebellion against the family schedules.

He walked along the street, which sprang to life as he went, other doors opening, ring of hurried feet converging from the side streets.

He had better keep a lookout for the pavement artist. It was quite probable that Hubert had been looking in the wrong place, a good proportion of the lost-or-stolen complaints proved to be cases of people looking in the wrong place. When had he last seen the pavement artist? He had an idea it had been late summer, somewhere in September.

It was round this corner, thought Harry, making the

10

turn. Three streets met, two of them directly intersecting. There was a small concrete island dominated by a green-painted metal urinal. The Inspector looked around. Until this relief job for six weeks had come up, the district had mainly been a handy place where he slept. The tube entrance was a hundred yards to his right, and marked the demarcation of predominantly residential and business property. He flattened himself against the wall. The stream of people grew broader as the seconds passed. As a whole the district was a dreary piece of late Victoriana, one of the last tidemarks of jerry-building before the impetus turned and devoured the outer suburbs and roared on in the twenties down the so-called arterial roads. Now people like Stanisgate had discovered that it meant thirty minutes from front door to desk, so its character had commenced another rapid change, the knobbly Victorian boots transmogrified into the gay central-heated slippers of Mrs. 1970. Except that a lot of it was incapable of easy renovation and stood with its "Diary of a Nobody" patina not yet wiped away or covered by bright paint.

A couple of tobacco shops, a branch jewelers, and an office-supply showroom heralded the beginning of the retail area.

Inspector James squinted between moving heads. The man's pitch had been almost dead opposite. He stared with surprise, his eyes fixed upon the florid Italianate architecture, three floors of it, with the oval windows heavily encrusted with dirt over what would be filagree underneath. You scurried off each morning to your work, he thought, and so you missed it. Then, again, did it matter? He thought it was pleasant to think of somebody ninety years ago managing to slap something up like that. Maybe some young architect, drunk with sunshine and the grand tour, had somehow slipped it past bearded directors. He chuckled and moved a little from the wall.

An elbow slapped him hard below the breastbone and he had a glimpse of a face momentarily furious as it went by in the crowd. Harry eased professionally into the flow, edging toward the curb, but it took him more than two minutes to gain the island and the other side of the intersection.

11

Here pedestrian traffic was much less; sheeplike, the flow took the slightly shorter sides of the quadrilateral.

He saw now that the side of the building he had looked at was inset eight feet from the flow of the pavement, flanked by the grimy bricks of its neighbors jutting out to the furthermost line of building. It was, he realized, the last building before the intersection on this side of, he hesitated, Turnam Street.

Although the flow of people was less, the pitch had been chosen shrewdly. The niche was protected against wind and he noticed that the plain concrete underfoot was free from the covering of grime which the backlash of the breeze festooned over the pavement. Harry looked carefully around. There was no sign that the street artist had ever been there. The ground-floor windowsill was about eight feet above the pavement, probably as the result of some sub-basement contrivance so esteemed during the days of its building.

Where the devil was the entrance? On the right was a taller, squat building which seemed to frown sideways at its neighbor. He walked left and turned right into the intersecting street, TURNAM STREET said the plaque opposite. There it was, an elegant portal up four steps, no longer whitened, and a double column of brass plates. The door, polished oak, was already set back, giving a view of the usual gloomy entrance.

He flicked his eyes over the plates. The most tarnished and largest read LOVERS AND SONS, TRANSPORT.

He goggled momentarily.

"Morning, sir."

"Didn't know you lived this end of the manor."

Sergeant Honeybody was short for a policeman of his generation, a bare five feet eight, but immensely broad of shoulder. His eyes, close set in a flattened face, had the calculated guilelessness of an old sweat. He had, Harry knew, been a little unlucky not to get a middleweight ticket to the Berlin Olympics.

"Oh, I don't, Mr. James, but I vary me walk through when there's time. Besides . . ." The pale blue eyes under the faintly scarred ginger eyebrows looked at the name plates. "I sometimes drop in to see Mr. Samuel

Lovers. I suppose you laughed at the name plate? Good advertising, he says."

Good man, Sergeant Honeybody! You found them all the way through, promoted until they did not want further steps. It was natural that Honeybody looked at him as if he was an upstart. The man he was subbing for was ten years older, wise in his ways and known to be.

Mr. Samuel Lovers, of course, would be a contact, one of the sergeant's own. In a way it was a tribute to the fact that his presence was temporary that it was mentioned at all. A contact was a contact, whether you were selling armchairs or police work, and you kept them to yourself.

"Perhaps you'd care to spare a minute to meet him? They've got a small warehouse in East Lane."

The double doors of Lovers were folded back, displaying a mahogany inquiry counter topped with telephone books. The sergeant walked past with his pigeon-toed tread and tapped at a plain door farther along the hall.

Mr. Lovers opened the door. The Inspector glimpsed a very tall pear-shaped figure topped by a massive head which although unbearded managed to convey the impression of genial shagginess.

He seemed glad to see them.

"The sergeant drops in for a chat occasionally, Inspector, and I regale him with any of the suspicions I may have gathered during my trudgings around the bailiwick."

Fruity voice, well-developed persona. Shrewd dark eyes inside the smile and side whiskers.

The sergeant started talking confidentially about something to do with trucks and backloading and Harry relaxed in the roomy Windsor chair. It was a comfortable office, with a touch of old-fashioned elegance. One felt one should look through the small windows at a courtyard instead of a neon sign.

"I was admiring this building, sir," he said when the sergeant and Lovers had finished their discussion, the former apparently pleased with what had been forthcoming.

"You noticed it, most people don't."

"It puzzled me."

"Ah, yes," said Mr. Lovers. "It was built by Jeremy, he

13

was the third son of the second Samuel Lovers. The Benjamin of the family in 1870, studied architecture under one of the Italian Renaissance fiends. The contemporary Samuel gave him his head, resulting in what must have been a minor scandal at the time. Of course, the family owned the entire district, more or less, so any complaints were doubtless surreptitious. Well, the young man died—lungs, as usual. The brothers erased the evidence as much as they could—rebuilt walls, remodeled windows, etcetera. That bit you refer to was not touched for some structural reason. I suppose you noted it goes eight feet in?"

Harry nodded.

"That was how the whole thing was originally built. Young Jeremy envisaged tubs of climbing geraniums."

Lovers snorted. "I sometimes wonder if the movement had spread what this district would have looked like—and the people—mandolins and love songs, eh?"

"Fascinating," said Harry, "these old family chronicles."

"Oh, that's all that is left, apart from this business. I'm a tenant, not the owner, y' know. But there's romance, like there is in every street of this dirty old town. The original Lovers dealt in pure."

"Pure?"

"Dog droppings. He paid ten pence a big pail and sold them for two shillings to the tanners. He rubbed it into the skins."

Harry saw the sergeant's slight consternation as he lifted his sturdy black leather gloves to his nose.

Lovers saw it, too, and laughed. "Fear not, Sarge, nowadays it's fixed by lab workers in white jackets. They probably use mustard gas and cyanide. Sweeter than the vi'lets. Anyway, that founded the Lovers' fortunes. Next thing, old Sam started processing himself, making the first genuine Russian leather in England."

The hirsute man rolled in his chair. "You've got to hand it to these Georgians, the guys who did Bonaparte over. Sam found out that it was an infusion of the bark of little birch trees that gave Russian leather the smell that people went for so he got the ingredients and started up.

14

At one time the Lovers exported more Russian leather than ever came out of Czardom."

"By the way," said Harry, "forgive the silly question, but what happened to the pavement artist who used to sit where the old building recesses?"

Lovers looked blank. "You've stumped me," he said.

"He was there last summer."

"Can't help," said Lovers. "Since I was a kid, there's been a succession of itinerants there—protected from the weather, I guess. Hot chestnuts, ice cream, I remember a Punch and Judy and, yes, I'm sure we've had pavement artists. I don't make the left turn outside the building, though. Car's parked further along this street and if I get a bus, it's directly outside."

"Not important," said Harry. "We run a kind of bank for idle inquiries."

He liked Lovers, he thought as he followed the sergeant outside. "I take the short cuts, Mr. James," said the sergeant, and proceeded to in a bewildering fashion, interspersed with a running commentary of sins historic, current and putative.

"Scobies." He jerked his thumb toward a neat two-storied house with net curtains at street level.

"*The* Scobies."

"Yeah," said the sergeant, "a nest of them, always more coming along onto the charge sheet. The grandmother lives there, not that she pays rent, so I hear."

Harry James recognized a church on the skyline. "Dubbers' Passage," said the sergeant. "All kinds of fakery. Anything you wanted, you could get around here, including half-crowns. That's all gone."

It was just after nine when Harry entered the antiseptic-smelling station.

"Like me to inquire about that street artist, Mr. James?"

The Inspector's sensitivity about his lack of regional experience struggled with his desire to put Dora's chore into Honeybody's capable hands. He most certainly didn't want the deadly little tag of being a man obsessed with street artists.

"It was just one of these little inquiries, sergeant. Noth-

ing to get on a time sheet. If you'd care to ask around, I'd
be glad, that's all."

He plunged into the work of the day and at eleven was
thankful to take a taxi to inspect bank premises.

Back at twelve-fifteen, he leafed through the previously
emptied in-basket, which had mysteriously filled.

"Mr. James."

Harry looked up.

"A young woman left these," said the sergeant. "A Miss
Stanisgate." "These" were a square envelope. Inside were
two photographs.

The flimsy, torn paper had, in thick greasy penciled
characters, "Two of the clearest of the missing pavart, per
Hildegard. Hubert."

Once upon a time, thought the Inspector, a good photo
was bang on, sharp so you could see the pores. Hubert had
captured the laciness of the building—better than it
actually looked, with somehow the essential London griminess well and truly nailed down by two uncompromising
plastic dustbins. The background, consisting of ten
painted, unframed canvases, was vague and the figure in
the foreground more so, the essence of artist you might
say, taken when the nip was in the air, duffle coat drawn
in at the neck and slouch hat pulled low, impression of a
large, bulbously inclined nose and shaggy eyebrows. What
looked like an outsize cigar box for the receipt of dona-
tions was crazily out of perspective.

To hell with the Stanisgates! Harry shuddered to think
what went on at the place where Hubert worked. Even
the note with artsy-craftsy scrawl, when he knew that
Hubert was surrounded by natty little portable type-
writers, and as for letterheads, Dora habitually wrote her
shopping lists on Blood, Cupping and Fulsome notepaper!

"Is that the pavement artist, sir?"

"Ah, yes." Harry tried to keep the annoyance from his
voice.

"None of the lads know much, sir." Sergeant Honeybody's voice was bland. "There was one there, that's all. I
phoned up the pubs. You get a fellow in like that, you'll
find they know him in the public. Has a drink and
changes the small coins there. It's a funny thing, the

16

nearest pub is a quarter of a mile. Three licenses deceased over fifteen years, the teevee and all that. I phoned the six nearest, no good. Mind you, if he had to go a quarter of a mile, he might as well go five miles. Young Spence was up that way, so I had him give a quick look into the nearest shops, six of 'em. Blank."

The Inspector grunted, pushed the half-plates to the vicinity of his filing basket and showed such a disposition to discuss more urgent and arduous business that the sergeant soon mentioned his impending lunch hour. During the afternoon Harry went his rounds.

Sergeant Honeybody had a husky baritone capable of a surprising range of intonation that sometimes worried Harry. On his return he followed Harry into his room and assumed a tone which the Inspector vaguely associated with butlers in the films.

"The Yard came through about that other matter, sir —the pavement artist. I told them you were working on it and that we had two photos. The chap who rang sounded ready to fall off his chair. They sent a car round immediately for them. You're to ring extension seventeen."

Harry decided that the voice and the half-hooded eyes betokened respect. Reputation depended largely on flukes.

He dialed the number on his direct line.

"Just a minute." He didn't recognize the voice, but immediately there came through the raspings of Superintendent Hawker, his own taskmaster.

"Where did you get that second sight?" The Superintendent was as affable as usual, which meant that he sounded as though he had discovered a very sick kitten in his bowler hat.

"Coincidence, sir. My landlord, who's advertising, had taken the shots and wanted to find the man to get a publishing release."

"I suppose your overwork is gross as usual," Hawker said in querulous disbelief. "Shove all the strayed doggies and stuff on to the office boy and come over. I'll be in my own room."

Harry thought rapidly. Nothing that couldn't wait. He gave some instructions to the sergeant.

17

In a way, he thought, as he inhaled the smell of floor wax outside Hawker's door, it was good to crawl back into the comfortable womb. The Superintendent was annoying in speech and uncertain in disposition, but Harry supposed he was a father figure.

"What the hell are you grinning for?"

"I'm sorry, sir, I was just thinking you were a father figure."

"A good father chastiseth." Hawker showed yellowing teeth. "Listen to me. A fortnight ago I got a call from the Sûreté, a fellow named Wolfe speaking. He just said that there was a French citizen named Albert Brun, born in Casablanca, 1920, alias Bergin, Brune and Botin. No fingerprints, no photo, sallow-faced, black hair, five feet eleven. No record of scars. Believed to be a street artist in Finsbury Park area. General 'manner of life and associates' report wanted.

"A queerish one. However, we give Paris queerish ones at times. First thing I checked aliens—no record. Further check with Minny Labor—nowt. Can you imagine someone asking the Minny if they could come here and draw pictures on pavements!

"Over to the divisions. Now, we had a bit of luck. Guy Fawkes night with the cold in the air, a man had keeled over outside a pie stall. Got tomato sauce down his clothes. He got up before anybody telephoned for an ambulance and said he was all right and that his knee went.

"The pie clerk is a fellow named Jody Dorking. There are two of 'em on—the place has a reputation. He says that the man was white and panting and bent like a bow.

"One of the people—you can eat them there or take 'em away—had just swallowed a king-sized steak-and-mushroom and he says his car's over the road. He's named Carr, a young fellow who works in a betting office nearby. He takes the fellow home, a three-minute drive. He lives in one of these studio flats. A room, a cupboard with a sink and two gas burners, and a bit of something you stick over the single bed during the day if you're fussy.

"It's let 'with service,' except there ain't no service, really. It's just to make it easy to get people out.

"Carr says that the man had straightened up and went up the flight of stairs okay. So that's that.

"The rent book says 'payment weekly on Sundays.' In fact every fortnight a stooge of the owners sets up a card table in the hall at five P.M. on Fridays and waits there until midnight. Takes seven quid and scrawls in your book.

"X. collapsed on a Wednesday and it wasn't rent day until Friday week. He was posted as a defaulter, first time in twelve months. Next day the owner and his minder let himself into the room with the passkey at seven A.M. That's a good time to collect your money—the flesh is very weak.

"In this case it was cold. Coroner's work!

"For all the marks he'd left on life he might have been a fly on a plastic tile. Rent book with the name of Mr. Brown and a P.O. savings book with seventy quid in it and the signature Frank Brown. The handwriting people say that he started to write the specimen signature as 'Franc,' but fudged it over."

"Income tax?"

Hawker glowered and tortured his voice into a falsetto. It was apparently his belief that anyone who ever thwarted him was a eunuch. " 'Aow deer no. Ai'm sure we carnt surply information to the perleece abawt returns. Aow dear no.' It took the boss four hours of going round to permanent undersecretaries to get the word there was no return of a Frank Brown, pavement artist, of that or any other address.

"Well, I rang Paris. I described the corpse. There was a longish silence, and then the fellow said that it hadn't been anything important but thank you."

"Might be a political affair," suggested Harry, "one of those French cases where all the documents disappear. L'affaire Brun!"

"I thought it was cleared up," said Hawker, who disliked other people's humor. "Surgeon's report indicated some damage to the heart, general debility, malnutrition,

19

a damaged liver and chronic bronchitis. Cause of death, general debility and cardiac failure, confirmed by the Coroner. But then the other reports came piddling in. I'd sent a non-urgent request to supply names of all pavement artists to all the likely divisions immediately I got the call.

"Listen!" Spatulate finger, jutting from the old man's mottled hand, pierced the air. "Five screevers, that's the old name, had disappeared from their pitches and another had got himself killed. Two in North London, one in the East End, and two around the city. The man who died was working a South Ken pitch.

"The men were simply non est. They were there, they displayed their wares, and now they are not. Nobody knows their names except that one might, might, be called Fred. The fellow that died was one Alfred Castelano, and we know that because he had a P.O. savings book with forty odd quid in it. The address was a common lodging-house where they had no record. Found in a road in Hammersmith, head smashed in, traces of duco. Hit and run. Here's the photo."

There had been a lot of work on the head, Harry realized, and the face looked as unreal as a sixteenth-century portrait, arched eyebrows, heavy eyes.

"Same as the other?"

"Oh, yes, nothing, no income tax, no nothing, no friends, no h.p."

Harry knew that Hawker was reputed to be able to sing obscene songs like a citizen of Dijon. You didn't become a Superintendent without language qualification. He said, "Castelano, one of the Spanish variants for brown-haired."

"I suppose you've been taking these tapes that teach you while you sleep."

Nevertheless for some reason Hawker was pleased.

"I don't suppose," the old man said, "that two people named Brown are a coincidence even if one spells his name in Etruscan?"

Harry had long since discovered the value of silence in dealing with Hawker. He kept mute.

"Har," said the Superintendent, "once upon a time, I

20

used to say my methods were irrefragable—in fact I invented the ruddy word—but now the machines are taking over, you get a new logic."

Harry saw that the old man was brooding. There had been a time recently when the speed of return transportation by jet from Australia had confounded an ingenious Hawker theory.

"Consensus of opinion"—Hawker jerked his thumb at an invisible committee—"is that it's coincidence—a drifting trade. We have got this Hammersmith boy on the blotter, and that's a case. I'll give you some help over at the division. . . . There's a fellow come back after sick leave, young Barker, as gormless as you. But he's weak through his pile operation, or whatever he had, so you'll have to put in some time there. You've got a good solid admin sergeant."

"I thought Barker fractured both legs when the car turned over, sir." Harry knew his deadpan annoyed Hawker.

"I apologize to you both," said Hawker. He smirked, "I'm sure you'll give him the utmost consideration.

"Your brief is to look into, one: the apparent disappearance in your division of a pavement artist, from which may follow, a: that there is some kind of seasonal coming and going, like swallows, or, b: they have been frightened off. Two: Is there any connection between the deaths of Brown and Castelano."

In the big property room Harry got out the two boxes marked Brun and Castelano. The report, between cellophane covers, was on the outside. The clothing could have come from anywhere, none of it new, none of it old or foul, moderately laundered, probably at a launderette service. Quantity basic, two trousers, one coat, one overcoat, four shirts, two sets of underwear, three pairs of socks, six handkerchiefs, one tie, one pair of shoes, one suitcase.

"*Tch.*" Harry pursed his lips. Hawker had spotted it of course, for the inventories were exactly the same. He compared the clothes, different materials, different sizes.

Plastic bags contained personal possessions, coins, notes,

comb, shaving gear, a packet of corn plasters. The post office savings books would be with the public trustee but, yes, here were relevant photostats.

Brown, John. Ingoings, he jotted it into his notebook. Thirty pounds, forty pounds, seventy pounds, thirty pounds, seventy pounds, forty pounds, seventy pounds, thirty pounds, seventy pounds. Total four hundred and ninety pounds over seven months, with outgoings of four hundred and twenty pounds.

Castelano. Eight months, totaling five hundred and seventy pounds, with outgoings of five hundred and thirty pounds. There was a neat little note in Hawker's writing, "All inpayments cash."

He looked at his watch, four-twenty, and returned the boxes to the civilian clerk.

Everything to be learned if you knew where, thought Harry, consulting information and getting an elderly voice called Mr. Potter.

"Just a minute." Potter sounded dubious. "There's an entry under boat race favors, kewpie dolls, plastic novelties and fancy goods. It doesn't specify pavement artists, but it's as near as I've got—I see it's got fancy chalks and painting books. Thomas Handy and Son, Fourteen Sheepwalk, N. one."

There had been no four-legged sheep in Sheepwalk for many years and the black buildings looked as though they might have preceded the invention of cloth, thought Harry, as he found Thos. Handy on a board between an exporter of toe wax, a metallurgical consultant and the reticulation officers' union. It was a large basement with rows of racks, a boy at a counter counting plastic combs, and a large man whom the boy addressed as Perc.

"Mr. 'Andy, the boss, 'as 'is office there," said Perc, jerking his thumb.

Mr. Handy was small and dark and wore large glasses. He sat in a glass-partitioned office, half concealed behind box files. Harry raised his voice and tiptoed so that his eyes looked over the front glass wall. "I wonder if I could ask you some questions?"

The bland face tilted and a pair of hands wrenched and

tugged at a sliding glass panel. Eventually it slid back a few inches and a refined voice emerged and told Harry to enter.

"Rilly," said Mr. Handy. "Pavement artists! Thet's the sort of fringe, you know." He twinkled at Harry through his glasses. "We're more in the entertainment business now, quite diversified in interests, rilly. My great-grand-papa started the business. He used to export used clothes to the Irish market, very large it was, I believe, and then he went into warehousing for the eyetinerant salesmen."

Through the window the Inspector saw the warehouse-man lumping a huge cardboard carton on his shoulder. Keeping it in place with the fingers of one hand, he rapped on the glass with the other.

Mr. Handy wrenched the slide back a fraction.

"These come in from Smith. I'm putting 'em up in grosses." Mr. Handy nodded rapidly.

"My word," said Harry, "that must be awfully heavy." He might be able to wangle a quiet drink with Perc.

"Light us a fevver." Perc threw the carton an inch or two off his supporting hand.

"What, uh?"

"Jye bells," said Mr. Handy.

"I see," said Harry at a loss.

"Joy balls," said Perc. "You know as a kid . . ." His free hand made a flapping motion.

" 'Ere." Perc jammed the carton against the partition and unslipped the folded cover. " 'Ere." His thick fore-finger, callused from snapping twine, twirled a garish paper and tinsel ball dangling on a piece of elastic.

A memory of an hour's bliss and beauty stirred some-where in Harry's mind.

"Still sell," said Perc, "kids'll still cry for 'em. Trouble is that there're fewer places where they're sold."

"I was asking Mr. Handy," said Harry, "if you did any business with pavement artists."

"The ole screevers, not so many these days! No, we don't do nothin' with em. They're a special class. They don't mix with the street sellers, kind of what you might call maladjusted to society, like you see on teevee. Keep

23

themselves to themselves." Perc managed the feat of roll-
ing each eye a different way to indicate the degree of
maladjustment.

Wishing goodbye to Mr. Handy, Harry sauntered
through the warehouse. He winked at Perc, licked his lips
and raised his arm in the beer drinker's salute. Perc's busy
hands were packing the joy balls and he barely glanced up
as he said, "Public of the Cross Keys at six oh five."

Harry filled in the twenty-five minutes and managed to
arrive at the Cross Keys a minute behind Perc.

"This is on me," he said, putting a note on the
counter.

"On the Guv'ment?"

"On your bloody tax!"

"Now you're talking sense. 'Ere's a friend of mine, sir,
Mr. Sugar, that might join us."

Mr. Sugar looked very ancient and Harry wondered how
anybody in the Welfare State managed to have no teeth.
The old gentleman seemed to have cotton waste in his
mouth, which blurred his talk and impelled small spitting
motions of his lips.

When they cradled their half-pints, Perc said, "I beckoned Mr. Sugar over because he knows the street people,
right back to the cat's meat and muffin men."

Perc listened and translated. " 'E says his granddad was
one of the old tossing piemen. Eighty-two Mr. Sugar is,
and his son looks after an office not far away. Now, old
dad, the gent wants to know about the screevers!"

Through a pint and a half of mild-and-bitter and a bit
of rather good Welsh rabbit from a steam container behind the bar, Mr. Sugar gave his conclusions via Perc. No,
said Mr. Sugar, the screevers didn't dodge about. Lazy
like, they got a pitch and stayed there like pudden in an
empty stummick. They had usually come down in the
world, like a teacher who takes to the drink. Yes, he'd
known some good ones with the chalk. There was a fellow
once near Hammersmith Bridge who could draw a slice of
cod with parsley sauce so that dogs tried to lick it and he
had to cover it with a bit of chicken wire. He died when
he slipped under the old tram after some toff gave him a

nicker and he got pissed. But they started to draw on bits of board or paint on canvas.

Perc chuckled. "What'll they think of next! Old dad says the minders worked out a way to collect from the screevers. They'd drop some oil on the paving stones unless they got paid their dropsy. That way the poor buggers couldn't use the chalk for a year or more on that particular pitch. Couldn't stop it. No law agin a man droppin' a bit of oil and scuffin' it with his shoe. So they started to draw on board or paint on canvas.

"And the old dad says that there were men who started up letting out the gear at so much a day, so that every deadbeat got into it, and for a time the whole lay collapsed. Not many about now, at that."

Harry got back to the Yard at eight.

There was a slip in his in-basket to see Photography.

The darkroom chief pushed over an envelope. "Mr. Hawker's out, but he told me to give you a copy." Harry spilled the half-plates out.

"Gosh, you've done a job!"

"Oh, you put 'em right up and then reduce. Marvelous! However, the bloke's disguised, as you'll see. We think he's around five eleven and pretty thin."

Harry studied the print. The screever had a loose-fitting coat with shoulders that were probably padded. The high lapels were partly concealing the chin and the hat, a canvas fishing hat, pulled low over the forehead. Squinting, Harry thought the eyes were deep set. The mouth was a thin gash. Broad nose, but cotton wool or facial putty could produce that effect.

Interesting, thought Harry, though probably not as the public thought of it. You couldn't disguise yourself from somebody who really knew you, not even with a top plastic surgeon at your command. "Really, Harry, what have you been doing to your face?" was the inevitable end to that kind of thing. You could, however, prevent yourself being subsequently identified by people who did not know you, hence bandits with false noses, stockings over their heads.

"The paintings, now," said the photographer.

25

Harry flipped them. Just daubs, his mind still pondered the formless face.

"Look, Inspector." The technician's finger jabbed. "When I saw that, I spotted something out of place." Harry saw a woman in nineteenth-century clothing bending over a chest of drawers, her head exploding into flecks of light from an open window.

"The rest are bloody awful. Stuff an eight-year-old wouldn't draw. But this. Damn it, I'd say a copy of Matisse and not a lithograph either."

The technician shook his head. "I even got the boy to check the stolen paintings list from Interpol, nothing remotely like it, but it's funny."

Harry stowed the packet in his brief case and made his way to the tube.

His fiancée had found the Inspector his lodgings and altogether he was not dissatisfied. As his Elizabeth had pointed out, girls could, and did, share small flats, but men were not successful sharers, and men alone in flats got into mischief. Altogether the Stanisgates were admirable hosts, with their own preoccupations which allowed no real thought for or annoyance of a third party. And in spite of Hildegard, Dora Stanisgate, whose father had been some kind of official to do with slaughterhouses, both knew and could obtain wonderful meat. He paid for bed and, also, Hildegard's breakfasts, but Dora Stanisgate would provide emergency meals at what he, and more importantly Elizabeth, considered very reasonable rates. Harry thought it might be due to Mrs. Stanisgate's fascination with her infra-red grill, but however.

"Hubert phoned he'll be back in half an hour." Dora Stanisgate was reading *The Making of the President*. "Did you know that Kennedy lived on soup?"

"Doted on petite marmite," said Harry.

"It says tomato or clam chowder," said Dora, doubtfully. "Though I read somewhere he had a French cook. Béarnaise sauce. Hubert likes rocking the saucepan. It's tournedos. I don't know what we'll have with it, but there are frozen peas and Hubert said he'd get some old Cheshire."

"As admirable as ever, Dora," said Harry, unfurling his

26

paper. You must admit, he told himself, that it was comfortable at the Stanisgates'. He believed that Leicestershire Stanisgate mainly lived on spaghetti somewhere in Soho, while Hildegard, of an evening, either ate quite mouselike at the table or else, presumably, took a tray up to her room, where she played her tapes up until eleven o'clock curfew.

Dora had triumphed again as far as the tournedos were concerned, Harry thought benevolently as he helped himself to cheese. It struck him that it had been a very quiet meal, Dora no doubt composing once again telling points for her manifesto at next year's council election, but Hubert had been silent through his sauce-making and latterly had not let forth the usual grumbles of a day in retrospect.

"Oh, thanks for the photos, Hubert!"

"Ah," said Stanisgate, much too offhand, "it was just a reminder. Did you locate the old boy?"

"Is he that old?"

"No," said Stanisgate, "it's just that one thinks of these fellows as ancient. He didn't look young."

"He's vanished," said Harry. "Some evidence that he might be dead."

A curious series of emotions flickered over Stanisgate's ordinarily not very expressive face. Shock, mainly, thought Harry. It was rather odd. He supposed Hubert had been counting on some cash.

"I suppose that if he is dead, you can use your photos for advertising."

"What? Oh, yes, I suppose so."

Harry put through a check call to the station and decided to turn in.

He had just taken his shoes off and was wiggling his toes when the extension phone by his bed rang. The Stanisgates did not care for telephones, and Dora was frankly afraid of them, so they usually solved the problem by keeping the extension switched through to Harry's bedroom, where the bell could generally not be heard elsewhere. For Harry was the annoyance of coping with breathless inquiries from Stanisgate's office about missing blokes.

27

"A very funny thing's happened down Merge's Alley, sir, that I thought you'd want to see," said the night sergeant.

"Funny things down alleys fascinate me, Sergeant. All right, I'll be along."

"I've sent the car on its way, sir."

Harry was waiting at the gate as the blue Morris drew up.

He got in the back seat. "Fill me in," he asked the young driver, "the sergeant seemed overcome."

"It is rather funny, sir. A stolen car—at least it looks obvious—got jammed down Merge's Alley, between a dwelling and the opposite wall. It's a poor area, the houses on one side are condemned and unoccupied. I've sent out the usual requests concerning the car—a sixty-four Chrysler, big fishbowl—and got a truck there with lights. Here we are."

Harry clambered onto the roof of the pickup truck. By some optical illusion Merge's Alley seemed to broaden until it connected with the farther street. In fact this broadening occurred for the final fifth of the distance, distracting the eye from narrowing in the middle of its length.

Harry gazed over the heads of the crowd at the rear end of the Chrysler, firmly embedded between the two walls.

Harry checked his watch. Eleven-fifty. There were in the region of three hundred people, packed round the police cars, thronging Merge's Alley.

He went back and switched on the public address system.

"There isn't anything to see. Please move on and do not obstruct the police. There's nothing to see."

After ten minutes the crowd had dwindled to thirty morose people who carefully walked at a snail's pace up and down the alley.

Harry got down and walked toward the rear of the car. The driver said, "We were cruising back to the car pool at eleven-twenty, sir, when we came up behind this car, which was nearly stopping. We had the sign lit up, and the Chrysler took off. It must have been in perfect tuning, the way it went. The driver turned the wheel over and

28

somehow got it into the alley. We stopped and there you are."

Merge's Alley consisted on the left-hand side of a row of one-storied houses—two up and two down, plus kitchen, scullery and a lavatory tacked on the back as a monument to progress. On the right was a high wall. Behind were the backyards of a condemned row, evacuated of tenants, and awaiting the fruition of a development scheme.

Harry looked through the back window of the gray car. A large, fat face met his, uncoordinated in features and woebegone, with small dark eyes like a trapped rat. Next to him, kneeling on the front seat, was a girl, thin-faced, mousy hair worn long, sniveling.

An elderly constable jerked his thumb at them. "'Is name's Williamson, sir. Eighteen last birthday and 'angs around with one of the smart crowds." The constable's voice was fruity with contempt. "And now we'll see how he likes a detention center. 'Er, Etta Pilsworth, sixteen and a good 'ome with teevee and their own washing machine. But, no, she 'as to 'ang round the espresso bars! If I know it, Mrs. Pilsworth'll warm 'er arse for this little goings-on."

The maiden's face dissolved in a blur of tears and the boy's pudding face became tragic to the verge of imbecility.

The constable walked away a few paces and lowered his voice. "They're oright as they go sir. Joy-riding, two or three times round the block, that'd be it. 'E works in a garidge and wants to impress his bird. Must have left it unlocked with the keys in it."

The Inspector felt a faint sense of harassment at the pressure of human problems.

"I want to get out of me 'ouse," bawled a voice.

Harry looked up. A red face, suffused with ire, a great chest clad in a striped shirt and garlanded with braces, appeared out of a first-story window. Harry saw that the side of the car effectively covered the entrance.

"Can't you get out the back way?" he called.

"There's no back way in this bleedin' 'ovel what should 'ave been condemned years ago," said the stout man with relish. "I just want to get out of me own 'ouse."

"Why don't you go back to bed, sir. It'll be fixed by the morning."

Harry watched the thoughts chase through the red-faced man's mind, but aid reached him in the form of a high-pitched woman's voice.

"There y'are Merv. Why can't you do what the gentleman says and come to bed like a Christian."

The stout man turned as though stung and Harry saw his forehead hit the top of the window frame hard.

Back at the police cars the Inspector was told that there was still no report on the Chrysler. He swore to himself.

There was a carroty-haired man who ran the local towing service. He grinned with the amiability of one who had sighted an expensive job.

"We might work a cable right round her and try to inch her backwards. Depends on the force she was driven in. It's like a cork in a bottle."

"We'll have to get her out." Harry's mind was preoccupied with the appropriate regulations.

"Tell you what," said the man. "That wall on the right is pretty well rotten. It would come down easy, like peeling a banana. If we got it down for ten feet or so, we could move the crate over a few inches with jacks, and then she'd come out easy without injuring the house on the other side."

He saw Harry's uncertainty. "The council acquired all that right-hand side. It would only mean getting hold of somebody in the Surveyor's office."

"We'd better take a look."

The Inspector shinned onto the top of the Chrysler. Glancing up he met the red-faced man's simmering gaze. There was a quart bottle and a glass on the windowsill, but for the moment the volcano was recruiting its energies. He swung a leg over the seven-foot-high wall and looked down into what had been a series of concrete-covered, pocket-handkerchief-sized yards, now split as weeds improbably forced life up between cracked intersections. The garage man had been right; as he swung the other leg over, he could sense the frailty of the wall. He jumped to the ground. There was a smell of age and unwantedness and a faint undertone of old drains. He

30

looked at the wall. With care and working from the top it would not be a difficult matter to remove it a few bricks at a time. A sharp tap and the calcified mortar would crumble. An old piece of canvas sheeting lay against the wall, raised up a foot. Harry put his foot on it.

"Christ!"

He stepped back and raised the edge of the canvas.

As he straightened, he met the eye of the red-faced man, who was setting down his glass.

"Perhaps you can tell me, sir," the man said with elaborate sarcasm, "when I'm to be allowed out of me bleedin' 'ouse. And, if it ain't . . ." He met Harry's gaze squarely and stopped.

"Constable," Harry called.

"Sir."

"Listen carefully. Tell the plainclothesman to bring some tools here so that we can break through into the house. Then you call the Yard and notify a case of homicide, and then call the local surgeon."

The plainclothesman brought an assortment of levers. There had been some attempt to board up the back door and festoon it with barbed wire, but the years had baked and frozen it.

"Hardly need all these," grunted Harry, as he tore and ripped at rotten wood and metal. "Careful now."

Hinges awry, the old door wobbled drunkenly and fell outward. Harry's pencil torch flickered against a brown-stained sink. They passed through a kitchen, into a tiny vestibule from which stairs led up, and through an open door into the front room. His torch showed torn wallpaper, indicating the passage of time and the forays of taste, from the original faded reds and what seemed to be animals twined with garlands, a mauve floral pattern, and, finally, the last embellishment of puce and yellow vertical stripes with a high gloss finish.

"It's coming in again, the wallpaper I mean," said the young plainclothesman. Harry was amused to note that the man spoke in a whisper.

The front door offered tougher resistance. When the hinges broke, wire kept it from opening far.

"Have we cutters?"

31

The man produced them from his pocket.

"Fine," said the Inspector as he severed the wire. "Now, what's what is a corpse in that back yard. Strangled. Cyanosed skin, tongue poking out. I don't think he's been dead so very long. Now I'll leave you here until the Yard team arrives. Use your torch to look around, but don't touch anything."

The surgeon arrived in a few minutes, an elderly man whose garrulousness covered and smoothed a lifetime of looking at the seamy side.

"Look at that." The doctor nudged him.

Now Harry saw that at each side of the neck, resting against the shoulders, was a piece of wood, roughly an inch thick. To each of these handles was attached a piece of white cord.

"The old thuggee method," said the doctor. "I was reading about it the other day. This fellow probably read it up too, wonderful thing education. If you use too thin a string, so that it cuts, you've got a struggle on your hands. With a suitable thickness, your man's unconscious before he works out what's happening. You note that it's synthetic fiber? Progress, lad!"

"Thanks, Doctor," said Harry. "Time of death?"

"Well now." The old man prodded again and looked up over his half-lensed spectacles. "It would not be after eleven-thirty and not before eleven o'clock."

"That's narrow, Doc." Harry looked somewhat startled.

"No, no. These things are only hard when you've two unresolved times."

"You mean?"

"I saw Mr. Huntingtower, as he was named, walking along Bridge Street in a great hurry at ten forty-five. That's about ten minutes' walk from here. He was wearing a black hat, by the way, which he seems to have lost."

"You knew him?"

"A little, not professionally on my part. He ran the Huntingtower Gallery, paintings, in Goughland Street. In fact he lived there. Rather good gallery. I'd say he was forty-eight, homosexual, well nourished, good conversationalist in a high camp sort of way. I've been calling in

32

there for three or four years, since he opened, and a customer to a modest extent."

"Did you speak last night?"

"I was coming back from a woman who suffers from mysterious back pains which occur after ten o'clock almost any evening and I wanted my bed. We just passed each other, that's all. I'm certain it was he."

Goughland Street, the "good end" of the manor, with reconstructed houses, several skyscraping flats with uniformed porters, and smart boutiques.

"In a hurry, Doc?"

"While I'm here, at least the committee can't have me up for not attending ladies with back pains. Besides, I like a good murder, lad!"

"There'll be a team from the Yard inside twenty minutes. But I thought I'd nip round to Goughland Street if he lived there. Do you know if he's got a house-keeper or anything?"

The surgeon shrugged. "No, but his manageress is called Spotting, Miss Dolores Spotting, and she lives in one of those big blocks of flats along Goughland Street. Bed sit. Though now they call it a 'luxurious studio flatlet!' Hah!"

Harry walked back through the house and out the front door and through the rusting front gate. Opposite were the great impersonal blocks of municipally owned flats. Useless to expect anybody there to have noticed anything happening in the abandoned houses, snakeskins shucked off in the social progress.

He walked round to Merge's Alley, two minutes by his watch, going fast. The crowd was back. Useless to make any real effort to disperse them. He walked along looking for the police driver and found him with the constable. "Move along, sir, please! Don't create an obstruction, please. No, madam, we're only doing our duty!"

One thing, thought Harry with satisfaction, the Yard squad could deal with the wedged car. He noted that the red-faced man now had some competition for his strategic window. A small woman competed with one elbow and a skinny, elderly male neck bobbed back and forth over a beefy shoulder.

33

"I'm going to Goughland Street," he told the police driver. "I'll take the car."

Apart from the street-lighting there was nothing to illuminate the Huntingtower Gallery sign in neat, disinterested sans-serif lettering in silver paint over one small plate-glass window. It was on the corner and part of a seven-story block of flats, the ground level of which was dotted with shops.

He found a telephone box. Spotting, D. was listed in a block fifty numerals away. He dialed. Her voice was crisp and businesslike.

He told her that her employer had been involved in a serious accident and drove the police car to the street door of the apartment block.

At other times Miss Spotting would have been fiercely protective of someone, with her icy blue eyes and longish gray-blue hair. She was what the Inspector privately called one of the mauve ladies, competent to a potentially intimidating degree. Now she was shocked, not that that meant too much, the act of killing always, or nearly always, shocked, but mauve ladies rarely killed.

Miss Spotting had a deep, fluent voice and chose her words carefully. She had worked for Huntingtower for ten years, originally off Bond Street, where he had had a quarter share in a gallery. Since he moved to Goughland Street three years ago, she had done the work of manager. There was a junior assistant, a woman. When they had major exhibitions, they engaged temporary help. Huntingtower had not been in on that day, which was not unusual between exhibitions.

"Mr. Huntingtower lived above the shop, I understand. Was that his only residence?"

"Yes, in summer he rented a house in the country or by the sea and spent quite a deal of time away. He never went away during winter except on business."

"He owned the gallery?"

"Well"—she hesitated—"he had sleeping partners, so I believe. Capital employed varies a great deal, and Mr. Huntingtower had financial associates."

He parked the car outside the building. Miss Spotting

34

produced two keys from her purse and unlocked the two locks in the front door.

The cool grays and off-whites of the walls and movable partitions flickered as the starter of the strip-lighting was actuated. Seen under artificial light it was long, cool and well-bred, all things to all men.

"You put the pictures away at nights," said Harry eying empty walls.

"There is a basement vault," she said. "Everything is put in there. For any long-term storage we use one of the professional storage agents."

There was a basement which occupied half of the ground floor area and housed the vault plus toilets. The ground floor consisted of a small vestibule, the main salon, with adjustable display racks, and a considerably smaller minor salon at one end. There was a microscopic office which had in one corner a stairwell. Miss Spotting told him that on the floor above, likewise completely cut off from the rest of the building, was Huntingtower's private room, a bedroom, a large living room, domestic offices, and a large library.

Something had been worrying the Inspector and now his memory crystallized.

"Didn't you people make a complaint a week ago and then withdraw it?"

Miss Spotting looked somewhat embarrassed. "It was my assistant actually. The charwoman had told her that the bars over the window to one of the toilets had been tampered with and without checking she telephoned the police. A flappable type, I'm afraid. I was taking the morning off. Anyway, Mr. Huntingtower came down and found that it was some old damage that didn't matter at all. But by that time a policeman had actually arrived."

"Have you the key to the vault?"

"A duplicate."

"Very well. Could you make a complete inventory check. See that nothing's missing, however trivial. I'll go upstairs. Do I need a key?"

There was a door at the stairhead, but Miss Spotting thought it was never locked.

35

In this case she was wrong. It was, however, the usual cheap interior door. Harry hesitated and then got out his wallet. He winkled the sharp-edged celluloid under the tongue of the lock and with a quick jerk flattened it back.

Huntingtower's office was studied in its elegance and fine rosewood furniture. The Inspector noted a small wall safe. Only one painting, a canal scene. He peered closer and the image dissolved into tiny dots. Pointillism, wasn't it? Not framed, just on a stretcher propped against the top of the bookcase where it would be seen by anybody leaning back in the lavishly upholstered desk seat. The lounge was a little fussy, Harry thought, in spite of the ascetic lines of its Scandinavian furniture. No pictures at all. The bedroom was similar, except there were ten photographs, all of men. The big wardrobes and drawers were immaculately kept. The bed was made. Opposite was the library with tiers of filled shelves. The bathroom and the kitchen had both been cleaned.

He looked at his watch, a little before two.

He sank thankfully into Huntingtower's desk chair. The four drawers were locked. Prudent gentleman Huntingtower, thought Harry as he fiddled with a small steel pick out of his wallet. Nothing to safeguard at that. Files of correspondence, all strictly haggling business and accountancy, exercise books containing names of people to be asked to viewings, bank statements, a wallet with a fiver in one compartment, and a file with a solicitor's name on it. Contracts covering ten years. Huntingtower's name had been MacGlaishen until he changed it. A copy of a terse will leaving everything to a brother, address in Scotland. Huntingtower used a scratchpad and was evidently a doodler. Harry looked at what seemed to be rough sketches for layouts in the salon downstairs and various squiggles. At the bottom of the page, so vigorously written that it had scratched through the flimsy paper was "11.10. 20m. 20m."

Probably the result of a telephone call, thought Harry, making a note. It would tie in with the time of death. The figure didn't signify, the number of the row house had been forty-three.

There were heavy steps on the stairs. Miss Spotting

came into the room, and Harry realized what a well-built woman she was. In her early forties, he thought, her face white and strained under the light.

He got up and insisted that she take the desk chair, pulling a smaller, harder one from the wall for his use.

"Everything is as it should be," she said. "Fifteen canvases in the vault, and some figurines."

"Money?"

She gave a tremulous, rather ghastly smile and slumped forward in the chair, beads of sweat on her forehead.

He filled a glass from the water carafe, and she lifted it with both hands.

She waved away his talk of a doctor.

"No, no. I have a very slight cardiac complaint and, well, I worked with Paul Huntingtower for ten years. No, we don't handle cash, like very good tailors, you know. All checks."

"Huntingtower wasn't in the gallery yesterday?"

There was a slight trace of surprise on her face.

"No. We're having, were having, an exhibition in a few days' time, three very exciting painters from Barcelona plus some loan paintings en route to the U.S. Paul was dashing madly. It's a lot of work, catalogues, invitations, seeing that people really will come, and to cap it the canvases haven't actually arrived and Paul was nearly going mad on long distance. So he hasn't been around the gallery much. That was our arrangement, that I didn't worry him. Anything I did, he backed up. He was wonderful to work with."

"No enemies?"

"Paul? Oh, Inspector, one always thinks one's own trade is extra bitchy. You find bleeding throats around art alley."

"Caravaggio, was it, who killed somebody on a tennis court?" The Inspector spoke idly, his eyes on Miss Spotting's face. He'd better get the surgeon round, he thought as he saw her slack jaw and mouth. His hand stretched toward the handset.

"Inspector." Her voice was faint. "Look at that!" She pointed toward the canvas of the canal scene and levered herself out of the chair and walked round the desk.

"Great God in heaven," she said. "It's Georges Seurat." She stood transfixed, and then reached up and took down the canvas. She looked at the back and held it out to Harry. Pasted on the back of the canvas was a yellowed letterhead with ugly Victorian gothic type. Paul Pont, 8 Rue de Chevalier, acknowledged 3,400 francs received from Paul Belyavin, of Smolensk, for a painting of a canal scene by Georges Seurat. Aug. 12, 1879.

"My God," said Miss Spotting, not without reverence.

"Let's see," said Harry, "he invented this dot business, didn't he?"

She nodded. "Died 1891 in his thirties, small output. My God!"

"What's it worth?"

Her blue eyes flicked over him. "If I had the money, I'd give you thirty thousand pounds here and now and maybe retire on my profit."

"When did Huntingtower acquire it?"

"He didn't. I never saw it before."

"Umph." Harry thought that perhaps even the capable Miss Spotting might not have known all her employer's business. She read his thoughts.

"Look, Inspector, Paul wasn't in that kind of business. Or that kind of money. He had a flair for anticipating trends. We rarely handled anything over thirty years old."

"But he could have raised the money if it was offered to him cheap?"

Her face showed contempt. "You don't get Seurats cheap!"

"A forgery?"

"I'm not in Paul's class, Inspector, but I have been twenty years in the business. On the face of it, I'd say this is a very good Seurat."

Harry sighed. The back of the canvas and the wooden tighteners would probably take a print. He opened the largest, middle desk drawer and carefully laid the painting face up. He closed the door and fiddled the lock closed with his pick.

"We'll leave it here. I'll notify the solicitor tomorrow. His will leaves things to his brother."

She nodded. "I've met him. He's in the antique business in Edinburgh."

He drove her home. "By the way," he said, "in these nasty cases we have to ask unpleasant questions, sometimes about sexual behavior. Was Mr. Huntingtower a deviate?"

Expertly he watched her from the corners of his eyes and saw her flush. Everybody has these tender, unexpected mental edges, he thought, uncomfortable himself because of her discomfort.

"I think so," she said. "Well, yes, but Paul was not notorious. It did not, most definitely not, enter his business."

Back at Merge's Alley he parked the car. The crowd had dwindled from sheer fatigue to about seven, plus, Harry noticed, a couple of local newspaper reporters, harbingers of the flight of national swallows.

Men were attaching a cable to the jammed Chrysler and as he neared it, Harry saw that the back window had been removed.

"Neat, sir." It was the uniformed constable. "Took the glass out o' that big back winder and the two kids crawled out. I drove 'em 'ome, after taking their prints. The girl's parents were frantic about 'er. We can attend to that one tomorrow. The Super says he don't want the wall touched, so they'll just winkle her out like."

"It'll be damages if you 'urt my 'ouse."

The Inspector had forgotten the red-faced man.

The constable stared up implacably.

"I didn't know you were a 'ouse owner these days, Mr. Perkins."

"I got me rights," said Mr. Perkins, but his tone was halfhearted.

"Three times booked as drunk and disorderly in the las' two years," said the policeman loudly, apparently addressing the rear axle of the car. Somebody laughed and the red face disappeared from the window.

"I'll go round to the house. Who is it by the way?"

"Mr. Porterman, sir."

Chief Inspector Porterman, a bulky man of great authority, was not one of Harry's favorites.

39

It was part of Porterman's manner—act thought Harry —to greet only by the briefest of nods.

"All right, Mr. James, let's have it."

Harry opened his notebook and reeled it off while Porterman squatted on the seat of his car.

"I'll send a couple of searchers to the gallery tomorrow, but that end doesn't look promising, apart from that annotation on the scratchpad. I think he was killed pretty near to where the body lay. Safe enough. There's a coal shed in one of the back yards with new oil on the hinge and some empty boxes inside that might be used as seats. All those yards connect up by wooden doors. You enter the first yard by a door—in good repair compared to the rest of the work—and then you can move along from yard to yard. Very old houses these, by the way, right back to the communal la and water-tap days, originally condemned forty years ago.

"Now we've got the surgeon's identification, and that means Huntingtower got here at approximately ten fifty-five. Entrance to the alley is badly lighted, and a simple matter to slip through the master gate. There he was killed. . . . Two possible motives, sexual or stolen property."

"Anything on him at Records?"

Porterman, who was fond of thinking aloud and tended to monologues, frowned.

"Nothing, for what that's worth. Nobody saw anything in the houses across the alley, scruffy lot. We'll keep trying. Very well, thank you."

Harry went back and found they had got the Chrysler out. One side was badly scraped and the handles had been wrenched from the offside doors.

"Bit of panel work, that's all," said the police driver. "Nobody's reported it missing, sir."

"All right," said Harry. "Leave the keys in. I'll drive her to the station."

It was four o'clock when he parked the car in the station yard. The plainclothesman had been right, somebody had done a good job of working on the engine and he was thankful for the efficiency of the heater.

40

It was strange, he thought, how sometimes days went past before people realized their car had been stolen, on a par with the strange variety of unclaimed goods left in railway trains. Reluctantly he removed the keys and got out into the freezing yard. It might snow, he thought as he sniffed the searing air. Somebody better check the boot. He fumbled with his gloved hands and unlocked it. Two battered suitcases. He slammed down the lid and took them to his office cubicle.

There was a small stack of reports to countersign, and a phoned message that his substitute would take over as from 9 A.M. It was at five o'clock that he finished reading. He got up stiffly and reached for his overcoat. He hesitated, flattened the suitcases on the floor. Might as well see if he could clear the car business up.

The first was unlocked. It contained seven canvases on stretchers, the largest being two feet by three and a half. Nothing else. In the second were eight canvases. No documents that he could see, apart from various papers affixed to the back of the canvases.

He got up stiffly from one knee. Hell, over to Porterman! Only thing, he'd better report in person. His own rank was not senior enough to risk offending the Chief Inspector's sensitive ego.

The car was out until they fingerprinted it. Wearily he got his bicycle clips out of the desk drawer and went out into the yard in search of the ancient communal machine known as the dock green groaner to the men who used it.

He caught Porterman as the Chief Inspector was preparing to leave. He looked gratified as Harry swung off his bike.

"Ah, Mr. James, you shouldn't have worried. I've told your men to resume their duties. Nothing to guard here."

"Yes, sir. There's been a development, sir."

Porterman, Harry thought resentfully, disliked developments not of his own making. He listened distastefully.

"That, of course, might be motive."

Harry saw the uniformed policeman hovering discreetly in the background.

41

"Higgins," he said, "what did those kids say about the Chrysler?" The man drew his notebook out of his top pocket.

"Bing Williamson and Etta Pilsworth, sir. Coming home from the pictures at ten forty-five. Two hundred yards from here"—the sergeant gestured—"is a cul-de-sac. They both went up there, they couldn't think what for, and saw this car parked on the right-'and side. There're always quite a few parked there at all hours. The boy sees the car with its keys in it. 'E tries the door, unlocked. 'Nip in, Etty, and we 'ave a couple of turns round the block.' Mad on cars, 'e is. He's finished the second circuit and 'as slowed down to turn into the cul-de-sac when the police car comes up behind. The young fool puts 'is foot down, then thinks he can get down Merge's Alley, stop, and the pair of 'em run for it. At eleven-thirty a report comes in that there's a car stuck." A faint spasm twisted his broad face. "You must say it's a queer do, sir."

"Yes, yes. The usual procedures were followed?"

"Yes, sir, negative to date."

"Well," said Porterman, "I'll send out a couple of technicians to cover the car and the bags. We'll have to wait and see what 'Cars' turn in. And don't forget that this might be an ordinary robbery. There was no wallet on the body. So I'll want all your Violent List checked."

"Not many around 'ere," said the constable. Harry could have kicked him.

"Quite so. Quite so," said Porterman viciously. "You and the constable might have a look at the place where the car was parked. It just might be that it was smack outside the owner's house. And see where the nearest filling station is and check—if it's an all-nighter. Ah, well, thank you."

At the corner Harry stubbed his shin against the outsize, rusty pedal of the dock green groaner.

"Let me 'ave 'm," said the constable. "We're old friends that brute and me."

"No, no," said Harry, an addict to what he knew to be the pernicious theory that an officer could always do anything required of other ranks. Sometimes he thought the Italian generals had had the right idea.

"Y' know," said P.C. Higgins, "I bin on traffic around 'ere for ten years off and on. I never saw that Chrysler, as a local, you know. You get to know the locals. Waste of time."

Harry plodded along in silence.

"'Ere we are, sir, Rotherham Court. Used to be a private road with a bit of garden stuck in the middle, and a few big houses. Nursemaids and all that. Flats, now. Good class sort of thing. Couple of retired bookies live there." He gestured into the blackness beyond the street lights. "Retired people. Handy to town, good shopping around. They got garidges, but not enough, so it's street parkin'. But then somebody comes and parks outside the flats, and there's a complaint and you 'ave to tell 'em that it's free for all, and that they don't understand."

"Where did they find the car?" asked Harry morosely.

"About fifteen yards up on the right. About 'ere."

There was a gap in the parked cars long enough to accommodate the Chrysler. Harry looked up at the dark windows of the flats and wondered whether he should knock the tenants up. The sergeant read his thoughts. "Take it from me, sir, that car don't belong around here."

The Inspector shrugged and turned the bike round. He heard footsteps briskly rattling and somebody came into the light at the beginning of the road, hesitated and stopped. Harry quickened his pace and a man's figure turned to face him, his face in darkness.

"Have you lost a hat, sir?" said a voice he was sure he knew.

"Take the bike," he said to Higgins.

"I'm a police officer, sir. Oh, Mr. Samuel Lovers. We met this, I mean yesterday, morning."

"Today's my early day. We operate a small warehouse not far from here. Look at that!"

"That' was a niche in the gray wall. In it was the bust of a heavily bearded man. On its head, at a rakish angle, was a soft black hat.

Harry took out his pencil torch and directed the beam. The plaque read: "ERNEST MUFFIT (1830–1905). Vestryman, lifelong member of the Fabian Society. Tireless in the public weal. Erected by his friends."

"Ah," said Lovers with amiable loquacity. "This used to be a private estate. Old Muffit had his house here. He knew Bernard Shaw. Great campaigner for public lavs for ladies. Tried to erect one at his own expense in the British Museum. When the house went with the other houses, this wall was preserved by covenant."

Harry took the hat off. It was in good condition, but far from new, and by a maker who sold in thousands. He sniffed. Its owner used a quite strongly perfumed hair dressing.

"A man was strangled during the night a couple of hundred yards away. He was minus a black hat."

"Who was he?"

"Art gallery owner named Huntingtower."

"Not my line," wheezed Lovers. "If it had been a pub keeper, now! Oh, well, if you don't want me, I'll be off."

"When do you knock off?" Harry asked the constable. His watch showed six-fifteen.

"Now," said Higgins, "but don't worry about that, sir."

"I'm bicycling home," said Harry. "Would you drop the hat into the desk sergeant and tell him to phone this through to Chief Inspector Porterman." He scribbled quickly before the cold could numb his gloveless hand. He could not resist a concluding sentence: "The late Mr. Muffit was an advocate of public conveniences for ladies."

The Stanisgate house was not designed to accommodate bicycles. There were area steps to the sub-basement, now partly a sewing room for Dora and a disposal point for suitcases and junk. He wrestled the dock green groaner down the stairs, avoiding the animosity of the pedals, but receiving a nasty dig in the stomach from one handlebar. He rested it against a drain pipe, and was surprised to find that sweat was freezing on his forehead. He stood looking up the steps, deciding whether he should sleep or eat. Experience told him that the telephone would be ringing before ten. He decided to sleep, you could always snatch a pie along the way, when he saw Hubert Stanisgate briskly and noiselessly mount the three front steps, open the door

44

deftly with a key carried in one gloveless hand, and enter the house. The automatic greeting had remained unsaid by Harry, partly because of his astonishment, partly because there had been a well-defined air of surreptitiousness about Hubert. A woman, thought Harry. He remembered that the Stanisgates occupied separate bedrooms because of Hubert's chronic insomnia. Perhaps that was it. Hubert's insomnia drove him to tramp the streets. And, of course, he wouldn't want to rouse the house on his return.

Harry wriggled his cold toes and decided to wait a couple of minutes. It would be one of those stupidly embarrassing situations if he entered on Hubert's heels. When he did go in, he found himself moving as quietly as Hubert had.

His room was at the end of the long first landing, a roomy and comfortable place. The landing was well lighted, as Dora Stanisgate did not like the idea of a house in complete darkness. He opened his bedroom door and saw in the wall mirror facing him the door at the other end of the passage pop a quarter open. Round it peered the plump cheeks of Hildegard and above her mop of brown hair the long spotty face of her brother, Leicestershire. Woebegone, that was the word to describe their faces, Harry thought as he shut the door. Ah, well, probably old Hubert was straying from the marital fold. He took the "do not disturb" from a drawer and hung it outside. The door opposite was now closed.

Chapter 2

For once he was left in peace until nearly ten-thirty. He opened sticky eyes and took the handset.

"Good morning, sir," said Sergeant Honeybody. "You had an eventful night, I believe."

"What further horrors, Sergeant?"

"Well, sir, the lady in charge of the Huntingtower Gallery, a Miss Spotting, reported a breaking at the gallery."

"What?" The bedclothes slithered off Harry's chest as he sat up.

"Yes, sir," the sergeant said imperturbably. "There was a picture which you had locked in a desk. It had been forced and the picture taken. Entrance appears to have been through a basement window leading into a gents. It looks as though the bars outside had been previously sawn through, then puttied up and painted over. You remember we had a false alarm from the gallery last week."

"Yes," said Harry. "Any prints?"

"Thousands," said Honeybody cheerfully. "You know what it is with shops. It's driving Bill Murphy mad."

Thousands of man hours wasted every year, thought Harry, on fingerprinting and identikit working, just because in the odd case it provided vital evidence.

"All right, I'll be in in twenty minutes. Get me in a pie and a cupper, please, Sergeant."

He showered and hauled the dock green groaner up the area stairs. Nobody ever stole the groaner, although it was traditional to place it in positions notoriously tempting to bicycle thieves.

As he parked the bicycle in the yard, he saw two men working on the Chrysler.

46

They shrugged mournfully. "Plenty of dabs from those kids, but that's all. Not a skerrick of anything. Probably vacuum cleaned inside regularly. Smudge marks from gloves and, look at that." The senior man pointed his finger at the driver's mirror, which had been unscrewed and placed upon a sheet of white paper. "Free from prints. That means a pro job."

The Inspector went into the comfortable fug of the station. You nearly always got a print from the driving mirror, even experienced thieves fell into that trap if they drove a car for long.

He shaved with an electric razor, ate a gluey pie, drank his tea and read the reports.

The three men on the Huntingtower Gallery robbery had done a shipshape job, but there was really little to report. Somebody had removed the grill, pried up the window, wriggled over the sill—large window—gone up the stairs, opened the small downstairs office, which was unlocked, and gone up the stairs, forcing the door.

A friend came on the telephone. "The report will go to Woof-Woof"—Harry remembered that this was Porter man's nickname—"but I thought I'd keep you abreast—that reminds me, how is your beautiful young woman these days?"

"Abreast of the stormy seas of life," said Harry.

"Fine. Well, that crate's got a peculiarly anonymous history. Bought in Paris last year, duty free with export plates, by a Yank named Sims. It seems he went round Europe in it—did around twenty-seven thousand miles. He brought it to England and sold it to a Bournemouth firm. Of course, part of the deal was that they had to pay customs duty. Exit Sims. The firm altered the steering over, registered it and sold it to a Mr. George Brown, who paid cash. The car people dealt in insurance and they gave him a comprehensive for one year. A Mr. George Brown, address being a hotel who have never heard of him. At least four George Browns are on their register over the period and we've checked them all.

"The manager of the Bournemouth firm doesn't know whether he got a sight of a driver's license. Probably so hypnotized by those crackly banknotes."

47

"Thanks, Bob, same for you some day."

Sergeant Honeybody came in, smiling happily. Harry wondered what domestic felicity, or happy quirk of digestive processes, produced policemen like Honeybody. Generally sergeants, now he came to think of it.

"Didn't want to worry you, sir, but Mr. Porterman would like to see you at the Yard at two. Meanwhile, sir, I checked the Violent listings."

Thank God, thought Harry, for sergeants.

"It's clear, sir! Berty Strout, Arty Williams and Billy Taverner are all nicely under the lock. Art Bailey is minding at Southampton and was there last night, big and beery as ever. Percy Strider is in hospital—checked on 'im myself. Suffering from a hernia where Berty Strout kicked him last year, dog eat dog, eh? But no organized violence around here and hasn't been since the old race gangs."

"There's the Scobies."

"Ah, that's the family home. The Scobies don't do anything violent in the borough; not unless you tried to take one of 'em, then you need half a dozen men and a car, but that's natural."

Harry tapped the V file, list of violent criminals known to work, live or sojourn in the division. Honeybody was, of course, quite right, it was a modest recital compared to some others.

"Who would you use for any strong-arm work?"

Honeybody's thumb nudged the file. "Most of those boys only get vicious when they're in drink. They get worried and knock back half a dozen scotches and then a word's a blow. Or inside, they might brood until they went for somebody."

"I'll see the Scobies."

"Who'll you take, sir?"

"Take? It's only a step, I'll walk round."

"I'll come with you, sir, I know the district, all fiddly little streets. It's quite a little warren, Mr. James, and the young Scobies all climb like cats. The neighbors are in with 'em, afraid to be owt else."

Harry dredged his memory. The old grannie, a disgraceful eighty-five and still reputed to drink a bottle of gin on occasion, lived there. The progenitor had been a

48

certain "Stick" Scobie, the nickname having been acquired in connection with his technique with pieces of lead piping. Stick had passed on in 1936 in Dartmoor, in his late fifties, having spent around eighteen years of his life under lock and key. Nevertheless he'd left six boys and a girl, all living. Now there were fourteen grandchildren, eight of which were boys between seven years (shoplifting) and twenty-five (demanding money with menaces).

"They get rheumatism as they get on," said Honeybody. "It slows 'em, but makes their temper worse."

The row house had neat white lace curtains at its two street windows.

Harry knew that their presence had undoubtedly been known within the house. The door opened almost simultaneously with his ring. It was Bonar Law Scobie, third son of Stick, who had been a high Tory politically. None of the Scobies gave much hint of the ferocity of which they were occasionally capable. Although possessing a certain hardness of physique, they would not stand out in any crowd. Bonar had the simian Scobie cast of countenance. Harry wondered if there were blue-eyed monkeys as he met the sharp eyes under the massive, scarred eyebrows.

"This is Mr. James, Bonar," said the sergeant.

Scobie flicked his seamed face toward the darkness of the hallway and beckoned. Evidently Stick had possessed the lower-middle-class virtues of his generation, for the parlor was worn dark rexine and horsehair stuffing and a smell of furniture polish. A faded ormolu clock, supported by a muscular manikin of flaking metal, drooped its hands hopelessly at six-thirty. Next to it stared a china owl. Harry looked at the bookcase and recognized the brownish-red binding and gold lettering of the collected works of Charles Dickens distributed by a cultural newspaper tycoon in the thirties.

"Well," said Scobie, "what brings you two here?"

His voice was flat and unremarkable except for a tiny hint of inherited Yorkshire.

"A man was found dead in an alley, Mr. Scobie."

"Strangled with cord," said Scobie and waited.

It was the Inspector's cue to confront Scobie with the

fact that the method of death had not been mentioned in the press reports, but he knew that there were a hundred gossiping ways in which the fact could have reached Scobie. Silently he offered his cigarettes round.

"Nothing to do with us," said Scobie, sounding a little more friendly. "I don't suppose even a fancy copper'd think the old lady was mucking about with cord. So there was me, Fred and young Elvis—'e's Kitchener's son. We 'ad a feller seeing us named Coates, in the car business. We went to the Lord Littelton about seven and had some grub, except Elvis who stayed with 'is gran. We played darts until half after ten and took some bottles and a bit of fish 'ome. Fred and me were talking to Coatsey until late, say about three. In the end Coatsey wasn't feeling like doing any drivin', the fish disagreed with him"— something like a smile crossed Scobie's face—"so we put him to kip on the sofey and the two of us went upstairs.

"'Ere." He wrote on a piece of paper with a pencil stub. "That's Coates's address and phone. He had some tea about ten and took off."

"Oh, well, thanks, Mr. Scobie. You know how it is."

"I know how it is, all right."

They went into the dark hall and heard Scobie fumble with the latch.

"I've seen Arthur Mace around," said Scobie.

Their departure was a matter of brief nods. Harry and the sergeant were nearly back to the station when the latter said, "That's the first time I knew of a Scobie dobbing anyone in for free!"

"Who's Arthur Mace?"

"Never heard of him but there must be very bad blood there."

The loyalty of thieves was a very complex business, thought Harry, and beyond a point it did not exist. But the Scobie family would set a high price on information, higher than the police could usually pay. This was hate.

"I've heard of this Coates fellow," said the Inspector. "If it's the same one, he receives stolen car parts. I'll see that he gets looked into."

"The Scobies knocked off their first car in 1920—old 'Stick' nearly got away with a T-model Ford parked on the

downs on Derby Day. I happened to read it in his record."
Sergeant Honeybody spoke as a connoisseur.

Harry got a taxi to the Yard, arriving outside Porterman's room at five to two, too late for a quick trip to the canteen.

Eventually, Porterman listened to his brief recital, drumming his fingers on the blotter.

"The fact seems to be, Inspector, that what could be a priceless objet d'art"—the burly Chief Inspector evidently relished the phrase—"may be said to have vanished from police custody. I shall have to ask the legal department just how far our liability would extend in case of a suit for damages."

"I deny that it was in my custody at any time." The Inspector realized he had made a mistake. He should have taken it without comment.

"To have it in your hands, to place it in a drawer upon your own responsibility, is not custody?" Porterman gave a barking laugh. "And, of course, no precaution was taken to keep the premises under observation."

Harry half lost his temper. "And no procedure exists whereby such observation could be justified on the work sheet."

He gave glare for glare.

"Well," said Porterman, "I shall be attending the conference at three and I shall have to raise it."

It was an efficient checkmate. Porterman frequently alluded to his presence at the three o'clock conference, one of the series by which the Yard is governed. As it was, it left the Inspector in the position of a junior civil servant and Porterman a visitor to the Privy Council.

He went back to the cubbyhole he shared with three other men. There was a memorandum on his clipboard. From Superintendent Hawker: "Awaiting your report re pavement artists. Pray do not overstrain yourself. E.H."

Sullenly Harry made his way to the canteen. On his feet all ruddy night and shirty fat men and shirty memos!

He took a cab to the apartment house where Frank Brown, possibly alias ·Brun, had been found dead. It looked clean enough: the linoleum on the stairway was uncracked. He consulted his notes. The owner was a Mr.

George Bell, who lived two streets away in an old-fashioned but snug flat with a lot of Queen Anne style furniture and some mauvish reproductions of Cornish lanes hung up in the living room. An elderly gas fire mumbled in the fireplace.

Bell ushered the Inspector in with a crablike, beckoning kind of motion, his gaze fixed on the wall-to-wall carpeting.

Harry found a chair.

"It's about the man found dead in your rooming house on November fourteenth."

"I had the Coroner's officer round." Bell had a querulous voice, tinged with self-pity.

"Yes, I read the file. You could not contribute anything. I wondered whether, on consideration, anything had occurred to you?"

Bell shook his head, and his eyes slid past Harry, who followed the direction of the glance. In the corner farthest away from the window sat a fat woman who could have been Queen Anne herself. Peering sideways, the Inspector got the impression that she was shrouded in black, with black bobbles fringing a high-necked dress over which peered a lardy, impassive face.

"My wife," muttered Bell. "No, there's nothing."

One acquired an instinct about these matters, thought Harry. Bell was concealing something, probably something quite unimportant. He lay back in his chair and surveyed his shoes. From the corners of his eyes he saw Bell shift uncertainly in his seat.

"Do you have more than one apartment house, Mr. Bell?"

"Three," said Bell, reluctantly.

"Well, I expect there are occasions when a little co-operation from the police comes in handy."

"I'm always full," said Bell. "Always full. If one goes, the room never remains empty more than a couple of days. I give a fair deal at a good price. Well conducted. No women allowed, excuse me, dear!" He flicked his eyes toward the fat lady.

"You give service?"

"There's service for the asking."

52

"So you really can't tell if women go in there or not." The Inspector automatically followed the old police adage to keep 'em talking.

"The other tenants'd pretty soon tell my manager. You see, the walls are thin and the other fellows wouldn't like it, jealous you might say. Excuse me, my love!"

"Well!" The Inspector made a snapping sound with his notebook and Bell's head swung round to his wife. Harry could not detect what signal passed.

Bell scuffed the carpet with one shoe. "Well, Inspector, since you put it that way, there might be a few things."

"Let's have 'em."

Again the half-surreptitious glance toward the wife. You could see who held the reins there, thought Harry.

"You see," said Bell in a flurry of words, "we advertise in the papers and on shop boards telling people to apply for vacancies between six and seven, and I usually go there with the manager to size the applicant up. My record shows that Brown moved in on January seventh. Now sometimes there is a fair turnover and over the year I see a lot of faces." Bell seemed to like the phrase because he nodded and repeated it. "A lot of faces. But I remember hesitating about Brown. It was on the tip of my tongue to say the room was taken. He was a frightened man, Inspector, a frightened man."

"What of?"

Bell twitched his shoulders. "I suppose I thought the police."

"How did he impress you generally?"

"Oh, he was shabby. It was cold as it is now and he was muffled up. The room had been vacant two days and I didn't want to hang around in the cold, so I let him have it. Never saw him again until . . ."

"Was he English?"

"He spoke very hoarse," said Bell. "He might have been a foreigner now you put it in my head, and if I'd have known, of course he wouldn't have got the room." He glanced at his wife as if for approval.

"I think you've left the important thing until last," said the Inspector.

"Yes, well," said Bell carefully. "On the fourteenth of

53

November my manager reports Brown as a defaulter. That's what is the whole secret of my business—never let them get behind. We let ourselves in, and, of course, there was the smell." Mr. Bell ran a finger round the inside of his collar.

"I told the manager to get the police and a doctor. While he's gone, I saw a piece of paper in the corner and I put it in my pocket."

"Well," said Harry, "I hope you've still got it."

There was a long silence. Finally Bell got to his feet, took down one of the pictures and fumbled with a small wall safe.

"Here." He placed a five-pound note in the Inspector's hand.

Harry cleared his throat.

"You have to remember," said Bell, "that he owed me a week's rent in lieu of notice. It clearly says in the rent book . . ." His voice trailed off.

"Oh, I don't suppose anybody's going into a song and dance about it. We'd better both initial it. Take my pen."

"There's something on the other side," said Bell when they had finished, "a name or something."

Harry had it gripped in a pair of tweezers—fivers held prints quite well—and was putting it in a cellophane envelope. He peered through the protective cover. There was a thick black greasy scrawl. He examined it under a glass. It looked like, "peril à corps," which made no sense in French except the initial word for danger.

He nodded to Bell and his expressionless wife, told him they might ask for his fingerprints later, and rather gratefully left the flat.

He found the pie stall where Brown had collapsed. The attendant, Jody Dorking, remembered the occasion well.

"The poor old sod went down like he'd been hit. We got him up and he was puffing and blowing and sweatin'. Doug Carr took him home."

"Was he a foreigner?"

Dorking laughed. "My mum and dad got Viennese accents you could cut with a knife. Result is that foreign accents don't register with me. I'm so used to 'em. He didn't say much. Always had a double steak-an'-kid' when he came to the stall, generally three or four times in a week, and tea to wash it down."

The Inspector located Carr at the betting office. He was busy and grunted at Harry while he checked a pile of slips.

He didn't notice much about Brown. Just wanted to get him home quick.

"Foreigner?" Carr shrugged. "Could be. He kept saying 'All right, all right!' or 'No, no' when I wanted to get him to a doctor. He got out, said 'Thank you,' waved me back and went up the stairs under his own steam. I waited ten minutes and drove off." He poised, his pencil in the air. "Best I can say, Inspector, is that he was hoarse and spoke very fast, gabbling almost."

Harry found a telephone and established that the D.D.I. who had handled the death of the second pavement artist was in.

"In my not-satisfied file," said the D.D.I. wearily. "I talked to the pathologist and he said that he felt—although it was almost impossible to demonstrate—that he had been run over more than once. It's a quiet little street with very little traffic. You could say that someone coshed him, put him on the road and went over him a couple of times with a car. The forensic lab came up with the thesis that it was a very heavy car or a truck. But it was raining like hell—a point in favor of an accident—and the tire marks had been washed off the road. Alfred Castelano lived in the really cheap kind of gaffs, places where they don't know nuffin. Aged forty-two, so the path bloke said, and very powerful. Five foot seven and wiry. He could have been a Latin by his coloring. Anchor tattooed on his right forearm. That's all except he must have felt the cold by the amount of clothes he wore."

At the Yard, Harry dropped the five-pound note into the laboratory, where it would be lifted on fingerprints and photographed. He walked to his cubicle and unlocked his private portable typewriter, a birthday present from his fiancée. Its touch, he thought gloomily, was already ruined by a succession of strange two-fingered typists. Useless to lock it, really, as there was hardly anybody around who couldn't pick a simple lock. But he did wish they would not slop tobacco ash over the keys.

He fingered out a report to Hawker and found a messenger. His in-basket was clear.

The telephone rang, and it was his fiancée.

"Where have you been?"

"About forty-eight hours straight in the public interest."

"I despair of the prospect of raising a family," she said primly. "But what's this I hear of you finding *Naked Majas* all over the place?"

"The most titillating picture I found showed a cat—I think it was a cat—sitting in a cornfield. How did you know?"

"The Hairy Friend rang me, all mysterious. On his way to see you."

"He's not! I'm home to one of Dora's steaks, I hope, and then the 'Do not disturb.'"

"All right, dear, you'd better rush."

Understanding woman, thought Harry, as he got out his overcoat. The Hairy Friend was a mutual acquaintance by the name of Blenkinsop. If he had a Christian name, Harry had never heard or seen it. Blenkinsop was art appraiser to several insurance companies, retained by both Yard and Customs. Get out quick and disconnect the telephone, he told himself.

"So long!"

He was halfway along the corridor before he was caught by the moon-faced Inspector who assisted Chief Inspector Porterman.

"Glad I caught you," he puffed. "Conference in old Hawker's room in five minutes."

Harry shrugged and thought of what divorce detectives were supposed to earn.

"At the conference they gave it to old Hawker for God's sake."

"Gave what?" Harry snarled in spite of himself.

"You *are* nervy. The Huntingtower case. Portyboy reports to Hawker who takes it to the conference."

Harry felt a sense of relief. He had become accustomed to the nuances of reputational ups and downs. Any complaint about his handling of the Seurat painting was up to Hawker. He wondered if the old fellow had gone out to bat for him. Probably, almost certainly, not.

"Hawker gets the cuties," he said aloud.

"What? Oh, yes. Portyboy's livid. Especially as the Hawk seems getting past it?" Bland eyes surveyed Harry within the lift.

Harry made his smile thin. "Hawker specializes in cases with a lot of apparently unrelated factors. His logic is still all right."

"Oh, quite."

They walked in upon Porterman, his bulk very erect in the second-best chair, Hawker at his desk, and the Hairy Friend, who waved away introduction and squeezed Harry's shoulders, to Porterman's manifest disapprobation.

Blenkinsop sometimes had his hair trimmed, at that mainly from perversity, and Harry supposed a pair of shears limited the Niagara Falls of the beard, which generally froze at around eight inches. Eyebrows, ears, and even, Harry had recently noticed, the nostrils yielded a hirsute black crop, through which a pair of large brown eyes peered and the tip of a jutting chin, cleaving through speedboat fashion, defied the suspicion of chinlessness. Blenkinsop said his appearance attracted women.

"Well," said Hawker, "it warms my heart to see old friends reunited. The point of this meeting is in twenty minutes' time. Meanwhile I just want to record that Mr. Blenkinsop, who is our expert on the subject, has examined the fifteen paintings found in the back of the Chrysler car and thinks that there are two paintings of the Venetian school, twelve Post-Impressionist and one Flemish school. If so, of an insurable value of around one million pounds."

"So," said Blenkinsop, "I remind you of the remark in one of Huxley's novels. 'My period is from the death of Macpherson to the death of Keats.' I'm fallible."

"Precisely!" said Hawker. "The quotation is 'from the invention of Ossian to the death of Keats.' Some accuracy will aid us in these quagmires." His cold eyes flicked to the electric clock.

"Well"—the Hairy Friend rolled with the punch—"I shouldn't have stepped out of my discipline. Sorry. To elaborate in non-literary language, I am reasonably certain of authenticity, but there are specialists covering each artist and to those the paintings must go, in addition to the lab tests. I am an expert on the Flemish school. There was a painting by the younger Breughel, entitled the *Four Children of Wim*. For some reason a Russian ambassador presented it to the Russian Czar Alexander II. From there it reached a high-grade civil servant in Smolensk, and it vanished without trace in the Revolution. Probably burned to heat a pot of cat-and-turnip stew like so many others. Except here it is, I'd stake my reputation, plus the fact that the lab people confirm the probable age of canvas and pigment."

Blenkinsop licked his lips, tongue poking through the undergrowth. "As for the one who got away . . ." He looked at Harry, who thought that Blenkinsop was thoroughly aroused.

"The Seurat?" he asked.

"Yes, perhaps I put it in an offensive way." Blenkinsop had a soft heart.

Harry shook his head.

"Well, if it was part of the same corpus, I'd say probably genuine. Miss Spotting thought it was. I would not take her word without corroboration. She's read the books, attended the lectures and the galleries, been in the business for some years, but I would not accept her identification."

"Umph," grunted Hawker, his eyes on the clock. "Now, you'll be aware that if this stuff is stolen, it represents a staggering amount of money. In reference to you, Chief Inspector, its garoting potentiality is to be considered. I circulated this matter, as it stands, to various governments, not to Interpol. As the result, you will hear the views of a representative of a friendly government. You, gentlemen, are all here in an official capacity, and Mr. Blenkinsop as a paid adviser. It is an affair of state and any divulgence, now or at any time later, would be dealt with under the Official Secrets Act. I am putting this on official record. So secret is it"—Hawker showed his dentures—"that I am

58

instructed that you may not even know the identity of the friendly nation. You will therefore disregard a rather strong Boston accent."

Harry, interested, saw Porterman writhe slightly in his seat. Hawker quite frankly leered.

There was a knock at the door. Hawker, famous for his theatrical sense of timing, opened it personally. "This, gentlemen," he said, "is Mr. Jarvey." He briefly introduced each man.

Mr. Jarvey was a comfortable, soft-voiced man apparently in his late fifties. His face was white and plump, but a pair of shrewd, skeptical brown eyes surveyed the room over half-lensed spectacles. "I understand you've had the usual warnings. Actually this seems miles away from espionage, but we don't like the other side knowing exactly how much we do know about what goes on in their countries.

"The background is that the wealthy Russian industrialists in pre-Revolutionary days were great collectors of French painting, and they had the foresight to buy a great deal of what was then avant garde stuff, everybody from Manet onward. On March 6, 1921, the Council of People's Commissaries decreed, 'All movable property of citizens fled outside the confines of the Republic is declared to be the property of the U.S.S.R.'

"This and subsequent decrees were upheld by the English High Court in 1928.

"The British decision was a case brought by a Russian princess. She lost but it made the Soviet Government particularly sensitive about the possibility of future claims. So the hundreds of pieces of artwork, which were not acceptable to the communist theoreticians, were not sent abroad and sold, for fear that their original owners would claim them.

"A great deal of it is carefully stored away out of sight. Now, you will excuse me if I go over some elementary ground. During the Revolution literally thousands of great mansions throughout the country were declared to be museums. This was actually a shortcut way of nationalizing them, but museums a lot of them actually became.

"Now." Mr. Jarvey slapped one fleshy palm on the table

59

by Hawker's side. "Most of the prize items were scheduled, catalogued and sent to the great national museums, who censored them and put the unacceptable loot into the strong rooms. However, just imagine the curator appointed in some one-horse town in the country, where some industrialist had a country home. The curator knows just enough to get rid of anything that isn't a realistic landscape or is religious in subject. I'm talking about the early twenties. A lot of stuff got pushed into cupboards or in storerooms in gatehouses. Over the years it has steadily been stolen and a man named Obermann and his associates have put their rubles into its acquisition. There are about a hundred canvases or more involved, we think."

"All modern stuff, eh?" boomed Chief Inspector Porterman, and Blenkinsop made writhing motions.

"Most of it would have been painted since 1870," said Mr. Jarvey, "except a few, and those in fact very choice. It is believed there is an El Greco. Anyway our information as to the contents of the parcel came from an Italian industrialist who does a lot of business Moscow-side. They mistook their man and he told us. They showed him some photographs but unfortunately he was too scared to find out the whole story. He suspected a trap."

"Who's this Obermann?" demanded Porterman.

"Nobody on our side has ever seen him. The Italian I mentioned was contacted by a couple of women, good-lookers—psychology at work." Mr. Jarvey allowed himself a little smile. "There may be an individual named Obermann, or it may be a cover name for the"—he hesitated fractionally—"association."

Harry tried unavailingly to catch Hawker's eye. Good smooth work, the shying away from "gang" in favor of "association," keeping Obermann and friends just within semantic respectability.

"We'd like to get closer to Obermann," said Jarvey. "Maybe we have something he wants and he has something to trade. So far it's no dice. I've had a guy dressed up like an oil millionaire with a yen for art who's been sitting around Berlin until he's got corns on his ass.

"Just to round this briefing off, we always tend to think that in these totalitarian outfits everything and everybody is ticketed to the nth degree. That's not quite so. In fact there are more nomadic types behind the Curtain than ever were in front of the damn thing."

"Why should this man desire foreign currency, sir?" Porterman intoned.

"There's a tidy demand for hard cash behind the Curtain. A fellow who has made a little pile would rather bury Swiss francs than his own stuff, in case he ever has to run for it, as one consideration. The governments employ squads to keep foreign cash out. Some comes through East Germany, a bit gets back via the fishing fleets, and a bit from the tourists, but *that's* actually brought in at a premium as a matter of policy by secret police agents.

"Obermann and his merry men are traders. It could be that this money would be used as stock and traded."

"I suppose," said Harry diffidently, "that the affair could not be Government inspired?"

Porterman looked disapproving.

"A good point," said Jarvey, slowly. "But times have changed since the twenties when they were that hard up. Even with all the calls on their philanthropic purse, the amount a batch of paintings represents isn't the price of a few satellites."

Porterman looked as though he had encountered a bad, but somehow titillating smell.

"I'm not sure," Harry persisted, "that I've got your point regarding the 1928 English court decision."

"Well," said Jarvey, "it did occur to us that if they decided to move the stuff, they might bring it here. You see they don't know what might happen elsewhere, but here they are protected to the degree that nobody they approached might seek the original owner or his heir and bring a case. It's one door bolted."

"It seems to me that the Customs would present a very considerable, a very stout door," said Porterman, smiling.

"Christ," said Blenkinsop. "You put some junk in the back of a camper, about fifty canvases on stretchers, put painting gear around and give your corduroy pants a lashing of paint, and you just drive across any frontier."

"Would not the paint look old?"

"You can overpaint, though that means careful strip-

61

ping down afterwards. But you can layer the original with plastic and then paint over. The new stuff peels off with about the same effort as peeling a banana."

"We have all heard of the collector who will buy a stolen article for her personal delectation," said Porterman.

And come to prayer, dear friends, thought Harry. Aloud, "I suppose this kind of hot stuff goes cheaply, eh, Blenkinsop?"

The art expert looked owlishly through his hair. "This is not Bill Bloggs trying to fence a gold watch with a name engraved, Inspector!" He sounded annoyed.

"At least I presume the watch would go," said Harry. "You could pop it in your pocket and not keep it under the mattress."

"I won't be goaded," said Blenkinsop, "by the rude constabulary. However I shouldn't really have to tell you that collectors are not as ordinary men, within the confines of their interest. A private individual who pays twenty thousand pounds for something to hang on his drawing-room wall, and a lot of people do, is activated by motives which don't necessarily cavil at buying something stolen.

"But I must bring something to your attention. There are some paintings, well-known ones, that have strange histories. I could take you to a very fine Flemish painting that has changed hands violently several times."

"Well," said Porterman, "if you're going back to feudal times . . ."

"My point," said Blenkinsop, "is that if you had the chance of buying a good painting, of dubious provenance, there is a certain chance that the passage of time will plaster the transaction with a patina of respectability."

"How do these things go?" asked Porterman. "There's no title, as with a house or a car."

"You have a receipt, describing the painting, believed in good faith to be by so and so. You see," said Blenkinsop, "a lot of these paintings have been out of circulation for fifty years. Some are well known, some have been seen by privileged experts in the interim. But a great many superb examples, which may be among your Mr. Obermann's swag, were last heard of in 1880 en route to Russia. If they were produced, with any evidence of authenticity . . ."

"There is a point," said Mr. Jarvey, "that these paintings, so clandestinely held, could scarcely be proved to be part of the Russian State, that is if they have been shrewdly picked. They will appear, as it were, from nowhere."

Porterman shook his head like an aggravated bull.

"Well," said Mr. Jarvey, "that about winds up my contribution, with just one last addendum. We got information that an Englishman was involved in the operation, a man who had been in Europe as a member of the armed forces in 1945 and was known to be crooked. Unfortunately that's as far as it goes, no verification. Well"—his neat gray hat appeared in his hand—"that's my contribution. If anything turns up, perhaps you'll let me know through channels, Super." The door shut softly behind him.

"What is the position regarding these paintings?" said Harry. "They are not stolen property, more like treasure trove in fact."

"That's an ingenious piece of weaseling," said Hawker appreciatively. "If the worst came to the worst, we'll call in the Coroner. Meanwhile I've got it down as lost property."

"And are you up on Huntingtower personally?" the Inspector asked Blenkinsop.

"Huntingtower, that was an adopted name, by the way, came of a long line of Scottish bagmen. In other words he was as shrewd as they come and as cautious as a man can be and preserve some movement. You know that on paintings he specialized in contemporary or near-contemporary stuff. Dealing in well-established fields is more like banking these days and takes the capital. But he was a very good judge of a painting, was the late Huntingtower, and I want to be there when they sell his library."

"The sort of man who would deal in dubious matters?" asked Hawker.

"I thought you'd ask that so I inquired around. In his gallery he hadn't much chance of being dishonest beyond the usual puffing and canvassing and slowness to pay. In his younger days he dealt generally and my information is that he wasn't too scrupulous as long as the risk was small.

"Well," concluded Blenkinsop, "I'll bring four men along tomorrow for a session with the paintings, all of them about top in their speciality."

"There's something about paintings, particularly valuable paintings, that brings out the tiger in newspaper editors," said Hawker. "And I don't want to see two-inch headlines."

"My God!" said Blenkinsop, "we're all in the same boat. Nobody who gets his living out of this business wants to see a hundred masterpieces suddenly appearing."

"Is the strange young fellow worth listening to?" asked Porterman when the door closed.

"The Customs take his word," grunted Hawker. "Well, Frank, what's your plan of attack?"

"We'll trace that car if we have to tap every garage in the country. Secondly, I'll know everything that Huntingtower did over the past month. Third, I'm certain that somebody in Merge's Alley must have seen something."

As Hawker nodded approvingly, Harry thought that it was an ideal case for Porterman, a specialist in hard-driving organization. He doubted whether the burly Chief Inspector had played a hunch in his lifetime, but Porterman's case record was excellent.

"You, Inspector, will keep probing a little more into the two dead pavement artists, although their connection with Mr. Porterman's case is remote."

"I would imagine so." There was amusement in Porterman's voice and for once Hawker was mild.

"One thing, now it's on my mind. The five-pound note found in Brown's room bore both his dabs and those of Alfred Castelano, who was found dead the same day as Brown collapsed at the pie stall."

"Return of a debt." Porterman sounded mildly interested. "These fellows probably knew each other."

"Probably," said Hawker. "I want the Inspector to establish how well they did. Next concerns Arthur Mace, who's a thug in business in the Kensington area. I have no

64

doubt a superior kind of thug, in deference to the neighbors, but a chap who by all accounts would relish the strangulatory process. Unfortunately he was seen in Kensington between the hours of eight and twelve."

"Unbreakable?"

"He was in a casino gambling. Two thoroughly respectable people will swear he didn't move except for a couple of visits to the toilet. The staff concur. However, there's a sergeant in the manor who makes rather a hobby of Mace."

Harry knew that sometimes, perhaps for personal dislike, a policeman will exercise more than normal zeal in keeping an eye on a crook, sometimes sacrificing spare time to do it.

"He heard a rumor," said the Superintendent, "that Mace and a man named Polly Packer had a deal in pictures, very vague, in fact the sergeant originally thought it was dirty films, which were, in fact, at one time part of Mace's business. I'd like you to see him this evening, he'll be reporting to the local station at eight. His name's Crook and his record is A-one. I'll be working until all hours, so you can telephone me."

As he walked to the tube, Harry thought wearily of food. His ears stung with the cold.

The sergeant was a spare man with a gray-looking skin and deadpan expression. His voice had gravel in it.

"Arthur Mace would be about the most vicious fellow who ever passed through my hands."

Harry stared at the blown-up colored photograph on the desk. The eyes were a washy blue-gray and held the camera incuriously. Longish nose, firm chin, under thin lips and a lot of wavy, golden hair. No feeling of personality came through, but Harry thought he would probably impress as handsome. Six feet two, said the chart. Forty-four.

"Spends a lot of money on his hair," droned Sergeant Crook. "Going very gray underneath that dye job. Two terms under lock, demanding money with and assault with intent. He came out six years ago."

"Nothing since then?"

"He had some cash stowed away, enough to set himself

65

up. He bullies himself into a lot of percentage situations. There are about five toughs who work for him off and on, all animals."

James let the sergeant proceed in his own way.

"I don't suppose I've met another man I hope will be worked off by a hangman. Arthur's got brains, otherwise he'd be some cheap boy around the greyhounds. But he knows how far to go."

"Any leads on him?"

"We've got nobody who's near to Arthur. The usual run won't open their traps about *his* business."

"What about this man Packer?"

Crook's laughter was like tins being dropped on gravel. "The inimitable Polly Packer. I've taken him twice. False pretenses, 1957, acquitted. Conspiracy to defraud, 1960. He was bloody lucky to get eighteen months, the judge was doting."

"I don't remember it."

"Fundamentally, the old Spanish prisoner approach, the corpus being a load of tungsten illicitly acquired from U.S. strategic stores and en route to China. Four greedy mugs from Manchester put up fifty thou in the hope of making half a million. Only for once one of them had second thoughts and went to the local police station. Polly provided all the documents—they were beauties, some of them in Chinese; Cuban warehouse receipts, bills of lading, two assayer's reports. The mugs were blinded by science. I thought that the idea was Polly's, but the judge thought he'd played a minor part. He came out and started a direct mail business. You know, a million ladies' corsets acquired from the War Office and yours for twelve and sixpence each. We had a look. With a bit of charity you could say it's honest. He's got a business brain has Polly but he can't resist a dishonest penny. You know the type, slavers after a mug like a dog with liver!

"All I know," continued the sergeant, "is from a man named Ted Fry, who hawks roasted peanuts. Cunning as a lavatory rat, silly as a five-bob watch; nobody takes notice of Fry, like talking in front of a lunatic! But he's got this amazing memory and he rattles it back to me. Then he's

66

forgotten it, just like bringing up his breakfast. I take my own little tape machine. Here."

The voice was the slushy swallowing of Southwark, with some impediment of the speech. "You'll have to get the hang of it," said the sergeant.

Harry concentrated. The informer was talking about three 'ores who lived with a Mrs. Boggis and robbed drunken clients. It was not unlike listening to an avant garde American comedian, thought Harry.

"Got him?" asked Crook.

"Southwark, adenoids." The sergeant nodded and looked pleased.

"Sprays something horrid when he talks. I should get danger money." He manipulated the machine.

The voice referred to somebody called Langham. "He said this Polly Packer 'ad crossed Arthur, yes crossed Arthur, for ten thousand, yes crossed Arthur. Arthur was goin' to have Polly Packer cut up, yes cut up. The other, said go away I don't want the effing nuts, no, he says, no, Arthur won't want any cutting, it'll be the hard nudge, right over, the hard nudge right over. It's the pictures, the pictures. Shut up, for God's sake about them."

The sergeant switched off.

"Who's this Langham?"

"Langham? Oh, the Long 'un. He's the nastiest of Mace's boys. Long in the tooth now, maybe fifty. Real name is Percival Foot. Always liked violence. He's over six four and looks thin, a big fleshy face with brown blotches on it."

"I'll look him up."

"You won't get anything out of him. Ted Fry was peddling his nuts in the King of Hearts pub. It's got a couple of small rooms, cubbyholes really, where you get conversations like this. The landlord's in with 'em to some extent."

"So this Arthur Mace might be going to have Packer killed?"

"That's what they mean by the hard nudge."

"Who was the second man?"

The sergeant shrugged. "No good asking Ted Fry, it

only gets him confused if you ask questions. He either didn't see the second man or didn't know him."

"We could put this Long 'un under full surveillance," said Harry, doubtfully thinking of time sheets.

"Constable Smythe, a good young bloke, has got a bit of a string on the Long 'un."

"What did you make of this picture business?"

"Five years ago Arthur Mace was in with a mob who ran blue cinemas around Maida Vale. We never got Arthur, but we knew he had twenty per cent of it. Naturally, I thought, he'd started up again. It didn't ring so true about Packer. Oh, Polly's not fussy, but he's a bit of an artist in his way. Anyway, old Hawker said there might be some valuable paintings concerned. That sounds more like Polly. He's badly scared, by the way. I saw him today drinking a double brandy. His hand shook. That's not my old Polly."

"You're satisfied that Mace had a watertight alibi for last night?"

The sergeant waggled a file. "It's a hundred plus. I'll take you around to check if you want."

"Good God, no. It is only that it'd be so handy if we could just nick Mace."

"Yeah," the sergeant sighed. "There's been no alteration in Arthur Mace's behavior, apart from visiting a casino—he only gambles on a certainty usually. You see his front is a little coffee and sandwich place. It's a hole in the wall. Six tables and a big glass window and a coffee urn. The sandwiches are brought from outside; the jokers say he buys them secondhand from station buffets, they're that horrible. Anyway, there's an old woman who serves named Mrs. Martin. She's a widow of a man named Cat Martin, who specialized in breaking into flats. She was a shoplifter until every shop assistant in London could spot her. Anyway, Arthur Mace sits in an alcove at the back with the telephone. It works both ways. Arthur can have a word with the fly boys who come in, all aboveboard. Anyway, when any of our lads go by they flick their eyes to see whether Arthur's in and who he's talking to, and if he's not there, they tell me. If he doesn't put in his normal six hours a day there, I make it my business to find where he *has* been. Nearly got him twice, but he's cunning as they come."

Harry realized that, as sometimes happened, the sergeant was slightly obsessed on the subject. He was probably normally taciturn.

"Just between you and me a man named Scobie tipped me off that Arthur Mace was around in my manor. Scobie is . . ."

"I've met all the Scobies, including old Grannie," said Crook. "Which one?"

"Bonar."

"Ah, he's the worst. A few years ago the Scobies clashed with Arthur Mace. I never got the strength of it, but it was something about some hot fivers. The Scobies went to bat and Mace said he'd play 'em any game they wanted, and it was the Scobies who shut up. So it could have been spite."

Harry looked at his watch. "Any chance of taking a sight of these gentlefolk?"

Sergeant Crook showed the relish of a man being asked to display his stamp collection. "He could start off with Polly. He rushes around like a sweaty blancmange all day. In the evenings he gets back to his office."

"I'd like to see him."

Crook lifted the handset. "That you, Polly? Crook here. I'll be along in ten minutes."

He slammed the handset down amid tinny squawkings.

On the way he gave the Inspector a word picture of Polly. Polly Packer was a cheerful, smiling man who had made the beginnings of his fortune by retailing bottles of cocktail with an "alcoholic base" consisting of one pint of cider per seventy one-pint bottles of flavored water. Various nosy consumer bodies, which Mr. Packer was wont to attribute to the proliferation of the Welfare State, had been his bane, and via tasty concentrated mushroom soup made entirely from cornflour, an unfortunate venture, Polly had concentrated on forgery.

His Burgundy labels, sold attached to bottles of Chilean

Cabernet, sold steadily in certain quarters, as did his bottles of "smuggled" perfume and his line of model gowns from the salons of Europe's most famous couturiers which were manufactured in Aldgate by a good pal. He did quite a bit with faked binoculars, but had found the smuggled watch business overcrowded.

"I'll leave the talking to you," said Harry.

Packer was a big, rubicund man, fond of a lot of after-shave lotion.

"Well, Polly," said Crook, after he had introduced the Inspector, "how's the genewine Burmese ruby rings hocked by a visiting maharaja and hence going cheap?"

"Your mum should have took the pill," said Packer. In a way they were old friends.

"I hear you're in a bit deep."

A trace of red came into Polly's neck, but his smile did not alter. "I'm in the direct mail business, Sergeant Crook." His thick fingers prodded a red ledger. "I run me little ads and send them genuine disposal articles. Last month it was records, and now it's plastic chrissie trees and lambswool-lined drawers for your old grannie. Money back guaranteed."

"Where do you get all the stuff?" said Crook.

"If you knew that, you'd know all I know. But I'll tell you that not more than two hundred yards from here is a fellow who makes factory-damaged children's vests and 'is brother next door turns out slightly imperfect shirts."

Crook gave his dry laugh. "You're an entertainment, Polly, but that won't stop Arthur Mace having you razored up—that is, if he stops at the razor."

Packer breathed quicker. "I don't know anything about any Arthur Mace. And if you don't mind, I've work to do."

"You went a bit too far with Arthur Mace, Polly." Crook got up and strolled to the window. "He's gone now, but there was one of Arthur's minders across the street when I came up. Fellow named Stevie, big bald-headed man from Sheffield."

"All right, Crook, what are you after?"

"You tell us what you know about Arthur and the paintings."

70

Packer laughed.

"And we give you police protection. You have a new name and twenty-four hours' protection. You've got enough stowed away to retire for a bit, Polly."

"All right, Crook, if that's all you had to say, the two of you be off."

The sergeant stopped at the door. "My extension's nine, any time you want me, Polly."

"Well," said the sergeant, "I hardly thought Polly would crack. I'll give him until tomorrow, then lean on him a little. You never know . . ."

"Should we put a man on to him?"

"He'll keep to the lighted streets and be all right. He's got a place in a fancy block with a reception desk and a night porter. I'll keep him checked." Crook looked at his watch. "Ten. Usually Arthur Mace takes a drink in the Cross Keys about now. Regular in his habits. Hope he hasn't got bitten with the gambling bug." Crook sounded genuinely solicitous.

"Funny thing," said Crook, "I've seen two murderers drinking at the Keys. Didn't know that they were then, of course. In different years, but standing at the same part of the bar where it forms a kind of angle. It's a busy pub."

The saloon bar was almost full. "Good service and food at reasonable prices," said Crook. "First-class landlord. Evening, Bert." They ordered two light ales.

"Talk of the devil," said Crook. "He's at the angle of the bar."

Harry recognized the man from his photograph, although the camera had not captured the bold hardness of the face, which in repose seemed to wear a faint, knowing leer.

"Who's the man with him?"

"A small-time club proprietor. Arthur owns a percentage of his joint and provides the chucker-out as his contribution."

Harry sipped his drink, and felt a nudge in his ribs.

"Packer's just come in."

Harry looked round cautiously.

Polly Packer had the faintly unreal look of a normally

71

abstemious man who had taken a couple of stiff ones under his belt.

He walked up to Mace and started to speak. Harry saw that the crowd at each side squashed back, performing the apparently impossible compression of rush hour tube passengers.

From behind his *Evening Standard* at the end of the bar the landlord saw or sensed something that sent him walking calmly toward the center of the bar, his eyes touching the sergeant's as he passed.

Crook walked over, unhurried, a middle-aged, gray-faced man, big-shouldered under his quilt-lined raincoat. Harry followed, deliberately allowing a couple of yards between them.

Polly Packer had finished what he had to say. Arthur Mace topped the plump man by six inches, but tilted his head so that his flat blue eyes slid over Packer's head. The fluorescent light made his hair like crinkled gold paper and waxed his smooth pink cheeks. He smiled, a smile of pure evil.

"I've been insulted by experts, Pol. Why not shove it and have a drink on me? Why, you're shaking!"

"I'm not." Polly had taken the bait and flushed as the cruel eyes dropped and leveled with his. He turned, and then looked back. "My," said Polly, "you *are* looking yourself this evening."

Harry saw the bigger man hesitate and wince, and then smile broadly and fixedly as a professional boxer will after a hurtful punch. Packer stuffed his hands in the pockets of his thick overcoat and walked to the door. Tension went from the air like a deflated air cushion.

They went back to the warm remnants of their ales. The sergeant's eyes were fixed clinically on Arthur Mace. "If he goes out now, I'll take him anyhow," he said. "Sus."

Mace, however, continued his interrupted conversation until closing time, and Harry learned that the sergeant was a widower with a grown-up family and lived in a boardinghouse run by a retired colleague.

They waited until the bar emptied. The landlord conferred with the potman. "He took a cab, looked like it had been ordered. Have a quick one on the house."

Harry took a rum and peppermint.

He said goodbye to Crook and went back to the station. Sergeant Honeybody told him that his deputy had left around nine and that it had been quite a day with a couple of drunks, one drunk in charge, a reported shop-smashing and a stolen car.

In the Inspector's room Harry telephoned Hawker.

"We'll have to consider putting Mace on the special list," said the old man. "Tomorrow's Sunday. Take it off, go punting on the Thames with your young lady."

Harry gazed at the gas fire and protested that there were some things he had to do, at least in the morning.

"Take it off," said Hawker. "There's times to let things stew and I feel it's now. Let Porterman pry around Merge's Alley. You go out and get some fresh air."

"Have you any idea what the temperature is?"

"In my room it's a nice 72. Goodbye."

There was a school of thought that said that Hawker dozed at his desk in winter and in summer slung a hammock on the roof between the radio masts.

He was conscious of the agonizing throbbing of his feet, which had never been quite the same after his first spell of traffic duty. His young woman had warned him that she could never marry a man who hacked his feet with razor blades and with one thing and another he hadn't seen his chiropodist in two months. It was pleasantly warm in the room, the desk chair well upholstered. The only damned thing was his feet. He seemed to remember his father swearing by mustard baths for aches and pains, not that there was a chance of either.

Wait! He'd picked up a couple of things for Dora Stanisgate the other day and what with one thing and another, he looked in the bottom drawer and found a small package. Tin of powdered oregano for Hildegard, and for Dora a bottle of Dijon mustard. It was mixed with stuff, he thought, and hardly as strong as the good old English yellow powder, but it still was based on mustard. At the back of the station was a sink and a gas jet.

He put on the large kettle, washed out the dubious-looking iron bucket. Carrying the bucket into his room, he pried the top off the mustard and with the top of a pencil winkled about half of it into the bucket.

Presently he went out to get the kettle, feeling a pleased anticipation of a man who has improvised his way through all obstacles.

"No thanks," he said to the hovering Honeybody, "I don't want the coffee essence."

He poured the boiling water in the bucket. Cautiously he added water from the carafe and tested it with his forefinger.

He removed his shoes and socks, checked that there was a towel in the desk.

He immersed his feet, ankles crossed and closed his eyes. Presently, he knew, the water would become cold and the beastly business of drying begin, but the moment was bliss and he started to think of food.

"It's Mr. Filder, Mr. James." It was Honeybody's butler voice. "He's a retired schoolteacher, sir, and . . ."

"I apologize for the hour, but bis dat qui cito dat."

Twisting round as far as he could, he saw butter-fair hair, a thin face and glittering glasses. He remembered such faces from childhood, "learned," his mother, an uncomplicated woman, had always thought. He must have pushed past Honeybody, thought Harry, which was strange in itself. He started to rise, found his ankles rocking ominously and found himself smiling vaguely as Mr. Filder trotted smartly past the desk.

"May I sit down, Inspector?"

"Oh, certainly, Mr. Filder."

He thought he registered the sound of the door closing and experienced a hateful little thought concerning Honeybody. Better brazen it out.

Filder sat close to the desk, so that actually his face was not more than a yard from Harry, who prayed that the ex-schoolmaster's feet would not knock over the bucket. The water seemed to have become tepid and he blamed Honeybody for opening the door.

"Here, sir." Mr. Filder smartly whipped a piece of

paper from his breast pocket. "To save time, sir, my own particulars and a brief statement."

Harry looked at it. Mr. Filder had placed the black hat on the head of the bust of Mr. Ernest Muffit. Somebody named Ashur-bani-pal had brought the hat out of Merge's Alley.

Honeybody's idea of humor! Probably the local Harmless Maniac. There was usually one who had somehow attached himself to a station. Ashur-bani-pal? King of Babylon or Ur, somewhere along that line, remembered Harry.

"Ashur," he started to say.

"Come here."

Mr. Filder moved and there was a scrabbling noise. Bracing himself on the desk, Harry managed to rise a few inches. By Mr. Filder's foot, attached to a green collar and lead, was a small black dog, memorable by the fact that it possessed an abnormally large and bony hound's head, out from which two large brown eyes stared expressionlessly.

"Good fellow, good fellow." Mr. Filder stooped and patted. "Ashur is hampered by an almost total incapacity to express emotion, like his illustrious namesake. He, my Ashur that is, is a most affectionate, playful fellow, given to little efforts of retrieving, such as running away with my shoes."

"Ah," said Harry. The water was definitely clammy. "Now, sir, when was this?"

"On Friday at approximately eleven-forty. I should explain that Ashur and I have an arrangement. All through the year we go for three-quarters of an hour's walk at eleven A.M. and twelve P.M. The rest of the time he is content with my small garden and this explains my presence here at this hour."

"And you placed the hat upon the bust of Mr. Ernest Muffit?"

"I was perturbed. It was not windy. I could not conceive where Ashur could have found it. I went to the entrance to the alley, and looked down it. It was deserted."

"Are you sure, sir?" Harry felt something brush against

his shin and some disturbance in the water round his ankles.

"Perfectly, sure. I should explain. I was a master and latterly vice-principal for thirty-three years at the local central school. Your sergeant—a stolid, reliable boy with little enterprise—passed through my hands."

Harry's sharp hearing registered the unmistakable sound of lapping.

"I am an insomniac, at least of latter years. I cannot sleep until two or three A.M., which explains my nocturnal habit."

Harry wagged an ankle and felt his flesh impinge on a soft nose. He beamed at Filder in embarrassment. "You saw nothing out of the way?"

"Ashur generally goes down that alley as part of his routine. He trotted back—I was about five yards further on—and gave me the hat."

"You weren't looking back?"

The faint lapping noise had started again.

"No, sir, but Ashur invariably dives down the alley. And had the hat been on the pavement I would have seen it. Now, sir, the hat was an artistic kind of hat in good condition, hardly belonging to Merge's Alley. I walked along with it and I remembered Mr. Ernest Muffit's bust. No disrespect was intended—in fact my father and he were friends—but the hat would be seen there, you comprehend, and possibly by its owner."

"You have been most helpful, sir." Without rising Harry attempted to make suitable little bowing and scraping movements.

Mr. Filder gave his thin, vague smile, withdrew Ashur-bani-pal from underneath the desk and went out.

Harry slipslopped over the linoleum to the door. The key had obviously long since disappeared. But there was a bolt, which on manipulation proved to be fractured.

He opened the door a little. He could hear Mr. Filder's reedy tenor exchanging pleasantries with the sergeant's bass baritone. Suddenly there was the violent explosion of sickness on the part of something.

Harry dried his feet and donned socks, shoes, overcoat and hat as fast as he could. He left the bucket for the cleaning detail to make what they would of. He opened the door cautiously. There was no sign of Mr. Filder or Ashur-bani-pal, but somewhere out back near the cell block the sergeant was roaring for cleaning utensils.

Chapter 3

For breakfast Hildegard had cooked the pork sausages in white wine and honey and the Inspector couldn't help wishing she had left them alone. Hubert Stanisgate ate herrings rolled in oatmeal and fried, which he declared he had eaten every Sunday of his life and please God he would do so until death. He repeated this statement with a disapproving glance at Hildegard, who was in the agony of surreptitious glances that affects inexperienced cooks.

"You couldn't have had 'em before you were two," said Leicestershire Stanisgate, who was fond of facts like his mother.

"Don't be too sure," said his father. "In the fishing village puking, puling, mewing brats, just off their mother's breast, ate mashed, tritated boiled herring. And why put honey on a perfectly good sausage?"

"People don't want to read about ordinary fried sausages," said Hildegard, slightly sullen.

"That's the trouble," said Hubert. "So instead of coming home to hearty steak and kidney pud, their husbands eat bits of shin of veal stewed with tomatoes and garlic and a dash of British port."

"That is nonsense," said Dora. "You know as well as I do that people are far better nourished nowadays, and as far as nutrition is concerned the average Italian . . ."

Hubert good-humoredly boomed across the table, "There isn't an average Italian, except the maitre d'hotels. Anyway, what say we finish the cards. Then there's the addressing and I've lost the list."

"I wrote it out on green foolscap."

"It doesn't matter whether it was on a red bowler hat. It was in my pocket and then it wasn't."

"I'll get last year's cards and the address book and work it out again," said Dora placidly.

The demoniac collective energy of the Stanisgates was at this time directed to making their own Christmas cards with pop art decoration. Hubert had brought home from work piles of *Realités* and other old magazines and a great tin of rubber solution. While the family toiled with scissors, he added the lettering in his quick professional script. When the Stanisgates operated as a unit, there was a concentration of purpose that the Inspector had learned to recognize. Though after he had gone upstairs to bathe and dress—he had overslept—he came down to find an unaccustomed desultoriness over the proceedings. Dora was frankly thinking of something else. Lacking experience in the arts and crafts, the Inspector kept to the role of bystander. Presently Hildegard muttered that she wanted to look at the plants. She was attempting to grow a variety of fresh herbs in pots in her room and to that end meddled with the central heating to her father's considerable annoyance. Leicestershire, who had started in some function with commercial teevee, said he wanted to talk to a friend about a program and disappeared. Hubert's busy pen had ceased to mark the cardboard and he was staring out of the window. With anybody but the Stanisgates, Harry would have forecast a family row.

The Inspector was due to lunch at his young woman's and he left early.

After lunch and the washing up—previews of domestication—Elizabeth turned up the electric fire, with its artificial yule log that for some reason blinked and flickered disconcertingly.

"Central heating for us," said Harry. In six months their financial background would be marriageable. It would be nice every night to talk to his wife about work. He talked to her now and, as was her way, she said nothing immediately.

Miss Elizabeth Holland for some years had suffered under a blight. Now it was her avowed intention to get unblighted.

Just now she switched on the player and danced the

Kazachka, mainly to spite Harry, who invariably fell over when he tried.

"You know I can't *see* the Berlin frontier," she panted.

"I may say," said the Inspector, "that the *Kazachka* is more revealing than the can-can, which is, as you may know, banned in seventeen American states."

"Lecherous voyeuring copper," she said, "why do you never take me to disgusting night clubs as a witness?"

"I never got that kind of work, Liz," said Harry. "God knows I'd welcome it."

"And an immoral hypocrite!"

Later, Elizabeth smoked a cigarette and said, "I said about East Berlin, you couldn't take canvases over it like our Hairy Friend said."

He had forgotten that she had spent her holiday in Germany this year.

"I prefer it east of the frontier," she said perversely and he did not respond.

She looked him in the eyes. "You'd thought of that?" she said.

"I thought of the old joke, about the French thinking a Picasso was a plan of the Maginot Line. Blenkinsop being less than frank, I wonder why?"

"You'd shop your own mama."

"I wish she'd quit driving that car," said Harry, who worried about his mother.

"I'm sure you'd take her a tract on visiting days," said Elizabeth. "I'll put tea on."

To the Inspector's dismay Elizabeth was committed to a business party and it was his rule not to attend such functions. He rather disliked as being undignified the public role of fiancée, particularly when it so often prompted the addendum, "Oh, yes, the one in the police." So for want of anything better to do he returned to the Stanisgates' about six with vague ideas of catching up on his reading and joining in the supper which the Stanisgates ate at 9 P.M. on Sundays.

He wandered into the living room with his book. One light only was on, beside Dora's armchair. He dropped into another and reached out and switched on a reading light.

"Oh," said Dora, "I didn't hear you come in, Harry."

She really was a very nice person, Harry thought. "Where's the kids?"

"About their mysterious business. Hubert went out after dinner. He's due back."

Something was clearly troubling Dora. The desire to talk was something a policeman learned to recognize. He hoped to God it wasn't one of these domestic things.

"I'm worrying about Hubert, Inspector."

"In what way?"

"Perhaps I should say that I'm worried about his being worried. After twenty odd years of marriage, you sense these things. I wondered if you'd noticed it?"

"Why not ask him?"

"I should have, but I didn't and then you get a kind of tongue-tied situation. The children feel it, I think. I hate him being worried. If it was my political activities, I'd quit them tomorrow."

What the devil can you do, thought Harry: say outright, "Dora dear, there's probably a little blonde with a big balcony, somewhere in his office."

Aloud he said, "Of course, I understand that advertising is a nerve-wracking business."

"I suppose you are right," she said. "He's been working until eight and nine at night for the past month."

Harry was relieved when the telephone rang.

It was Porterman's heavy, deliberate tones.

"Sorry to break in on your Sunday, Mr. James, but could you see me at the local station house? It shouldn't take long."

Pompous old bastard, thought Harry. Break in on his Sunday, indeed, as though he spent every Sunday in leisured ease.

However, the big inspector was placatory enough when Harry found him in the Inspector's office studying a series of photographs.

"They went in that door." His forefinger stabbed a closeup of a wooden door. "Hinges oiled about two months ago, so the lab says, which means they were using the back yards for that length of time. It's about two yards in from the east end of Merge's Alley. See that"—a

81

closeup of a jagged strip of metal. "Part of some old fastening device. A blood smear on the end of it, twenty-four hours old when we found it, type is a rare one. Must have bled profusely. Tiny fragments of skin that the lab describe as from a blond with the type of skin that scratches easily.

"Now we sifted through that yard with a toothcomb. Imbedded in some muck just inside the gate—decayed vegetable matter and soot—we found six sheets of paper. The hypothesis is that somebody sustained this gash, and fumbled in a pocket for a handkerchief to staunch it. In the process this wad of paper fell to the ground—it's smeared with the same blood group—and got trodden in. Here . . ." Porterman produced photostats. Green paper, foolscap, with one hundred and forty names, some with addresses, written with ballpoint, probably a woman. "We were going to start checking when we saw this."

Harry was half expecting it. "Inspector H. A. James." The rather large but well-formed cursive writing was Dora's.

"It's my landlady's Christmas card list," he said.

"Good God in heaven!"

Porterman stared wildly at the ceiling, then said, "Respectable?"

The Inspector had the wild impulse to reply in the negative, but he said, "She's on a number of local committees and likely to be a councilor. He's an art director with what I understand to be a well-known advertising agency."

"I've never," said Porterman, "found myself in so many dead ends as with this case."

He sounded human and Harry fought back the impulse to like him a little.

"That ruddy car, for example, absolutely nothing on it. Nobody saw anything. Hmph. Probably nothing to do with the case, although the bloodstains . . . Mm, look, God knows I hate Sunday interruptions myself, but would you have a word with the Stanisgates? I take it that they're at home."

"Okay. I'll take a set of stats if you don't mind."

He found that Hubert had buckled down to the lettering. The children were not around, and Dora was consulting a leather address book.

"Save you the trouble, Dee," he said. "Here's your missing list." He watched Hubert's broad face and saw the sloe eyes switch to his and hold them. There was a strange expression on Hubert's face.

"So you got it back!"

"Got what back?"

"My wallet."

"Now look, Hubert, I'm talking as a copper. Would you mind telling me how you came to lose that list?"

Hubert's big hand reached over to the table.

"Stats, I see. I deduce the originals were found at the scene of a keerime, m' dear Watson."

"A mile away, at a place named Merge's Alley, the crime being strangulation of an adult male with a nylon cord."

"Don't play the fool, Hubert." Dora Stanisgate's soft voice was as sharp as it ever was. Hubert didn't like it and his smooth skin reddened around the cheekbones.

"It was in a wallet. I walked out of the Bleeders at one o'clock last Monday to have my lunch at the Bunch of Grapes. I usually try to be earlier because at one o'clock the city spews these horrible men with furled umbrellas and black overcoats. As it was, the tide smacked me head on, people shoving and pushing. When I was seated in the pub dining room I thought I'd look at Dee's list, as I'd promised. No wallet."

"Tell me about the wallet!"

"Haven't you got to caution me or something?"

"You bloody well know better than that," said Harry. "But if you want it that way, I'll tell you that you can phone a solicitor and get him here."

Dora's expression caught Hubert Stanisgate's eye. She looked very distressed in her pleasantly equine way.

"Sorry old girl. It was an old brown wallet six inches long and five in depth. I don't use wallets for notes: God's own gift to thieves. You've seen me enough to know my system of scattering it round my pockets. If you went through my wardrobe, you'd come out with ten quid any time—if old Dee hadn't got there first."

He cast an affectionate glance at Dora. "Last June when we took that cruise, I wanted a small trunk and I found an old one in the bowels." He jerked his thumb at the floor. "I turfed out most of the weevily bits, but there was this wallet. Hadn't seen it for years, one of the stupid things everybody gets given when he's about twenty. Well, I was in this cursed middle-class brolly and briefcase syndrome, like all the little swine with bowlers. That's because at the Bleeders the brains get back from lunch at three-fifteen and get rid of accumulated wind by writing memoranda which get on my desk at five-fifteen. So I take all this bumph home and read it in bed. Now this wallet has got a kind of pouch at the back extending over its entire area. It holds quarto sheets nicely when spread out, so I put the bumph in it and bring it back in that. I had to fold Dee's list."

"Any distinguishing marks?"

"Letter H in tarnished gold." The Inspector thought Hubert was reluctant.

"And you didn't report the loss to the police?"

"When one in six burglaries are solved, what chance is there for a wallet? You tell me."

Harry contrived to look bored with very little effort. A tough, he thought, looking at the big man. Hard muscle in spite of his forty-odd years. He managed a yawn. "Hubert, old man, I listen to that crack ten times a day, remember."

"Oh, sorry," said Hubert, embarrassed. "Well, I didn't report it."

"You've got a visual memory," said the Inspector. "Try to recall the robbery."

"I think it must have been when a very tall fellow bashed into me," said Stanisgate. "I had to look up slightly into his ugly mug. Big, flabby face and thin otherwise. I met types like him in the army—could fight like threshing machines, wire and whipcord, and liked it. I sort of caromed sideways and bashed into a little fellow, well about five foot eight. Let's see, one of those small gray houndstooth patterns on his overcoat, wide, very blue eyes. I said, 'Sorry' and he just grunted something. Over in a couple of seconds."

"Had you any knowledge of Huntingtower?"

Hubert cleared his throat. "I know maybe a couple of hundred painters, Harry. If I want to buy a canvas, I get it from the cow, not from some twenty-percenting milk-man."

Dora was wriggling in her seat in embarrassment and Stanisgate looked at his wife and sighed. "Who was it that married Truth? Ah, well, I once had drinks with him, along with thirty other people all sipping Australian flor sherry with half a sardine on soggy toast in the other hand. Four times. Fifteen years ago. Dee was still taking the money in her uncle's butcher shop—pound and a 'alf of Aussie 'ogget at one eleven three—and I was hawking stuff around the agencies with cardboard inside my left shoe. The kids went to Dee's auntie during the day.

"There wasn't any Huntingtower Gallery then. I think he was a general dealer, and he made a few bob as a lecturer on art. These fellows usually have two or three spiels they've perfected. He had one on the 'black' Goyas and another on Rubens and his world. Bloody good, although you could see he had a soul like a rent collector. *What* a memory! In the discussions afterwards—this was a club I belonged to, sherry, refreshments and a talk every Thursday—he could reel off half-page quotations from memory.'

The Inspector noted that Hubert was glad to talk. Let 'em, was the professional answer.

"One thing he had was a lecture on faking," said Hubert. "His speciality. Told us all about those hundreds of fake Millets in the Yankee galleries. Nose like a ferret. Well, that's all. Never saw him afterwards."

"Ever hear anything about him? His reputation?"

Hubert shrugged. "You know the old joke about dealers not caring to drink bloody marys because people think it's their clients' blood. Everybody moans. The dealers say they lose dough promoting no-hopers. Etcetera. You can give it up and sit at a cozy little desk at some place like the Bleeders with a non-contrib pension at sixty."

Stanisgate stopped and said he supposed the Inspector would want it all written down and signed.

"Good Lord, no," said Harry. "I boil it down to a dozen

85

lines for the Superintendent. It could be that at some time you'll be asked for a formal statement. By the way, for the record, where were you on Friday night between ten-thirty and two?"

"Enjoying my usual interrupted night's rest."

Harry felt rather than saw Dora's tension. Fancy skating by Hubert. He'd let him go for now, plenty of time to reel him in.

He looked at his watch. "If I spring a cab, suppose we go to the Yard and you look through our photos in case you spot the fellows. We'll get through by ten and I'll buy you a drink."

In the identification booth Hubert watched photographs—four hundred of them—appear on a viewing screen, one every ten seconds.

"All mod cons," said Harry. "Some of these are controls, innocent coppers."

"That's the little fellow," said Hubert eagerly. Harry stopped the machine and made an annotation which he handed to the messenger.

Hubert did not spot the large man who had barged into him. He declared he had seen nobody like him.

"Okay," said Harry as he left the booth. "At least we'll see who the other is."

"Old Joe Chenery, sixty last month," said the clerk from Records, peering into a large folder. "First conviction 1927—that's the year Lindbergh landed in Paris. Worked with racecourse gangs. If they didn't get it off you at the cards, Joe picked your pocket as you got out of the train. No record of violence, doesn't use a minder."

"What's that?" asked Hubert.

"Pickpockets work in crowds," said Harry. "They're nearly all unobtrusive people, men generally. Sometimes they have a minder. He's a big fellow and he jostles you so that you're off guard. Now if you spot anything wrong and open your mouth, he'll plant his fist in your bread basket. You double up while he yells, 'Man's fainted.' By the time you get up and sorted out, both of 'em are in the next parish."

Afterwards they had drinks and something to eat. He knew very little of Stanisgate, the Inspector thought, after eighteen months in his home. Concerning Dora he knew quite a lot, but under his casual façade Stanisgate was all reticence.

"Well," said Stanisgate, "now I've seen you fellows at work, I wonder how anybody gets away."

"Evidence," said the Inspector as he sipped his third whisky. Professional experience had taught him to hold his drink. Stanisgate, an erratic rather than a habitual drinker, showed signs of loosening his tongue.

"You see," said Harry, "the Director has to be certain there is a case to answer and his standards are high. Because a murder doesn't result in a day in court does not necessarily mean we don't know who did it. Similarly the five out of six burglaries you mentioned that aren't solved are sometimes known to us as being the work of some gang, but we haven't the necessary proof."

"Suppose a crook changes his identity, goes to another part of the country?"

"Well, if he's a crook, he'll come into police hands and his prints will show who he really is. If he went straight, of course he might get away with it."

Stanisgate ordered another round. Harry noticed his eyes were a trifle out of focus. Excitement plus alcohol was a dangerous mixture.

"I'm a great believer in names," Hubert said portentously. "You may wonder why I named my boy Leicestershire. 'Smatter of fact I said Worcestershire, but Dora howled like a wolf at bay. I knew a talentless man named Bill Hunter. Next thing was he called himself William Carmarthenshire Hunter and people fell over themselves offering him executive jobs. Another man called Harry Rogers took the hint and blossomed forth as Harold Lancashire Rogers and now he runs a Rolls. If you have a county in your name, you can't do wrong. The boy'll live to bless me!"

Harry discreetly ordered a taxi. The cold hit Hubert in the middle of a more complicated dissertation and he fell asleep. Evidently Hubert's recuperative capacity was considerable, because when he got out he was red-eyed but perfectly steady.

All the lights were on in the living room. Harry had a

tantalizing, incompletely focused mental picture of a painting he had once seen. Mrs. Siddons—or was it Bernhardt?—frozen in some drama, all outraged matronliness and clutching a boy and a girl.

Except that Leicestershire wore his fairish, slightly curling hair fashionably long and his Carnaby Street gear always gave Harry the impression of girlishness; whereas Hildegard had on pedal pushers and her prized leather topboots, purchased last summer in Lisbon, and which—so Dora had confided—gave her hell because of some metric confusion when she ordered them. On her knee crouched an alarmed-looking Skye terrier. Harry remembered that between cookery courses Hildegard assisted at a local kennel, from which on rare occasions she brought home some small creature for the night. On the subject of pets, Hubert was adamant. No animals should be kept in cities and even budgerigars should be returned to flutter in their native Australian bush. Harry believed without proof that Hubert did not care for animals.

Now that he was observing more closely, the Inspector realized that Dora's alarm was all for her children, the usual maternal protectiveness, thought the policeman in him dismally.

Stanisgate stood, legs apart, and shot his cuff up on his thick wrist. "Midnight. I've always said I don't care, but you have to get up next day."

"They were worried about you, dear," said Dora in low key.

The Inspector faced Hildegard's avenging forefinger. "He took you to the Yard," she said and her eyes flooded.

Stanisgate's voice was a trifle thick, but authoritative. "Good God, and I've always said I won't care what you get into as long as you don't snivel." His sloe eyes raised histrionically to the ceiling.

"They were worried about you, dear," reiterated his wife.

The Skye terrier commenced to whimper as Hildegard's fat tears dropped on his fur.

"I was," said Stanisgate, to the ceiling, "identifying some miserable pickpocket who filched my wallet."

Hildegard hiccupped and clutched the Skye terrier to

her bosom. The Inspector suddenly thought that she might be attractive if she lost a few pounds and you like the intense sort of girl.

"We thought he'd framed you." Leicestershire's voice wavered. He stared at the Inspector truculently.

"Now, my son," said Hubert, speaking softly, "part of the considerable sums paid for your education included instruction in civics. The police may or may not be stupid, venal and occasionally brutal, but they do not frame law-abiding citizens. Only idiots think otherwise."

It was a freezing moment. Then Harry said softly, "What did you think I was framing your father for?"

Hildegard's sobs had stopped at her father's words and she stared frozenly at the ceiling, while her brother's eyes were looking at the carpet.

Hubert's eyes met Harry's in an expression of sardonic amusement. "A protrait of Father Christmas, Inspector. Here!" He moved very fast for his size to the drink cupboard.

"Here, you Leicestershire, a brown ale, a taste you will grow out of! Hildegard, pour yourself and your mother this stuff you brought home last summer! Harry, try this white scotch the Bleeders gave me last Christmas, a job lot no doubt. Dee, open the Bath Olivers or some of Hildegard's doings. I shall sing 'Christmas in the Workhouse' in a reedy tenor."

Stanisgate had the knack of pouring out his personality. The emotional temperature rose suddenly to match the central heating. Even Dora smiled as her daughter poured some of the Bual which Hubert had rescued from her intention to put into cakes.

Harry drained his colorless scotch. "Goodnight all."

He hurried up the stairs. No doubt a conscientious man would have crept back to listen. As it was, he locked his bedroom door, wanting no early morning confidences should they arise.

"The stew," said Hawker on Monday morning, "is more watery than I would wish. One thing, your Polly Packer scarpered. Curious business. Sergeant Crook's idea of a good night's rest apparently is to camp outside the houses of criminals in his manor. At two o'clock he was

89

lurking inside a phone box opposite the flats Packer lived in. I suppose," said Hawker, "that he had a swag of meat pies and a crate of ale."

Harry waited. Hawker talked like this when he was worried. The old man's skin was grayish, and birdlike wattles under the chin looked flabby in the morning light.

"Ah, well," said Hawker. "At three o'clock a taxi draws up. Master Packer nips smartly out the door and that's that, leaving Crook a withered pea upon the vine.

"Packer told the driver he had an urgent business engagement. The driver said he took him to London airport. We think he got a five-o'clocker to Madrid. His name don't appear anywhere, but to a man of his resources that wouldn't be hard. No trace after that."

"No leads?"

"Nothing we could apply for a search warrant for. He had no current woman living in, the rent's paid to the end of the quarter. Crook, who was rushing about all yesterday like a goosed dowager, unearthed Packer's clerk cum bookkeeper. Over the last week Polly settled up all his debts, past and future.

"When you get a man like Packer doing that, it means he doesn't want any kind of warrant out for his extradition. At the moment he's clean."

"Except perhaps for his passport." Harry usually acted as devil's advocate.

"First catch your hare," grunted Hawker. "Besides, those bloody passport things are the dickens."

"Money?"

"What the hell do you think he had in his suitcase, spats and a dicky? Anyway, Master Packer would have his pelf in Panama or Lebanon like all the fast boys. I'd like to know why he ran. Oh, I know he ran the chance of being cut or worse, but why?"

Harry said nothing and Hawker massaged his blotter with his spatulate fingers. "Porterman's going crazy. All these reports"—he indicated the pile of yellow flimsies—"add up to nothing. This man Stanisgate, your landlord, and his cursed Christmas list, tch. Know anything about him?"

"Not so much, sir."

"No personal involvement?"

"I like the family, but no."

"Well, get me a detailed report. Another thing, the pickpocket, Chenery. Porterman got him out of bed at five o'clock this morning. The usual case of amnesia, poor fellow can't remember anything about last week. Only thing is that the local boys say that Chenery's in the chips. When he's touched something good, he always gives himself away by living high, a good cigar instead of fags and scotch instead of Scotch ale."

"I can't imagine anybody getting rich by pinching Christmas card lists," grunted Harry.

"I'd have preferred to see Master Chenery fed a little cream instead of Porterman's technique," said Hawker. "He's having a protracted pub crawl on the strength of his earnings. You might take a look at him."

A copper was as efficient as his contacts, thought Harry. He had an acquaintance high in the advertising world. His friend said he'd call back about Stanisgate.

Chenery lived in Brixton and Harry caught a bus after having ascertained from a local sergeant Chenery's preferred ports of call, which extended from the Oval to parts of Herne Hill. Six bottles of sparkling grapefruit later, he found Chenery in a snug little saloon bar with two larger companions of genteel shabbiness who were prepared to listen to Chenery's view on life and the iniquities of insurance companies in particular. In return Chenery bought whisky. Harry stood next to them, ostensibly engrossed in the racing page. He ordered a light ale.

Chenery opened his wallet and Harry glimpsed a wad of notes. He thought with irony of the little pickpocket's reaction if his wallet should be lifted. Probably dog didn't eat dog.

One of the hangers-on made some remark about Chenery having come into money.

"And more where it came from." Chenery smirked.

The little man glanced round boastfully and their eyes momentarily met.

Harry saw the sudden narrowing of the guileless-looking blue eyes and knew he had been spotted for what he was.

He was certain that he had never seen Chenery before. A lot of thieves, over a lifetime of dodging, did develop a sixth sense about plainclothesmen, and a pub like this, at midday, would be filled with regulars all known to each other.

He grinned philosophically to himself in the mirror behind the bar. Chenery was muttering to his companions. They drained their drinks and without a word went out the door.

Harry thought that the big craggy-faced man serving would be the licensee, which proved to be the case.

"No trouble is there?" The big man reacted instinctively as Harry showed his warrant card.

"I just drove three good customers out."

The landlord served two new customers and returned. "I'd just as soon see the back of that little fellow."

"Comes in here a lot?"

"Oh, I reckon he's in and out of pubs all day. Generally comes in about this time for an ale. When he's flush, maybe every couple months, he'll give the scotch a good nudge. Then he's a bit obnoxious. You know, forcing drinks on people, wanting to be center of the stage."

"Who were the fellows with him?"

"Them! Oh, they usually have a couple of pints of mild each at lunchtimes. Both janitors in flats around here. Their wives do most of the work and they do the drinking."

The Inspector ordered another drink. "Does he ever have anybody with him?"

"No. Just a minute, it must have been a couple of weeks ago! He was in here about this time or a bit later, and a big fellow came in. Not much flesh on him, but going on for six foot four. Big pudgy sort of face. Black hair going gray. He sat down next to the little man and says something to him. They had a couple of drinks and then went off together."

"What day was it?"

"Let's see, I had a man from the brewery here. It'd be Friday week. Come to think of it the little fellow's never here weekends."

Harry knew that the weekends were Chenery's busy

days. Pockets filled with pay packets, crowds congregating.

The Inspector got a cab to Hammersmith and thumbed through his notebook for the addresses where Alfredo Castelano was known to have stayed. It was hard foot-slogging work. Generally the places were deserted at this hour and only the proprietors or the manageress were in the premises.

"With the best will in the world, Inspector," said one in a singsong Welsh accent, "I don't know 'em. They come and they go, like a sea. Yes, there's a few you get to know, the regulars, but I've got my hands full just keeping the place clean. . . ."

This was more or less typical as the Inspector plodded on. This was how the days passed, thought Harry. Once, as a sergeant, he had knocked at nine hundred and seventy doors to show a photograph of a small, murdered boy.

"I think I remember him," said one manageress. "He had the cut of a sailor and as my boy was merchant marine, I've a soft spot for them. But it was just a nod and a good morning. Oh, you get a few that wants to tell you their troubles but not so many."

"Scum," said another man, without passion. "Lived all their lives by cadging on the public expense. Hardly ever sober and those that are are half cracked, some of 'em licensed dope addicts just waiting for the doctor's surgery to open."

He kept on climbing icy steps and ringing bells.

"The gaffer's not in," said a small ginger-headed man. "He's lying his head off at the County Court."

"I'll come in and have a warm anyway if I may. I'm a police officer."

"You're welcome to sit in the kitchen awhile. I'm minding." There was a faint Highland lilt to the soft, pure vowels. In the grimy hall the Inspector saw that the man's left arm was a stump and that he walked painfully.

The kitchen into which he was led was large and not so dirty as he expected. The establishment evidently served some kind of meals. An antiquated coke-burning stove had its front opened so that the room was suffused with heat.

The man seated himself in a small rocking chair and picked up a sock which he proceeded dexterously to darn with his one good hand. Harry took off his overcoat and drew up a kitchen chair.

"The sod that owns this gaff," said the redheaded man softly, "physically resembles an old codfish. He has the mind of a half-stuffed parrot. He had heard somewhere that salt melts ice, so this morning at six o'clock he sprinkled it on the front steps. When I went out at six forty-five it had hardened like glass and I went down arse uppards. Twisted my ankle. Codfish is frightened I'll get legal aid—he'd have been groaning on Gerald Gardiner's doorstep by now. So it's free hoggings for yours truly for maybe a week. What rank would you be?"

"Deputy Inspector."

"You're young. Well, maybe they are learning. Perhaps you'll let me have your card. It'll terrify the gaffer into the trots—he's weak in the bowels—and maybe I can stretch things to two weeks. Not that I approve of you. I'm a Scottish anarchist, and that's different, as you are probably ignorant of such matters, from Stalinists, Trotskyites, the I.L.P. and old ladies in the Henry George Society."

"We do a short cram course," said Harry. "I even had to read *Fields, Factories and Workshops*. You know, summarize in three hundred words, writing on one side of the paper." He put a card on the table.

"I'm Joe Bliss," said the redhaired man with a kind of pride. "You got me tabbed over at the Special Branch. I hate you bastards."

"Surely," said the Inspector, "there are Marxist police, both Russian and Chinese, and police of every kind of persuasion. And by reason of your own arguments! Here we're not supposed to have any politics."

"And that," said Bliss, "shows just how bloody ignorant you are."

"Consider me withered away," said Harry, "and replaced by a female vigilante from the Primrose League. Man, you'd hang!"

Bliss smiled, but not very warmly. He sniffed. "Somewhere, the codfish learned something about cooking. He turns on an Irish stew plus dumplings—lamb flaps but very cheap and filling—and a pretty good beef stew, cooked very slow. It *is* beef; I've checked. Half an hour ago I poured in two cups of Spanish sauterne, as per instructions."

The Inspector saw that two large casseroles rested on asbestos mats at the top of the stove.

"Part of my compo from the gaffer," said Bliss, "is victuals. Join me."

Simony, or something, thought the Inspector, but was conscious of the acids gnawing at his stomach.

"Fine," he said.

And so it was. "A first-class stew," he said.

"It's not altruism," said Bliss. "The cod-faced gentleman knows he gets us in for good cheap grub. So he hasn't bought a mattress for ten years and God knows where he got 'em from originally. Some people say it was from a closed-down leper hospital in Sierra Leone. That's life, brother! Down the street there's a house where the mattresses are beautiful and not a louse in the place. But the food brings you down with ulcers after a week. On balance, I go for the grub."

They ate companionably until Bliss cleared his second helping away with his bread.

"Now, what was it you wanted?"

Harry took the postcard print of Castelano from his breast pocket and flipped it over the table.

"His name was Castelano, a pavement artist."

"What's he done?"

"Did you not hear? His skull got under the wheel of a car and we are looking for the driver."

Bliss fidgeted.

The Inspector said, "He was a poor devil that got done over, maybe on purpose."

Bliss looked at the stump of his arm and the Inspector realized that he was older than he had thought. "I get a pension for that," he said, "and live in these places. A matter of principle. I told you that I don't like you. But anyway a Spaniard is the guy in the photo, although it's a rotten likeness."

95

"Taken in the morgue."

"Tsch. As I said, he was a Spaniard and that interested me. I had a brother that was killed there in '37. I speak the language a little."

"You talked to him?"

"He had the accent. We were in a place in Putney. I said, 'Qué tal, hombre?' meaning 'what goes, pal?' and he gave me a shifty look. Next day he moved out. That's all right, I'd spoken out of turn. Funny old world, this."

"Somebody might have driven a car over his head; twice."

Bliss made a little whining noise. "I observe. I've trained myself. There were two of them, working different pitches." Harry passed over the picture of George Brown. He held his breath.

Bliss looked. "It's a leveler all right, but that's the second one. What happened to him?"

"He was in bad shape and he died in his room of neglect. I suspect he was frightened to go out."

"I'll be damned," said Bliss. "Here." He limped over to the cupboard and returned with two thick glasses. "The gaffer's gin, good Dutch stuff he says he has to drink because of the stones in his kidneys. I'll bleed him white, the old sod!"

The Inspector sipped. It was very good gin.

Bliss drank his in three quick swallows.

"Nobody looks at screevers. If you look in their direction you only see the daubs, not the man. Usually it's a tanner in the cap and a nice warm, benevolent feeling that you've done your yearly bit for the poor. I get around a lot. Oh, yes, I'm an agitator, you ask them at the Special Branch, and I use my eyes. These two men ran at least eight pitches between 'em. Used to nip around from one to the other, hopping around like sparrows, on and off the buses. At first I thought one of the takeover boys had rationalized the industry, as they say." The ginger-haired man wheezed with amusement. "Christ knows what they were up to, hopping about like that. Not money, because you get virtually nothing dropped in your cap if you aren't there. I checked that with an old chap who carries a tray of laces around. I thought of police spies, but one of them was surely Spanish and no cop ever got to look as seedy as the other. I thought they were up to something."

"You saw them together?"

Bliss had gone back to his sock-mending.

"They were generally like Box and Cox or those little manikins that used to pop in and out of clocks. But I saw 'em together four or five times."

"Where?"

"I'm not kidding about my politics." Bliss's cold eyes held the Inspector's steadily. "There are times when I have to meet one or two people and we don't want to be seen. You know enough to know that you either do that in a place where few people ever go, or else somewhere which is teeming with folk. I saw those two in both kinds of places, though they didn't see me."

"Go on," said the Inspector.

"I've maybe said more than enough. The gaffer's due back in half an hour and if he sees you personally, he'll have a stroke, with all he's got on his conscience. So what about going back to directing traffic?"

"My boss likes me to get nice signed statements in writing."

"That's nice of him. Look, now, Deputy Inspector, maybe tonight I'll write out a piece. What I've told you and anything else I remember. I don't like working-class battlers being run over. But on the other hand, maybe I won't and then we'll see what happens."

Bliss acknowledged Harry's farewell with the briefest of nods.

Back at the office, Harry reported to Hawker.

"Oh, ten to one Chenery's seen you somewhere. These fellows collect our faces, you know. Let's see about Bliss." The Superintendent made a telephone call.

"He's the real McCoy all right. On the potentially dangerous list. One of these tough, sentimental Scots. Construction worker, and a broken cable took off his arm. He was offered a job for life in the store plus a pension. Enough to live on. He took the latter and came south. He's currently suspected of circulating subversive literature to members of the armed forces. Hm. Anything on Stanisgate?"

"Not yet, sir."

"Well, don't dawdle."

His friend came through at seven-thirty.

"I had to give quite a bit of thought to your problem. Main difficulty was the aversion toward talking about an acquaintance to the police."

"We come across it all the time," said Harry. "Nobody splits to the headmaster."

"Luckily I know rather well a fellow who deals with Blood, Cupping. And I happened to be instrumental in getting him his present job. Even so, I had to give him a little thesis on civic duty. You don't know how convincing I can be in the course of morality."

"I know," said Harry, "but not about the morality!"

"Well, I sold him." His friend chuckled. "He'll remain anonymous. If you come over now, I'll have him ready to sing in five minutes. Note my professional terminology."

"That went out with Edgar Wallace," said the Inspector. "I'll be over."

The anonymous gentleman was very tall and bony, with thick black eyebrows that gesticulated according to their owner's moods which seemed generally gloomy. He stared under them at Harry.

"I understand you want a report on Hubert Stanisgate."

"Well, we call it a confidential profile. The file does not record the sources and in certain circumstances it is thereafter destroyed."

The man laughed without a great deal of humor. "We've both been schooled in double talk, Inspector. In fact you want a run-down on Stanisgate, warts and all. Huh?"

God of machines, thought Harry, protector of policemen, the tried approach always worked. Careful with the slight, embarrassed stammer! "Well, sir, that does, er, seem to, er sum it up, with as much background as possible."

"Well, my own position is that I've dealt with Blood, Cupping, Fulsome for four years. We use three agencies for different divisions.

"First the agency. Blood, Cupping . . ."

98

"Known as the Bleeders . . ." Harry said, attempting to establish some familiarity as he had been told in training lectures.

A thin smile greeted him. "No doubt there are office jokes as in every establishment. Anyway Major Blood, who founded them in 1928, died some time ago. Cupping is an accountant, very good one, F.S.A. Fulsome is getting old and a bit pompous, but he knows every inch of the road. Both of them know how to pick first-class staff. A good medium-sized agency which grows a little larger each year. I'll find out what they write. . . ." A bony arm stretched for the telephone.

"No, no," the Inspector said, "don't trouble."

"As to Hubert Stanisgate," said the bony man. "He was around twenty years ago as a freelance artist, at a time when there was a shortage. He learned fast and made a living, specialized on exploded drawings of machinery. Ten years ago he joined B.C.F. as a staffer and six years ago became one of their art directors. His reputation is hardworking competence. If they fired him, he could get a job next day. No drink problem. You know him, do you?"

"Yes."

"He's not a bad fellow, courteous to people under him, touchy with those over him. Doesn't suffer fools gladly, and of course the trouble with Stanisgate is that most people appear fools to him."

"Any special friends?"

"He knows a lot of people. We all do in this profession. My impression is that he keeps any close friendships outside his work. I think that people are often a bit afraid of Stanisgate; a certain brutal nonconformity. Oh, one thing. A fellow I talked to in the poster business has a dim memory that Stanisgate had another name when he first came to London, but couldn't remember what."

"You say 'came to London.' Do you know where from?"

The black eyebrows knitted. "Funny thing, just got that impression, and I don't know from where. His accent is standard, flattish London suburbia."

"Did he have a job before he joined the agency?"

"No. He was out of the Army. Cupping took him on on the strength of his artwork. I don't suppose it was a matter for references."

"And he's in no trouble?"

"Trouble? No, no! Except, of course, this domestic trouble."

"What might that be?"

"I understand it's a sick child. At any rate he's been taking time off over the past six weeks. One of the things in this job is that one often works long hours, but on the other hand there's more consideration in any emergency of this nature than in some other spheres."

Harry felt his face tighten and he instinctively leaned over the desk. "You are sure of this?"

"My dear Inspector, I spent two hours this afternoon in what I am sure are known as 'discreet inquiries.' As it happens, on two occasions the relevant account executive at B.C.F. has taken me through into Stanisgate's studio and explained that he was taking time off."

"Thank you, sir." He said goodbye to the bony man.

Chapter 4

At six o'clock came a thunderous knocking at the Inspector's door. When he huddled into his dressing gown—the central heating never really seemed adequate at that hour—he saw Leicestershire's long anxious face peering at him through the electric light.

"Didn't you hear?"

"I slept like the dead. Hear what?"

"There was a policeman hammering at the door and an old man in a car outside. The policeman said there is a superintendent in the car and you're wanted as soon as you're dressed. He said to tell you there's an electric razor in the car."

Hawker was slumped in the back seat of the big Austin and his eyes blinked tiredly at the Inspector.

"Joe Chenery's in hospital, badly cut. They found him lying in a side street a mile away. He'd been knocked about as well as having the razor. Expert job, he'll never look the same. Must have been doing a little of the black and the bloke wouldn't stand it."

Joe had a room to himself, with a uniformed constable seated in the corner. Hawker looked in and went to see the house surgeon.

"His face is in a bad way," said the young man. "Maybe they can do some plastic work later. He lost quite a lot of blood, but we put that back. And he was bruised around the loins and stomach, no internal injuries, so we think."

"So it's nothing serious?"

"Well." The house surgeon looked at Hawker as if seeing him for the first time. "At the age of sixty it's no picnic being kicked in the stomach and losing a dangerous

101

amount of blood. He's a heavy drinker by the signs, heart not so good."

"Can he talk?"

"Jesus," said the young doctor, "talk about swear, what a master! He's learned not to move his mouth much, and we took his choppers out, so he's not too distinct, but you can hear him!"

"Well, then," said Higgins briskly, "he's not seriously ill and can talk. So I can have a few words with him."

The young man looked as though he had been trapped. "Of course," said Hawker, "you'd be present."

"Well . . ."

"Tell you what," said the Superintendent, "get three chairs taken in there. You sit at the side of the constable and the Inspector and I'll sit by the poor old chap's bed."

The large guileless blue eyes peered from the swathing bandages. Hawker lowered himself heavily upon the chair.

"Well, Joe Chenery! You won't remember me, Jack Hawker!"

Hawker switched his face to look at Harry as he lowered himself into a chair. "Old Joe's one of the smartest. When I got out of uniform I was on the pleasure steamers with old Sloper Thom as my sergeant. Old Sloper Thom." His eyes flickered toward the bed. "Well, well, the dear old fellow's now eighty-eight and living at Worthing. On the pier every day. He did all right, because he bought some row houses in Highgate, which they replaced by blocks of luxury flats. Yes"—Hawker fumbled in his pocket—"I remember Joe Chenery likes a good cigar. These young fellows"—he eyed Harry with contempt—"'don't know what a smoke's like. Can't afford it. I remember when you got a lovely smoke for sevenpence. Anyway, here are half a dozen of the Green Upmanns that I keep for the Commissioner. Put them on the locker, Inspector! Well! Well! Time flies! Joe was working with Snouty Quinn, who ran the three-card lay. We used to chase 'em round the ship but Joe was much too smart for me. It was the old *Golden Eagle*, running to Calais, that I remember best. . . ."

Hawker's voice had the soft droning quality of a bluebottle in a meat safe and tiredness hit Harry so that he felt his spine slump and the words flow over him.

Presently he felt Hawker tap his knee. "Those were the days, Inspector. This mark got on board wearing horrible check trousers. If anybody asked for it, this fellow did. Anyway, Snouty Quinn, who loved a bet, said he'd have these trousers before they docked at Margate."

Hawker's eyes turned to the man in the bed. "Lord love us, I won't forget that. Snouty Quinn got his trousers half an hour off the Margate Pier, and there was the bloke with a blanket wrapped round him and a steward running around like a headless fowl saying he couldn't take it ashore as it was company property. Ah, well!"

There was a gobbling noise from the bed. The wide blue eyes were fixed on Hawker, who leaned over.

"Well, I'll be damned," said the Superintendent. "Of course, it was Sailor Bell who made the bet and got the trousers, Lord knows how!" He slapped his head with an open palm. "My memory's going. But it was the *Golden Eagle*, Joe?" The old man's voice had an appealing note and he cupped his ear to listen to the answering gobble.

"Well, at least I got the boat right," said Hawker. His neck swiveled abruptly. "Who did you, Joe? Who did you?" The voice was a little whiplash of sound.

Harry saw the lids come down over the baby-blue eyes. A kind of wail came out of the Chenery's open mouth.

The Superintendent talked fast and earnestly. "You'll be safe with us, Joe, we'll be guarding you day and night. And it won't do you any harm to keep in with us. . . ."

The old pickpocket thrust a naked arm out of the bed and made as though to push the Superintendent away.

"I think that's enough," called the house surgeon, but Hawker was already on his feet. Harry saw spatulate fingers reach out and pocket the cigars.

"When are you relieved?" Hawker asked the constable in a low voice.

"Midday, sir."

"You'll be keeping on until he leaves. It's important that I should know immediately if he lets anything out."

"He won't," said the uniformed man. "Scared as a rabbit when he sees a stoat."

Hawker nodded. "He might talk in his sleep."

In the police car he handed Harry a cigar. "The hypothesis is that somebody hired that little rat to do a job. When Porterman started talking about murder, Joe saw his way to put a squeeze on. So he got taught a lesson."

"I wonder why they didn't knock him off?"

"And have another murder investigation under way? As it is, there isn't even a complaint. The local boys will do what they can, but Chenery will walk out of that hospital and that's that. One thing, it's established that it's gang work. Chenery thought he could stand over the head, so a couple of boys collected him."

"Well," said the Inspector, "it could be that they were hired for this job."

"Who would you hire?"

"Well, last I heard the Fat Chap is still hanging around in the Brewer Street vicinity. You wouldn't even have to have much in the way of criminal connections to have heard of the Fat Chap. He'd fix up anything if the price was right."

"And you'd find yourself in the fire. The Fat Chap wouldn't rest until he found what your angle was. No, no." Hawker yawned and stretched and reached out to tell the driver to park when he found it convenient.

"I don't know whether you know, but I spent a couple of years in Paris after the war. There were a lot of bad men around, deserters a lot of them. I worked with the city force—the Prefecture—mostly. There was a lot of rivalry between them and the Sûreté in those days. They wouldn't even exchange information.

"Christ, it's a wonder I lived, all the drink I got through. It was hanging about in bars all day listening and I never did get the hang of spinning one drink out all day. In some places I'd be known to the barman and he'd keep a brandy bottle filled with the stuff the hostesses drank in the clubs. A dead ringer for good brandy, but non-alcoholic and tasting faintly ginger. Filthy stuff, but better than hob nails on your liver.

"Well, the Sûreté and the Prefecture are under one boss nowadays and they say it's sweetness and light. I thought to myself, There are some old men who get bitter as age creeps up." Hawker showed his big yellow teeth. "Not like me in my mellowed autumnal tints.

"So I went through the lists and picked a man I used to know. He hated the Sûreté then, and I heard that a Sûreté man had jumped over him last year when they were both up for commissionership. So I flew over at midday yesterday. If I'm lucky, I might find somebody who'll okay the expenses; if I don't, it doesn't matter. I had my best supper for ten years, just a bit of liver fried in butter while I looked on, a salad, a couple of rolls, butter and a big board covered with cheese. How can they be so bitchy when they eat that cooking?"

"It's the wine."

Hawker laughed through his cigar smoke. "The man I saw doesn't use alcohol and is a vegetarian. My God, he had a nut steak at this little place we went to."

"I wonder they served you with meat."

"You know the French! My friend just looked at 'em and they went out and came back with the liver and a bottle of wine. Probably run a knocking shop upstairs!"

It was always difficult for Harry to decide whether the old man was serious or not.

"I'd phoned this friend and he pretty well whooped for joy. He goes on pension next month and I gather he's already writing his scabrous reminiscences. God, what a lot! I'd telephoned him, and he'd got sufficient rank to get a rundown.

"Wolfe, the fellow who put through the original query, is the man they employ on occasions diplomatique, the kid glove stuff with a potential political sting.

"Anyway my friend rubbed his hands and used his rank to get me this story.

"Fundamentally it was the same story as Jarvey told. One, if the paintings are in France—and a lot are of French origin, remember—the Ministry of Fine Arts will fight like a tigress to prevent them going out. On the other hand, if they have crossed the border, well, the Foreign Office could earn a little gratitude by tipping Moscow off.

"As to the men involved, Bron alias Brown had the

nickname of Ten per Cent. That was his speciality, dealing in any kind of dubious articles on a flat percentage of the sale price. In the immediate postwar years he made a lot of money. The one thing that does emerge is that he was a physical coward. The other fellow is thought to have been christened Jesus Moreno and comes from Vigo. They breed seamen there and he was third mate on a freighter for a few years, becoming an expert smuggler, well known, an adept at moving things across frontiers. There was an association between the two men. Bron would accept some stolen article and find a market for it, say, in central America. Moreno would attend to the moving of it. This man Moreno, alias Castelano, was a tough physical specimen.

"Both were just about broke, so my informant thinks. Easy come, easy go. When he was flush, Moreno spent money like a madman and Bron had taken a series of tosses in property investment.

"Then this rumor came along and crystallized and grew. Moreno and Bron would be wealthy men if they pulled it off.

"You know," grunted the Super, "the French use informers to a much greater extent than we do and there are a lot of people who make a good living partly by informing, as well as the concierges. The information was that Bron and Moreno were working with an Englishman named Hubert Harcourt in the early stages of the deal, but that they had quarreled with him."

He fished in his breast pocket. "You read the flimsy while I enjoy my smoke. I telephoned Records at eleven last night."

Hubert Elderson Harcourt [read the report] was born in Bristol, January 20, 1921. He was the illegitimate son of the late James Elderson and the late Miss Maude Harcourt. Educated at two inferior private schools (now defunct) near Deal until seventeen. School certificate, distinction in art. Called up for Army Service 1940 (December). Described himself as an art student living at a Brixton address. Both parents deceased, no living relative. At various times promoted to lance-corporal. Behavior described as fair.

(Note. This man won the D.C.M. at Caen, August 7, 1944, citation mentioning extreme coolness under heavy enemy fire.) In army of occupation until January 1947. His name appears in the special dossier on black market activities. Quote, Harcourt is suspected to maintain relations with deserters engaged in criminal activities and to be a trafficker in petrol, unquote. Never charged. In December 1942 he was given leave. On December 16 he was arrested at Croyden wearing the uniform of a colonel, with D.S.O. and Bar. In his wallet were cards engraved Colonel Sir Hubert Harcourt, D.S.O. A local constable spotted something was phony and summoned the M.P.s. Harcourt made a brief statement that it was done quite innocently so he could have a better time over Christmas. The Army disciplined him but did not consider it much more than a prank.

No fingerprints taken, but his name entered in our master file and cross-indexed to "Impersonation."

Background to date. Extensive inquiries—see further —revealed nobody intimate with Harcourt, not any personal background. Description: 6 ft. 2½ inches, well built, very dark eyes, blond hair, no scars. He was remustered a lot in the Army, inference being that people didn't particularly want him around. Perhaps the best comment is from a former platoon sergeant who said, "Harcourt was an intelligent brute with plenty of guts."

In 1947 there were outbreaks of armed robbery. On March 3 two young clerks who had collected a small payroll walked down Marsden Street, Islington, turned a corner and were set on and menaced with knives by three men, who had parked three stolen motorbikes. However, both clerks shared the hobby of amateur wrestling. In the affray, one clerk was stabbed to death, but the other got a headlock on one of the thieves—Jovics, a Polish deserter. Of the other two thieves, one panicked, dived for his motorcycle, tripped and broke an ankle. He was A. Burton, an English deserter. The third man walked quietly down a side street and out of the picture. He went by the name of Robinson, but Burton had seen him in Germany and knew him as Hubert Harcourt. Jovics and Burton were hanged in Pentonville, May 27, 1947. Some attempt was made by counsel to pin the stabbing on Harcourt, although it was no defense. (N.B. Chief Inspector in charge thought Jovics did the stabbing.) Before execution, Burton—described as a man of low intelligence, easily led—said Harcourt, whom they met in a café near Fleet Street, talked them into the attempt. He said Harcourt kept their combined capital amounting to fourteen pounds odd.

No further record of Harcourt appears. It was concluded that shortage of money would force him to attempt further robberies, but his name or description appears in no further piece of information.

Procedure. Usual inquiries. All men taking new jobs, with special reference to the merchant marine, were checked over a three-monthly period. Result, negative. Periodic spot checks for twelve months. Negative.

"A damned rum thing, this report," said Harry.

"I would have said he threw himself into the Thames and got caught in one of the holes," said Hawker. "To disappear like that with a capital charge involved and every copper looking for him. . . ."

"Still livin' on his fourteen quid, no doubt. And nothing heard until now."

"Not quite that," said Hawker. "When I got home in the middle of the night, this report had been delivered, but an addendum had been phoned through, much to my old housekeeper's disgust. There have been four inquiries over the years, two from France, one from Germany and one from the F.B.I., asking about a criminal named Hubert H.—on one occasion—and plain Harcourt on another. Each inquiry involving some big robbery, a warehouseful of furs from Manhattan, a couple of truckfuls of optical lenses outside Bremen, another fur robbery in Paris and, eighteen months ago, the contents of a spice warehouse at Dijon. All very valuable and needing careful handling. I'd say he'd be a fence specializing in such stuff. Of course, we had nothing useful to provide. But it looks as if somehow he got a passport and operates a lot abroad."

Hawker stared gloomily through his side window into the pale, watery sky.

"Nine forty-five," the old policeman said listlessly. "Okay, driver, we'll get going."

Both the Inspector and the Superintendent were lost in their own thoughts for the rest of the journey.

As they got out of the car, Hawker said, "I'll put the word out about Harcourt. That kind of high-class fencing is usually planned around the West End. You've got a good source there, haven't you?"

"Yes, sir, nasty little man named Tosher."

"Well, I'll authorize anything reasonable for a lead."

"And I got a profile on my landlord, sir. I'll shoot it up to you before I go."

It was ten forty-five by the time he reached the shop that Tosher managed and the little man was just unlocking the front door.

The Inspector supposed that there would be no early demand for the piles of trusses, elastic stockings and two books on the history of flogging which occupied the window. It was rum, thought Harry, that all the famous places one reads about, in any capital city, seemed to have dozens of similar shops in streets nearby. Tosher had not seen him and he paused for a moment and tugged his overcoat closer.

A born informer, thought Harry, as he paused in the darkness of the shop and watched the little man desultorily flicking a handkerchief at boxes on the shelf.

A naked electric bulb lit up.

"Oh, it's you, Inspector."

Tosher wore dark glasses. Without them his eyes did not look pleasant. He was an alcoholic. The Inspector had never seen him drunk and incapable. Tosher's normal condition resembled anesthesia, his bodily movements jerky and profound. He had friends in every pub in the square mile, and during the day Tosher was constantly locking up for a quarter of an hour. For topping up, to keep the slight glow flickering in his stomach, Tosher used bottles of British port, which he periodically carried in a black Gladstone bag and concealed behind the boxes of rubber goods.

"Not busy, eh?"

"It brightens at night, Inspector, it brightens in the evening," Tosher said in his gray voice.

Harry rested his elbow on the table. "Ever heard of a Hubert Harcourt, or Hubert H.?"

The pain of the morning had made Tosher's pasty

forehead wrinkle. He reached under the counter flap and came up with a tooth glass.

In a series of jerky movements he reached behind the boxes on the shelf, withdrew a bottle, slopped three inches of dull reddish fluid into the glass and drained it. A fruity smell suffused the little shop and Tosher fumbled in the cash drawer and withdrew a bottle of chlorophyll tablets. He sucked one as he thought.

"I know a Percy Harcourt, stout build, drinks gin, who works in Fleet Street but, um, no, it doesn't ring a bell."

"It's urgent, Tosher. He's got some connection with hot goods."

"What's it worth to me?"

"The maximum, Tosher, and could be a bonus if I can swing it."

Tosher's thin fingers fumbled against the sticking plaster on his cheek. "Won't be much today—it brightens up in the evenings. I'll start making a few inquiries at eleven-thirty."

"Do that. I'll try to call in around nine."

Harry looked at his work sheet. Chief Inspector Porterman wanted him to go to the Huntingtower Galleries to check something with the manageress. "Because you know her," Porterman had explained on the intercom, but actually, thought Harry, as a device to obtain the services of somebody not attached to your squad.

Having seen it only by night, the Inspector had retained the image of a locked deserted building, and he was surprised to find the glass and wrought-iron door ajar and the sound of activity coming from within.

Inside were some dozen people, and in the air was the kind of subdued hum, punctuated by an occasional darting shrill cry, that the Inspector associated with cultural occasions. He recognized a neck and tapped a shoulder.

"Why, Harry." Blenkinsop's brown eyes looked round. "Getting cultural. Elizabeth been at you?"

"Don't be an ass, old man, but why all this?"

"An exhibiton of paintings by Barcelonians. They were flown in yesterday and Dol Spotting phoned me up for a preview."

"Any good?"

Blenkinsop's beard waved. "I'm not enthused. Too sophisticated I think, but they'll have their admirers."

"A word in your hirsute ear." Harry led him behind a triangle of plasterboard which acted as a background for a green figurine.

"I've been thinking, Blenkinsop, about your theory about dressing like a painter and taking canvases through customs lines."

Brown eyes looked at him shrewdly. "I forgot your Elizabeth went to East Germany last summer. Well, I said what first popped into my mind. Mark you, there's every chance that somebody like a painter would get through with a cursory glance. On the other hand, you might run into a spot check, and the Curtain countries would certainly take a close look. The canvas is obviously old when you look at the back. I'd say, Harry, that they would use some professional smuggler's trick, false-bottomed suitcases."

"Not like you to make misleading statements," the Inspector grunted.

"It rocked me a lot," said Blenkinsop. "Hell, man, I get my living out of paintings. What happens if a hundred masterpieces suddenly turn up? What does it do to values? No wonder somebody knocked Huntingtower off.

Harry refused to rise. "How is the authentification going?"

"Five of us have put in thirty hours each. Of course, only fifty per cent of the lab tests are through."

"And the result?"

Blenkinsop's forehead wrinkled in discomfort. "Well, the lab tests indicate nothing abnormal: pigment and canvas as they should be. As for appraisal, well provisionally we see no reason to believe that the canvases are other than what they purport to be."

"That's a mouthful of expertise. I'd like to see what a good Q.C. could do to you."

"Come off it, Harry." Blenkinsop's hands made little pawing motions. "It's our living and as explosive a parcel as was ever dumped into anybody's lap. There was a Tiepolo that was last heard of in 1741. . . ."

"I appreciate it, friend," said Harry, "but off the record?"

"All genuine, I'm afraid. Oh, old Horningham—he's been at it so long that he looks Italian—was churning around that the Tiepolo might have been painted by a student, but getting a decision out of him is like getting blood out of a stone."

"Who's that with Miss Spotting?" The Inspector had been watching a stocky man, with very broad shoulders, and a mop of white, curling hair over a very red face.

"Oh, apparently he's Huntingtower's elder brother and heir from Edinburgh. Man named MacGlaishen."

"I'd better introduce myself."

The Inspector walked over.

"What, eh what? Inspector! I saw a Chief Inspector yesterday."

"I was sent round to have a look. Good morning, Miss Spotting. I've a couple of small questions for you, if you please. Perhaps we should go in the downstairs office."

MacGlaishen followed them in.

"It's only a few minor matters." The Inspector asked half a dozen questions regarding Huntingtower's business associates. It took only a few minutes.

Closing his notebook, the Inspector said, "So you're going ahead with this exhibition?"

"Opens Wednesday. Remind me, miss, to phone the printer again. Yes, I'll be selling the gallery and it's easier to sell a going concern. My brother owned this section of the building."

Miss Spotting excused herself.

"He was younger than you, sir?"

MacGlaishen showed no resentment. "Thirteen years, child of a second marriage. We came from a croft originally. Grandfather and father were packmen, dreadful hard work and tramping in all weathers, but father scraped together a wee bit of capital. Paul was at school, and then the Army took him. When he got out, he found I'd looked after his little bit so that he had a tidy little stake. Not so big but a nice start for a young man. He wanted to go south. Maybe as well. Two brothers in the same business in the same place may not be a good thing.

Well, south he came with his bit of capital, and he didn't do badly on the whole. Though I think he would have done better if he hadn't specialized in pictures. But who knows," demanded Mr. MacGlaishen unexpectedly in his hard aggressive voice, "what goes on in the human heart?"

"No, indeed," said the Inspector, wiping his forehead with a handkerchief.

"Yes, it is hot, so I'll turn off the gas fire," said Mac-Glaishen, stooping. "People won't buy when they're cold which is why we have to spend all the money on heating. But today"—he laughed—"there's nobody spending.

"Where was I? Yes, to be sure. I deal in old furniture. Now I have a table, say a refectory. I might have paid too much for it, on rare occasions I have, but the point," said Mr. MacGlaishen, with a kind of hard passion, "is that I have a table, a good substantial bit of furniture, whereas that out there . . ." He shook his mop of white hair so that it ruffed like the crest of a cockatoo.

"You kept in touch?"

"Now," said MacGlaishen, "I don't write letters. What's the point in chew-chewing over five hundred miles. If I came to London, maybe three times a year, I'd drop a card and we'd see each other. Paul never came north. As far as correspondence is concerned, of course, when he was in general dealing, we'd do a fair bit together. Since he concentrated on contemporary"—MacGlaishen rolled the word contemptuously—"he was outside my field. Still, Paul had the nose. Quite often he'd write me about something he'd seen, and sometimes I'd say yes and then he'd get his trifle of commission."

"He didn't write anything about a painting by Seurat?"

"Seurat." Mr. MacGlaishen's cheek empurpled and he started in his chair. "What was the name? James. You'd be the man who lost my priceless masterpiece. Twenty thousand pounds it's worth. A bearded fellow out there told me. And you had it in your custody and lost it."

"Well, Mr., er, MacGlaishen," said the Inspector glacially, "that depends on who owned it."

"It's part of my estate!"

"If proven."

"Possession's nine points of the law."

113

"Not in England. Back home you'd better inquire of the Fiscal."

"Now," said Mr. MacGlaishen, after a few seconds pause, "why are we raising our voices? It's just—as you'll appreciate—that Miss Spotting told me what a plum it was. Well, no, there was no mention in his letters of any paintings. The last was about a commode, with the liner missing and heavily restored, which might have been partly Louis Fourteen. When they told me of his death, I flew down here, at my own expense, and no sooner had I gone than the local police came round and my boy gave them the file of Paul's letters. I'd have seen them damned."

"I'm sorry, sir, but you'll appreciate that in the course of our work we have to ask unpleasant questions. What was your brother's sex life, if you are aware of it?"

MacGlaishen's stout, pugnacious jaw dropped a trifle. "We didn't talk about *that*." Contempt underflavored with sabbatarianism tinged his voice. Then his eyes became alarmed, and his voice a husky whisper. "I thought she"—MacGlaishen's eyes sought the ceiling—"was familiar. 'Paul this' and 'Paul that.' Tell me, Inspector, there's no commitment, no common law commitment?"

"I'd be pretty sure not, sir. Meanwhile, I'll go upstairs. I believe we have two men here."

"That you have. It's been a rare eye opener. They looked under the lavatory seats. They are in the library upstairs. I told them that we'd want the downstairs cleared first. They are finishing up, I think."

Mr. MacGlaishen tramped remorselessly behind the Inspector as he opened the door leading from the little downstairs office to the stairway. Two young men in uniforms were in the library. The Inspector knew both of them slightly.

"What cheer?" he said.

"Phew, sir," said the eldest. "Two thousand volumes and we've taken a look see in each. We feel like a couple of book worms. Nothing. All shipshape and correct. Each book had an index card, only one missing."

"And what's that," said MacGlaishen quickly.

The constable proffered a card, and Harry read it over MacGlaishen's shoulder:

"*My Boulevard Years* by Henry du Cane Phipps (1st edition, John Lane, 1898). Du Cane Phipps, a third-rate portrait painter and engraver, was a remittance man, and an accurate source of trivial Parisian gossip between 1860 and 1890. Died Felixstowe, 1930."

The annotation was in very small neat writing.

"Miss Spotting says that he never lent books," said the constable.

"A man who lends books is a fool," intoned Mac-Glaishen.

Inspector James had been feeling a certain tiredness concerning MacGlaishen.

"Surely," he said piously, "there is an obligation to lend scriptural works."

"Inspector," said MacGlaishen, with no apparent rancor, "without this bit of an estate I'd sell up at a conservative seventy-nine thousand. I hope that at my age you are in the same position."

The constables stared pie-faced at the ceiling.

"Game, set, match, to you, I think," said Harry. "I won't detain you any more, Mr. MacGlaishen."

He watched the broad back go out the door.

"Well, Fielding, nothing spectacular?"

"No, sir, dead loss here. All records in good shape, all dealings on the up and up. He either destroyed private correspondence or didn't have any. Clean as a whistle." He waved his hand at the bookshelves. "I got the local librarian round. Some very valuable stuff among it. Old MacGlaishen rubs his hands and smiles."

"Hm," said Harry. "No leads."

"Never seen anything like it," said the constable with the authority of his twenty-three years. "No lead on the car, nobody saw anything. The Super's had the crime lab fairly groveling around. They *think* he came into the alley and was garroted. Must have been surprised, because he didn't struggle. Practically instantaneous. The old surgeon says it would be like 'slipping into a great inkwell.' Funny old devil! The Chief asked him, straightfaced, 'What color ink?' and the old chap said he thought a mixture of black and red. There must have been more than one, the lab boys think. They lifted him, carried him through the side door and left him under that canvas. The whole thing would take maybe a minute and a half."

Harry went downstairs. There were more people in the salon and he saw MacGlaishen bobbing and bowing and handshaking.

"Well, well, I'm surprised to find you in this gallery."

Harry smelt the perfume of good scotch whisky. He looked up to meet the pouched, genial dark eyes of Mr. Samuel Lovers.

"And I didn't know you connoisseured these arts, sir."

"Well, no, but I understand I found his hat. Had a reporter waiting on my doorstep when I got home. Told him there had been a white rabbit in it that got away. He didn't take it kindly." Lovers gave his infectious, booming laugh and the Inspector joined in. Heads turned.

"Plasticity," boomed Lovers, cupping his hands at an abstract. "Got that out of the Queen," he said sotto voce to the Inspector. "Frankly I don't understand it. Anyway, it's a gray dull day, and quite slack at the office. Saw you come in. I found all the bods are here by invitation, but a very charming lady told me I could stay."

Mr. Lovers smiled broadly at Miss Spotting who had come across to them. A womanizer, thought Harry, amused, as the smile crossed the boundary of a leer. Now he really looked at her, Miss Spotting had quite a spectacular figure, and seemed amused by Lovers, who looked at his watch and said, "It is two minutes to one, and I wondered if a drink and sandwich would be in order. I saw a pub along the way and perhaps. . . ?"

The pub was rather a hostile specimen of brewery Regency. Watching the burly man, the Inspector thought that a pub was his natural milieu.

Lovers expertly set down the three drinks and a plate of sandwiches. "I must say I prefer a pub to look like a pub and not a ladies' room in a film, but the sandwiches look rather good."

"Why your sudden interest in art, Mr. Lovers?" Dolores Spotting asked presently.

116

"Well, I suppose curiosity, but partly because I saw the Inspector in the distance going in and I had something to tell him. But by the time I'd crossed the road and followed him in, you both and another fellow were going upstairs. So I looked around and presently you came out and asked me what I was doing."

"Well, you don't look an art gallery type." Miss Spotting smiled.

"Perhaps that's as well. There was a fellow there like a dog in a thicket. Never saw anybody carrying so much hair about."

"You know," said Miss Spotting, "most of the people in the business look like bank clerks, really, so an occasional beard is rather pleasant."

Lovers caressed his walrus mustache. "I suppose I can't throw stones, but at least I have it clipped."

Harry left them to get another round.

"Well, cheers!" said Lovers. "What I wanted to tell you was that on the night of the murder I was walking back home. We've got a couple of contracts that mean that I stay up until about midnight on Friday nights, nip home and have three or four hours' nap, and away again at five on Saturday morning. Well now"—he gave his broad grin—"I won't say that my Friday evenings are arid, but I was sober enough. A bit late, maybe, because a fork lift had jammed. I would have been within two hundred yards of Merge's Alley—Merge was an ex-pawnbroker turned jerry builder in the seventies, by the way—when I saw a man walking very fast. He was about my height, or over six feet that is, and walked with this peculiar fast, loping action. Lope, I suppose that's the word. He came from the direction of the alley, and I saw him for maybe a second under a light, like a photograph. Big fellow, fresh complexion, big nose, wide-spaced black eyes, brown coat and odd-looking soft brown hat. Something made me think, You've been up to something, old chap, and then he was past me and going into the distance because he walked so fast."

"Could you fix the time and place?"

"The place, well, I imagine, yes, if I walked over the same ground at night. In fact I made a little sketch from memory. Here." He passed over a piece of paper. "As to time, well, frankly, when the grog's in, the sense of time is out. Normally, I let myself in my flat at ten past midnight, a couple of minutes either way, but what with the breakdown and my own fury resulting in recourse to the bottle I keep in my desk at the warehouse, well . . ."

"Are you . . ." The Inspector stopped delicately.

"A bachelor with no resident concubines. A lady comes in and cleans in the mornings. And the foreman at the warehouse went before I left, so as to the time factor you could cut me into ribbons. But I do remember this fellow as distinct as if he were here."

It was, Harry realized, heavily, a quite good word picture of Hubert Stanisgate.

"Well," he said, "I might get you to try an identification."

"I'd like that," said Lovers, earnestly. "I'd like to see the swine hang. This has always been a law-abiding district. In fact in the 1830s . . ." He broke off. "Sorry, but as you may have gathered I'm a nut about local history. Anyway, I hope it may help."

"Well, yes. You probably know enough about police work to realize that we willingly, or at any rate have to, work our way through hundreds of leads which prove dud. Anyway, in this one we're at the stage of welcoming anything."

"Bad, is it?" Lovers' mustache quivered in sympathy.

"Pretty foul, but often things change very rapidly in a murder investigation." The Inspector sighed and produced his wallet. He pulled out a group photograph taken by Hildegard with the imperfect Japanese camera she had bought in Gibraltar. "See anybody there you recognize, apart from me?"

Lovers peered. "My God, that *is* the man, the big fellow. Don't say I've made a fool of myself?"

"You are positive?"

"I'd like to see him, but, damn it, yes, I'm a hundred per cent sure."

"Well, thanks," said Harry. "Now I must leave you."

At the pub door he glanced back. Lovers was saying something to Miss Spotting, and she, head back, was smiling at him. He hoped that she would get back to the gallery before MacGlaishen had an attack.

There was a phone box at the end of the road. He dialed Blood, Cupping and Fulsome and was transferred to Hubert's extension. He glanced at his watch. It was two-fifteen.

"Who is it?" asked a cautious male voice.

"It's just a personal call."

"Well, I'm afraid he's out on business."

"Do you know when he'll be back?"

"I'm afraid I don't. He might be out all afternoon."

Harry gave his thanks. A colleague covering up if ever he had heard it. He got a taxi back to the Stanisgates'.

"Did you eat anything?" asked Dora.

"A pub sandwich."

"I hope Elizabeth disciplines you into regular meals when you're married. One thing about Hubert, I always know he loves his belly too much to skip a meal, except when we were first married and sometimes very broke. Anyway, I shouldn't talk, what with one thing and the other I often forget about eating now the kids are not lunching at home. I've got a big pot of soup."

"Hildegard?" he ventured. There had been a recent soup fiasco involving tripe and cider and Hildegard's tears.

Dora grinned. "No, my mulligatawny, which is very good even if I say so. Shall we eat in the kitchen?"

Dora's kitchen was large and elegant except for an irregular stain on the wall where Hildegard's home-made sauerkraut had mysteriously exploded one hot August night.

"She'll get over it," said Dora, "and start concentrating on simple things. The Mediterranean made her a bit dippy over garlic and things. I tried to tell old H. she was too young and impressionable, but he wouldn't have it."

"I was thinking," said the Inspector, drinking his soup, "how little I know of Hubert."

"He's a very reticent man in some ways. Hates what he calls personal questions. I don't suppose any kids know less about their father than my two, except those that get left on steps. Come to think of it I don't know much

119

except that he has no relatives and was born and educated at some seaside town."

"You married during the war?"

"Four months before D-Day. He had some leave. We'd met in 1943, the usual pickup at a dance hall." Dora giggled. "Old H. dances like a very pompous old sergeant on parade, but thinks he's good. Bless him! You know, I suppose many women fall in love after originally feeling sorry for the bloke. It was that way with me. He was always alone and proud and touchy, never with other boys who knew him.

"When we were married, we had to keep it quiet. He was on some assignment where they preferred to take un-married men and he didn't want to get turfed off it. It worried me, of course. I'd read about these cloak and dagger things."

"I suppose that meant you didn't get an Army allot-ment?" the Inspector said with deft casualness.

"No, though that wasn't a problem. I was in Uncle's shop—Lord, those ration cards!—and H. managed to get a few art commissions when he was on leave. It was not until the end of '46 that he got out and we talked it over and decided that he had to make sure of his basic techniques. That's half the trouble today, Harry. . . ."

"Don't get political, Dee."

"Sorry," she shrugged. "Anyway that's the story. He went to the Poly and I went back to the shop after Leicestershire was born. Flogging Aussie 'oggett as H. says. He worked like a man possessed. I've never seen anybody capable of such sustained work as H. Sometimes he sold something and we plonked the baby on auntie and really hit it up. Until I told H. that lamentably—because I was enjoying it—I'd have to take care of the purse. We bought our first house and nearly went broke doing it, but we survived."

Dora's face switched toward the door. Harry could hear nothing, but in a few seconds it opened. Hubert with what Harry thought was unconscious histrionics paused in the doorway, his big body filling it.

"Lor," said the Inspector, "the 'usbin'."

"Wot goes on 'ere," boomed Hubert.

"Yes, what does go on?" said Dora. "What's the provider doing away from the dark, satanic mill?"

Hubert tossed his hat on the workbench and slid himself onto a chair. "The sack! 'Mister Stanisgate,' they said, 'why is the stamp book filled with used cinema tickets?' and out I went."

"When he goes on like this, I know he hasn't eaten—makes him lightheaded." Dora worked with quick efficiency.

She gave her husband a plate of bread and cheese. "Take this and you and Harry eat it with two small glasses of stout each. In twenty-five minutes there will be breaded lamb cutlets, onion sauce and sautéed potatoes. I don't want to call more than twice."

"Not for me," said Harry. "Just stout and cheese."

Hubert poured out the two stouts and poised his face over the bread and cheese.

"No trouble, only an immense depression of spirits. I told the lad I was going home and walked out. No, no, nothing wrong with the work. The personnel Bleeder knows I could get more elsewhere so he treads delicately."

"Were you treading so delicately last Thursday night when you were near the scene and time of the murder?"

Hubert took a draft of stout, leaving a faint foaming smear on the fine hairs on his upper lip. He deliberately munched a slice of bread, and said, "Is this official?"

"I'm afraid so, Hubert. Look." He took out of his pocket a large scale map. "The red dot shows where the body was found. He was killed some time after eleven. At approximately midnight you were seen there." The Inspector's pencil dipped and speared.

"I've tried everything for the insomnia," said Hubert. "Hot baths and special tapes that hiss and wheedle under the pillow. But the only thing that sometimes does the trick is an hour's hard walking. I've got it to a fine art, dress, get down the stairs and out the door without a sound. I can't remember Thursday particularly, not to swear to." He drained his glass and poured another.

"No," said Hubert. "Not to swear to. All my damned nights run together in my mind. It seems to me that I sat down in the chair in the bedroom, took my shoes off and wondered if I was going to sleep or not. I read through some office stuff, decided I wasn't going to sleep, put my shoes on and crept out of the house like a great cat, as you might say."

"Do you remember being at this spot?" Harry poured himself a stout and thought it unfair that a character like Hubert had been able to marry a woman with such an impeccable taste where meat and cheese were concerned.

"Um." Hubert eyed the map without much interest. "Usually I automatically bear in a rough circle, thinking about all the things in my head. I don't *notice* things when I'm out at night. Usually after forty-five minutes I suddenly see a landmark and realize I'm five minutes from home. One time the built-in direction finder didn't work and I suddenly came into Hammersmith Broadway three hours later. Had to get a cab back."

"You're not much help."

Stanisgate frowned. "Believe me I'm sorry, but"—with a flash of his usual manner—"it simply didn't occur to me to keep a log book."

"Well," said the Inspector, swallowing. "I don't suppose it matters."

Stanisgate spoke suddenly as a person will who has had something worrying at the back of their mind. "Harry, is it possible to watch a person? I mean, stick on their tail all the time?"

"Sure," said Harry. "Total surveillance, it's called. The Americans have it to a fine art, microphones in the cistern, agents under the bed. Only trouble is that it costs a hell of a lot. We do it, but the authorization comes right from the top, and then it's mostly espionage stuff."

"Har," said Hubert morosely. "It may be significant, Sir John, that this nine-pound-a-week clerk runs two scarlet Jags and has thrice been found sleeping stertorously in the secret code room."

"Stow it, Hubert! I don't get that stuff. With me it's the clerk tickling the petty cash of fourteen pounds nine to pay a bookie. Anyway, are you saying you are being watched, perhaps by little green men?"

"It's them teevee waves what they send through my 'ead that worrits me," said Stanisgate. "No, it's just that I get a prickly feeling in the back of the neck. I'll swear I saw a little buck-toothed pismire on three occasions when I was coming home."

"The prickly feeling is the harbinger of the D.T.s.," said Harry, "and the way you were swigging scotch the other night I don't wonder. Next you feel things crawling down your chest."

Stanisgate did not smile. "How can you trap somebody who follows you?"

"Tiger principle; elephant ditto."

"What?"

"The hunter becomes the hunted. You somehow make a circle and come up behind him. Just tap him on the shoulder—if you punch him on the nose a beak will certainly fine you—and you say, 'Well, *really*, old man!' "

"I'd like to break his jaw. You sure it's not police?"

"I'm pretty sure I would know, and I haven't been notified. Sure it's not nerves?"

"I don't have any nerves."

"Divorce?"

"Inspector, I'm a very wise, or at least discreet, bird."

"Usually," said Harry, "people follow patterns. We know they live at A, get up at a certain hour and journey to B, eat at C, that kind of thing. That makes surveillance simple. Following people about for long periods doesn't really pay off." You are sure it's not that a jealous husband has answered one of those little ads about confidential investigations?"

"Quite sure."

"Then it could be serious. Nobody's going to take the trouble to keep a full-time tail going for peanuts. There would be at least two of them, perhaps three. Tell me, Hubert, are you making a formal complaint?"

"Can I?"

"Oh, sure. It's no offense in general to follow people about, but it can sometimes come under Annoyance and Molestation. Pity you weren't a good-looking girl, it's easier to get a conviction."

"No complaint!" said Hubert, looking down at his large, clenched fists.

"You know," said Harry, "if you've offended professionals, you're not in the Queensberry Rules. Doing over, as they call it, is a nasty and highly professionalized business. Don't be a fool. Kick the nearest, without getting off balance, and then run like hell."

"I've had dealings with violent men," said Hubert. "I know all about throat chops and stuff like that."

"Any Army sergeant instructor," said Harry, "would be five minutes work to at least twenty men I can think of, besides which they never go in unless the odds are three to one in their favor. Take my advice and sprint. I've seen you show a pretty turn of speed when we've been out playing with the kids."

"Thanks," said Hubert. "Not a word to Dee, mind."

As he spoke, they could hear Dora calling from the kitchen.

Back in his shared office, the Inspector wrote his reports and then became immersed in a file, sent to him by Hawker, on the incidence of damage in railway compartments.

"For you, Harry." The man at the desk handed across the handset.

"Mr. James," boomed the Chief Inspector. "This man Lovers is a highly reputable citizen, by all accounts, very old family. I'd take his identification as quite positive."

"That's how it sounded to me."

"This insomnia, is it genuine?"

"Well, the family doctor is also a personal friend. I've heard Stanisgate discuss his insomnia with him over the dinner table."

"Mm." Porterman sounded disappointed. "Nevertheless it seems that one could build up this condition as a kind of alibi. It's just a question of one's own word. It would be a possible asset to anybody likely to be questioned about why they wandered abroad at night. And, of course, there was this list found very near the body."

"He had an explanation for that."

"He seems to have explanations for everything. Oh, well, it could be coincidence, but I'm not fond of 'em. I'll have a couple of men tonight outside the house, from ten o'clock on. If he goes out they'll tail him."

"You noted that he appears to think he is being followed?"

Porterman gave a disgusted grunt. "A crude ruse to see if we were tailing him."

As he put the handset down, he doubted whether Hubert was that crude.

A messenger brought down a pile of memoranda from Hawker. Harry's mouth pursed as he read a red sheet marked "Priority."

My suspicious mind instigated the following inquiries.

Is the birth recorded at Somerset House of a Hubert Stanisgate of his approximate age?

No.

Is there a record at the War Office?

No.

Registered as a change of name?

No.

There seems to be no reason why he could not be Hubert Harcourt. To this end I got in touch with: Ex-Staff Sergeant Biderley, M.B.E. (who received it rather earlier than the Beatles). The sergeant had the pleasure of training Harcourt for three months.

And Ex-Private Jelf, who was in the same hut as Harcourt for four months. They will be in the reception hall at 6 P.M.

You are requested to confront them with Mr. Stanisgate. It is realized that this intrudes into your domestic life, but the tradition of the service takes precedence.

"Effing old bastard," said Harry aloud.

"Hawker?"

"Yeah."

The man at the next desk smiled sardonically.

"We poor bastards have to pick the words out ourselves, so we don't waste time being smart. But when you have the seniority to get access to the typing pool, why, man, you get sonorous, you get witty, you get sarcastic." The man slapped a palm against his forehead.

He got Elizabeth at her office.

"No meal tonight. Work."

"One of these days I'm going in to give that worm Hawker a piece of my mind."

"He'd like that," said Harry. "If you really want to pleasure him, bring a sjambok and lightly beat him."

"I'd pleasure him!" said Elizabeth. "It's a frightening thought."

"What? Beating Hawker?"

"No, that all coppers get slightly mental."

Sergeant Biderley was so in prototype that Harry had no need to use the public address system. The gym sergeants that the Inspector remembered, along with the smell of gym shoes, from his cavernous school gymnasium, had both had small waxed mustaches screwed into skewer points. Biderley was of the next generation and clean-shaven. But the neat, clean, almost birdlike motions were there, and the ramrod spine. The Inspector felt himself guiltily forcing his own vertebrae into place.

The sergeant had decided that a slightly sepulchral, firing-party demeanor was the order of the day.

"'Arcourt, Inspector? Frankly I'm not surprised."

"No?"

"I had thousands through my hands. You get to know 'em. Bad feller at eighteen, never any good thereafter. Knock 'em into shape all you want, but the leather'll always crack."

"He got decorated."

"So they said. I'm not surprised. He always 'ad guts, no question. When he started pinching—not the usual scroungin', pinchin' from 'is mates—I 'ad 'im up. ''Arcourt,' I said—and I was twenty-odd years younger and 'ard as the 'obs of 'ell—'if I catch you, it'll be the Glass House and I got friends there who'll be waiting to tickle you up.' He laughed! 'Catch your 'are, Serge,' 'e said." Biderley grinned. "I 'ad to 'and it to him. 'Catch your 'are!' I said, 'I'll 'ave you by the short 'air, boy, and we'll see 'ow you squeak?' 'E smiled. Could have booked him for dumb insolence, but I didn't. If he'd been the sneaking kind I would have, but 'e just stood there with the leer on 'is face. I made a mistake, sir, in being soft. I waited to catch 'im on somethin' big—somethin' like a twelvemuncer—but it never 'appened. 'E 'ad brains, did 'Arcourt. Wot's 'e done now?"

"Wanted in connection with murder."

The sergeant shot his dentures out between his lips and sucked them in. " 'E 'ad guts, no question."

"Calling Mr. James!"

Ex-private Jelf had arrived five minutes late. His aspirates were impeccable behind his cockney whine. A small man, bundled up in a shabby overcoat, he delved among the dandruff that flaked through his eyebrows and visible hair.

"You never passed through my 'ands?" said Sergeant Biderley, after Harry had introduced them.

"No, Serge," said Jelf, huskily. "But I knew Bertie the Bastard, that's what I got asked to come here for."

Jelf smoked and coughed in the taxi and showed signs of feeling disappointed.

"We are a bit short on police cars," said Harry.

"I don't want to get into anything," said Jelf.

"Do your dooty," said the sergeant, "and let 'them' do the worryin'."

"How well did you know Harcourt?" asked the Inspector.

"So, so."

"When was the last time you saw him?"

"August, '42." For some reason Jelf sounded sulky. "I say," he said, "can you handle him?"

"There won't be any rough stuff," said the Inspector.

"Then he's not Bertie the Bastard, that's for sure."

"A violent kind of man?"

"Suppressed, but always there," said Jelf, scratching an eyebrow and releasing a tiny snowstorm of dandruff. "He had this bluff, damn-your-eyes sort of manner, aping a gentleman like, but if he was really mad and thought he could get away with it, well, the boys were all scared of him and we had some tough cases."

"No peculiarities?"

"When he was thinking, he used to scratch away at his chin."

"No scars, so the record says."

Jelf chuckled. "I reckon he's got one on his foot. He went for a man one night. Over nothin', some bird or other had knocked him back and Bertie was in a black mood. He'd just given the other fellow a crack in the stomach to relieve his feelings. He knew exactly how far he could go without getting on a charge. Well, this fellow, can't remember his name, had a glass in his hand, and when he saw Harcourt coming he dropped it on the ground. Harcourt had his boots off and one of his big feet came down smash on the glass. I never knew so much blood could come out of your foot. The M.O. put in four stitches. Of course, Bertie swung the lead, said he'd cut a ligament, but the M.O. wasn't having it."

"I wonder why Harcourt didn't desert," said Harry and the old sergeant snorted.

"Bertie used to say that there was no percentage in being on the run, too many things against you so that a man got desperate and the M.P.s got him. No, he said it was safer inside. You know he used to break into shops?"

"No."

"Well, he wasn't a blabbermouth and the few chaps who knew wouldn't talk. He had a rule that he never went near the shop except that one time when he broke in. So he needed some chaps to go in and spot where the till was, what the stock was like and that sort of thing. He used to work the medium-sized shops, and he's supposed to have gone through a jeweler's one time."

"A wonder he got away with it."

"A lot of people got away with things during the war," said Jelf sagely. "However, though Harcourt never chummed up with anybody, always kept you at arm's length, there were people who thought he wasn't too bad. He always had money and was generous with it. I remember once when I was broke and an eight-hour pass came through. 'Alec,' Harcourt said, 'here's a quid I've got no use for, take it.' Things like that."

"Was he married?"

"Bertie the Bastard marry?" Jelf gave a wheezy laugh. "I'm sure the records had him down as single. Oh, he was attractive to women. Used to go dancing whenever he could."

"Good athlete," said the sergeant. "He could beat anybody we had between a hundred yards and 'alf a mile. Been really good if 'e'd trained."

The taxi drew up and the Inspector told the driver to wait.

"This won't take long, just follow my cue."

The long lounge contained Leicestershire Stanisgate, who nodded before immersing himself in what was, all too obviously, a teevee script. The Inspector glanced round. Hubert sat erect in the Windsor chair appropriated to his use, reading a thick folio book.

"Oh, hallo, Harry."

"Hubert, let me introduce Mr. Biderley and Mr. Jelf. Mr. Stanisgate."

"Forgive me if I don't get up," said Hubert. "This great tome's both valuable and borrowed and I don't lug it about more than is necessary."

"That's quite all right, er," said the sergeant, and for a minute the Inspector sweated.

"Mr. Stanisgate," said Sergeant Biderley after a split second.

"Quite all right, I'm sure," whined Jelf as a kind of descant.

"We three have an appointment, but I've got to get some papers from the bedroom," said Harry.

"Sure," said Stanisgate, face impassive. "Better take your coats off. I like this heating on the moderate side, but the family consider themselves hothouse plants, so there we are."

Harry went to his bedroom and sat down for two minutes, then returned.

Sergeant Biderley was sitting relaxed, a man who through his life had acquired the knack of seeing things accurately from the corners of his eyes. Jelf sat, squirming uneasily, his small eyes constantly drawn toward Stanisgate, who sat immersed in his book, ridges of concentration upon his broad forehead.

The Inspector gestured, and Jelf shot into the protection of his overcoat. The sergeant moved stiffly and stood momentarily staring at Stanisgate.

"So long," called Harry.

"Bye," called Hubert without raising his eyes.

"Wait until the cab moves off," instructed the Inspector as he opened the front door.

"Well?" he asked.

Jelf avoided the Inspector's eyes.

Sergeant Biderley popped his dentures.

"Those eyes, the way he holds his head, and the voice remind me of 'Arcourt. The build, too. 'Arcourt could have developed like that, although I thought 'im the type that gets quite a bit of fat on 'im later in life and that fellow back there ain't. I wish I could have seen 'im get up and walk."

Jelf nodded in agreement. "One moment I thought it was him and then I didn't. I thought that fellow might have been a bit taller than Bertie. And when Bertie sat down, he slumped right down in the chair. This fellow kept his spine straight. Still Harcourt must have turned out very like this fellow. His hair was a bit lighter, but sometimes the hair gets darker."

"Can I put it down that it could be Harcourt who you saw, but that you're a long way from being positive?"

"That's about the ticket, sir," said the sergeant.

Jelf agreed.

"He showed no sign of recognizing either of you."

"One thing Bertie was proud of was the way he could control his face," said Jelf. "Even if you saw him doing something, he could look at you so innocent that you doubted your own eyes. Besides it's been a long time, and he's not the only one to change."

" 'E'd recognize me," said the sergeant grimly. "Any man I 'ad up like I 'ad 'im up remembers my face on 'is deathbed. I've known men who passed through my 'ands thirty years ago to turn pale when they saw me again."

Both Jelf and the sergeant wished to be dropped at Charing Cross, where the latter proposed a beer at a pub where he proved to be well known. The sergeant exhibited a vast capacity for whisky chased by beer and Jelf, a rum drinker, possessed a rather trying store of corrupt limericks. It was therefore a little after nine, and with a stomach uncomfortably bloated by bottled beer, that the Inspector called in on Tosher.

The informer blinked at him and indicated the rickety shop chair. "Sit down."

Tosher turned off the light and shut the door. Through the window the Inspector watched a couple walk rapidly along the freezing street and shivered.

"You gave me a nice assignment!" said the informer's lifeless voice.

"You know the score and the perks are goodish."

"There should be a good bonus," said Tosher, and Harry remained silent.

"I only got something by a fluke. I asked around, and there are more Harcourts than you'd realize, but none of 'em the kind of fellow you asked about. It was pure fluke. I was drinking with these two fellows—dealers they call themselves, but they're not fussy. They were discussing that jewel robbery two weeks back, and I popped up with 'I suppose Harcourt will handle it.' They looked blank so I started to spell it, 'aitch.' My word!" said Tosher, "that did it. I'll have a great bruise on one arm where one of them grabbed me."

The Inspector sensed rather than saw movement within the closeness of the little shop. There was a clink and the sound of pouring and his stomach rebelled at the fruity, winy smell

"Well," said Tosher, " 'what the hell's this about,' I said. 'Take your hands off me!' One of them says, 'It's for your own good, Tosher. Nobody talks about the Big H.' 'I'm frightened of nobody,' I said. 'People who talk about him end up in hospital or maybe at the bottom of the river,' he said."

Harry heard the glass clink again.

"Take it easy on the rotgut, Tosher."

"I know my capacity, Inspector, I'm on maximum, but under control. I'm frightened. My hand is shaking, so I know. You're thinking that I've got booze tremors in my hands, but this is real shaking like ringing handbells.

"No," said Tosher, "when I get my teeth in, you can't shake me off and I was on these fellows like a leech. I told them a friend had a warehouseful of hot transistor sets and there was money in it for me if I could find a fence. All right, bit by bit I got it out of them. Nobody knows the Big H., he's a voice out of a telephone. He only touches the very big tickles involving stuff that is specialized."

Once more glass and bottle clinked.

"I nearly had them out of their minds," said Tosher without inflection. "They went out of the pub and there was little Tosher trotting beside 'em. They go into another boozer and I'm alongside. Finally one of the big bastards whispers that he's heard, *heard* mind, that you go to the Whisky an' Club. That's . . ."

"Yes," said Harry, "I know all about that place."

"They try to push me around and they always end in quad," said Tosher, obscurely, clinking again. Harry heard the sound of something soft falling to the ground, the pile of surgical corsets, he surmised.

"Yes," said Tosher, after a few seconds of heavy breathing. "You go to the Whisky an'. There's a waiter there called Ted Johnson. You slip him the wink you want to speak to Big H. and you give him a phone number. And perhaps you hear." The informer's voice was as precise as ever, but the words were widely spaced.

"I went there," said Tosher, "got a member's card. They know me. I asked one of the barmaids and she said he'd left four weeks ago. I went and sat down and crosschecked with a floor waiter. He said Johnson had gone, come into some money. Well, I sat there for a slow one and then I got frightened. Somebody was watching me, I could feel it."

There was a thud. The Inspector put on his pencil torch and located the counter flap. Tosher had collapsed on top of the pile of corsets. His dark glasses had become pushed up onto his forehead and his bloodshot eyes blinked in the torch's rays. Grunting, Harry hauled him up and into the chair.

"Legs gone," said Tosher. "They won't come back until morning. It's the fear."

"It's the drink," said Harry, feeling the cold clammy sweat on the man's brow. "Suppose you go into hospital, Tosher? I'll have you in a police ward."

"No," said Tosher, "I worked it out. The only secret that's safe is something that nobody else knows but you. I should know *that*. No, I worked it out while I was seated in that club, frightened to move. A tourist party came in, thirty of 'em. In the flap I wormed out and into a cab. I had him stop on the way and phoned the owner and told him I was going off sick. There's not much during the day—it brightens up at night—and he's got an uncle who'll relieve.

"Get me a drink! Two inches."

The Inspector rummaged and poured. The tooth glass knocked against the informer's teeth as he swallowed.

"Put me in a cell tonight and tomorrow get me to Paddington by eleven. I got a friend in the West Country, runs an ale house. He understands me. Somewhere in the West Country," said Tosher. "Licensed to sell cider and perry. Nobody knows."

The Inspector felt Tosher's pulse—thready but not weak.

"Where are your keys? I'll lock you in the shop."

Outside the small spill-off of people from the bright lights walked smartly along. There was the smell of fog and ice in the air.

He instinctively glanced to his left. In the doorway of a shop with its window filled with extractor fans stood a large man, probably six foot three or more, registered Harry. His face under the black hat was mottled in brownish marks. The Inspector moved on. In the next doorway, a shop with opaque windows, stood a smaller, snappily dressed man, with a keen eager face with a razor scar down one cheekbone.

Harry moved out to the curbside, stopped and turned round. The big man had moved onto the pavement, hands in the pockets of his shapeless overcoat. There was a faint, glistening anticipatory leer on his face. The smaller, scarfaced man padded neatly out of his doorway.

This is where you run, thought Harry, and as he did so, the first faint spots of snow drifted down. Pivot and run. God knows where the nearest phone box is.

From the side turning ten yards ahead loomed a helmeted figure and the Inspector gave a yell. Checking his stride he turned and saw the backs of two overcoated figures walking rapidly in the opposite direction.

"You on this beat?" he asked the uniformed man.

"No, sir, I'm taking a short cut home. A constable isn't due down here for another thirty minutes."

"Inspector James. Get me a car and a driver, priority urgent. I'll be outside a shop eight doors down."

When the car arrived, Tosher, with docile confidence, let the Inspector and the driver carry him and deposit him on the back seat.

"Don't forget me bag," he said.

Harry found it under one end of the counter and looked in it. There was a pair of socks, a clean nylon shirt, rolled up, and three bottles of British port, plus a quantity of florins and half-crowns and a few crumpled ten-shilling notes. He locked the shop and took Tosher to the police station, where he outlined his needs to the sergeant in charge.

He left Tosher, clad only in his long, grayish combinations, on a small truckle bed in an unlocked cell.

"Get in touch with me when you're ready, Tosher. We'll see you are all right for money within reason and I'll arrange for the desk to give you a tenner to start you off."

He sought the sergeant and explained matters. "Try to get some food into him, on the expense sheet. Steak and egg, or something like that. And get the surgeon to take a look at him around nine-thirty; I'll have a car round for him at ten."

The Whisky an' Club had changed hands so many times that the Inspector did not know who was its present owner. Its reputation had fluctuated with its ownership, now up, now down, and once it had narrowly escaped closure. At the moment it featured on the itineraries of various conducted tours of London nightlife, and bewildered foreigners found themselves ushered into its grim sleaziness and regaled with the establishment's champagne cocktail, which had no foreign connection at all, and a small piece of lardy pastry with a tinned shrimp on top.

A watery neon sign with a couple of letters missing indicated its existence at the end of an alley, ending in a cul-de-sac. It had the advanatge of being within a few minutes of Oxford Street, which was probably the only reason, thought Harry as he dismissed his cab, why anybody made the walk between the ranks of dustbins that decorated the alley.

The doorman was short but very broad and wore a fixed smile.

"Member, sir?"

The Inspector ran through his memory. "Tommy Burke, isn't it? I gave evidence against you in 1963!"

The man grunted something.

"Who's the boss now?"

"Mr. Robinson, sir."

"All right, where does he hang out?"

The man flapped his hand. "His office is at the end of the bar."

Inside, a wave of scented steamy heat and cigarette smoke was like a slap in the face. He remembered MacGlaishen's theory that people did not buy when they were cold.

The swing door led directly on to a small hatcheck room and then into a long bar with stools, the plastic leather a trifle worn and cracked even under the subdued, pinkish light. Altogether the Whisky an' needed a facial. Harry remembered an old saying that here you could see the most elderly strippers in Europe.

There was no element of surprise, thought Harry. There never was in these places unless you obtained a warrant and arranged for three young men to charge through in wedge formation. Burke would have some means of contacting the boss.

God knows why there were twelve people in the bar, determinedly gay, thought Harry. He watched a man order a martini and felt like telling him to avoid ordering mixed drinks. The two women behind the counter flicked hostile eyes toward him.

To the right a swing door led into the club proper. At the end was a deserted gallery which the Inspector thought originally housed a band. Now what had been a dance floor was covered with tables. At the end was a small stage on which stood an elderly fat man in a red foxhunter's coat, striped trousers, wearing a clerical collar and a deerstalker hat.

"Norom. That's stoopid spelled backwards," he was shouting, "but I never saw snorom like I see 'em now. Can't you talk? Lost your slimy, bifurcated tongues and your dirty, lying habits?"

About fifteen people sat at tables talking. Only one, that Harry could see, looked toward the fat man.

"Look at 'im," shouted the comedian, sweating profusely, "'im in the secondhand topcoat, peddling filthy postcards. I tell yer, he's got . . ."

Harry looked round and caught the fat man's eye. He stopped in mid sentence, turned and went through a small door at the end of the stage. There were sometimes, the Inspector thought, advantages in looking like a copper.

It was strangely quiet after the fat man's bellowings, and the Inspector saw that a great many of the tables were also silent and that eyes were covertly watching him. Only a handful of people behaved normally. Harry rather wished he had telephoned for a rundown on the place.

He reached out and tapped a small gray-faced waiter on the shoulder. The man looked at him with an expression of conscious rectitude.

"Want a table, sir?"

"What I want is to talk with Ted Johnson."

"Mr. Johnson quit five weeks ago, sir."

"Know where he lived?"

"Couldn't tell you, I'm sure, sir."

He went back into the bar, but just as he reached the door he caught sight of two men in the far corner of the room, one conspicuously tall and the other with a scarred face, the two he had seen near Tosher's shop. They sat silent, cigarettes drooping from their lips.

He walked to the far end of the bar and tried the small door.

"That's the liquor store, sir," called one of the barmaids. The doorman had misled him. In fact the office was situated with a common wall shared with the tiny entrance hall and cloakroom. There would be some simple hatch device enabling doorman and manager instantly to communicate. It was with considerable annoyance that he wrenched the door open without knocking.

136

A very white-faced man in his thirties looked at the Inspector over a small desk.

"Inspector James, C.I.D."

"Ah, yes, we're always pleased to help the police. I'm Mr. Robinson."

"When, for instance, have you helped the police?" the Inspector snapped.

The man hesitated and stared. "Well, I only meant . . ."

The Inspector looked at him hard. "Heroin?"

Robinson curled his top lip. "I'm a registered addict."

Keeping both hands in his pockets, the Inspector stared down at him. "You had a waiter here called Ted Johnson. I want his address."

Robinson delved into a drawer and produced a folder. Difficult to tell with addicts, the behavior pattern tended to be unpredictable, but the Inspector thought that Robinson was in a state of funk.

"No," the man said, "we have no Johnson on the staff."

"Now, now," said the Inspector, "you said you like to help us. I need not remind you that we help people who do help us." He paused and let the sentence hang in the air. "And of course we don't feel bound to do anything beyond our duty for people who obstruct us. Johnson's been gone for some weeks."

Robinson licked his lips. "I took over four weeks ago."

"You the manager?"

"Owner."

"Well, look up the records."

"I'm afraid the previous owner took them with him. I started fresh, as it were."

"Who was the previous owner?"

"A Mr. Sylvester."

"I suppose you have some vague notion as to where he lives?"

"I dealt with his solicitor. Mr. Brass, of Carlton Mansions."

"In the club is a man about six foot four with a pudgy, sallow blotched face. Know him?"

"I'm afraid I know very few of the customers."

Without another word Harry marched out.

He wondered whether Hawker's curious nocturnal habit still kept him at the office. The old Superintendent had been a widower for many years and inhabited a gloomy, heavily furnished house at Wimbledon which he seemed to avoid as much as possible.

"Yes, I'm still here," Hawker said briskly over the telephone. "I've got Porterman with me, but if you really want to be a night owl, I can see you at one."

The Inspector spent the intervening forty minutes in Records. The tall, blotchy-faced man was Percy Foot, alias the Long 'un. The summary on the outside of the cardboard file read, "Born 1910. Seven convictions involving violence. In 1953 sentenced to seven years for armed payroll robbery. Separated from wife and six children, but pays maintenance. Very dangerous man fond of violence. Moderate potus. Fond of betting on greyhounds. Usually has a mistress living with him."

The smaller, scarfaced man was one Simeon Lewis, a onetime silver ring bookmaker now warned off the turf and the greyhound tracks. Two convictions for demanding money with menaces.

A precious pair, thought Harry. He remembered that the blotchy-faced man had been mentioned in connection with Arthur Mace. That might be an angle.

The file on the Whisky an' was a collection of grimy and sordid facts. The man Robinson was believed to be a man of straw, but, said the annotation, the lease had a mere five months to go and the owners would not renew. Leafing through the depressing chronicles of the club, the Inspector had one piece of luck. A man had been attacked outside the club and amid the collection of statements was one made from Edward Johnson, a waiter, of a Kensington address.

Harry called the local station and the night sergeant amiably agreed to send somebody round. It did not take long before the call back. "A dead duck, I'm afraid," said the voice. "Respectable rooming house. Small bathroom and alcove for cooking, separate front door, you know. The Johnsons were there two years, kept themselves to

138

themselves and paid the rent on the knocker. They left four weeks ago and the landlady got the impression they were emigrating, but she wasn't interested."

He went to see Hawker and found him at his desk with a cigar cocked at a jaunty angle. The lines and creases of exhaustion had gone from his face. The Inspector had noted this peculiarity with many of the "heads," this power of recuperation. He wished he knew how the old devil consistently got away with so little sleep.

Reading his expression, the Superintendent said, "I get about seven hours sleep out of the day, enough for my age. Plenty of times when the door's bolted, I've got my head down. I take it in small doses, an hour at most. And I can sleep anywhere, standing up in a shop doorway if need be. When I joined the force you had to put in long hours if you wanted the promotion road. Many a time I've put in fourteen hours on my feet and then in for a four-penny shave and twopence for hot towels before off again. Anyway, let's hear from you."

He listened, occasionally wrinkling his long upper lip, his cold, obsidian eyes fixed on the Inspector.

"You're not the only fellow with an informer," the Superintendent grunted at last. "There's some bits in the Receivers Files on this Big H. business. Not much concrete, except that he doesn't operate very often, which might fit in with the theory that he's got an international practice. Six years ago there was forty thousand pounds' worth of machine tools that went off and a rumor turned up that it was fenced through the Big H. Three years ago it was a load of pelts landed from Russia. We're pretty sure that they never came on to any European market, so it probably meant they got to the States. There again the rumor was that the Big H. fenced them on commission. Stolen goods thought it was the usual romantic nonsense. You know . . ."

The Inspector did. The criminal world had the same tendency toward mystique as every other profession, including the manufacture of tales about super crooks and super coups.

"I had Sergeant Crook in here. Oh, this fellow Polly Packer turned up in Egypt, under his own name and a bona fide passport, William Aloysius Packer, for heaven's sake. Seeing the pyramids with a lady American tourist to help him. According to Interpol he's behaving like any other well-heeled tourist and has opened a dollar account with one of the banks. Anyway, there's nothing we can do. If we flew somebody out, Packer could, and probably would, tell them to jump in the Nile. Then I'd get a please-explain from the Auditor-General.

"Crook, of course, is nuts about Arthur Mace being Jack the Ripper, Peter the Painter and the guy who pinches girls in crowded lifts. Remember that! Now, two things have come in about that Chrysler that was jammed in the alley. When you get to my age, all cars look alike except some are bigger. However, I understand that there are only twenty of that model in the country. Every solitary copper in the country has been asked. Ten responses, eight poorly evaluated and the remaining two checked and found simon pure. Now Sergeant Crook is sure that sometime four months ago he saw this car stop near Arthur Mace's flat and drop him off. A very powerful-looking man who the sergeant saw briefly and could not identify was driving. How would you evaluate that?"

"I know about Crook and Arthur Mace, but my money would be on the sergeant when it comes to facts."

"Humph!" Harry could not tell what was in Hawker's mind.

"One thing, Inspector, and thanks to my evil mind. I called for the file on Castelano who they found smashed in Hammersmith. The rain had obliterated most clues, but there was the impression of tire treads on his left hand. There was a peculiarity in one of the treads, a star-shaped cut. The offside back wheel of that Chrysler matched it more or less. You could argue that there are tens of thousands of those tires around and statistically others with similar faults are around, still . . ."

"I suppose Crook thinks that Mace is Big H.?"

"I suppose there's the outside chance. Nobody knows his origins or what he did during the war, if anything. The superficial description is okay. He was charged in 1950 as Arthur Mace and given three months for attempting to

140

suborn a stableboy. We checked his prints—no previous record—and made out a file card on him. He could have been this man Harcourt. If I committed a murder and was wanted," said Hawker, "and I knew the police hadn't got my prints, I'd go to Northern Ireland and commit a nice little offense that would put me inside for a couple of years.

"No, no, the trouble that gripes poor Crook is that Arthur Mace is spending his days in the cubicle at the back of his coffeeshop, engrossed in some kind of ledger, and there he stays until he goes straight home or spends an hour in one of the gambling hells. It worries Crook. He's frightened that Mace might be going straight." Hawker showed his yellow front teeth.

Harry watched the Superintendent get up and walk to the window. It was during these late night sessions that Hawker's mind shot after his half-formed hunches.

"I had a bad fifteen minutes with the Commander. He don't like it, too many sensational possibilities. Fortunately, the crime reporters so far regard it as being the usual middle-aged gay getting done over in an alley, back-of-the-paper stuff. I spent some hours checking and picking brains.

"The nub is several million pounds' worth of paintings, less those found in that Chrysler. Even Porterman, poor devil, has accepted that, if for no other reason than he has no alternative. The men I talked to were unanimous that in this kind of job the stuff is kept away from the receiver. He's rushing about arranging transport and the sale. It's too risky on many counts for him to keep it in his back room.

"That means," said Hawker, "that accommodation has to be got. When the move is okay, the stuff will be shifted pronto, but until then, if I'm right, it's in some hired warehouse, garage or room, and where do you do for that? Only one man."

"Elephant!" said the Inspector.

Mr. Elephant was a solicitor, but was always careful to emphasize that he was not in practice. He had a couple of rooms on the fringe of Mayfair with "Investment Services" on the door. Some people thought the real brains were those of Fuller, his clerk, a small cockney with a red knobbly face.

"If you're going to make a living out of skulduggery," said Hawker, "accommodation is your big problem, so you go to Elphant. He and his backers—I should imagine the names of the syndicate members might make funny reading—lost a lot when the soliciting law changed—stuck with expensive head leases and no ladies to bring in the money. My honest old heart bleeds!

"Those are the fellers that will make my old age one of regret. The untouchables, the stinkers. However, Elphant has developed sidelines. You want no-questions-asked premises for whatever purpose and you see 'my man Fuller.' That feller we found making pep pills in his private lab, he got the premises through Elphant."

"Would Elphant talk?"

"My sweet flaming oath." Hawker sounded awed. "Take a clean young public school boy, put him through courses!" The old man's bony hand whacked down on the blotter.

"Have a nice cozy chat with him, Inspector!"

Harry was always forgetting just how malevolent Hawker could look.

"I started on a beat in the old East Division, three coppers together. We had a superintendent on the premises in those days. His name was Smart. We'd wheel them into his little room. Wham. You'd hear their head hit the wall. Old Smart would say, 'Caught his toes in that worn lino. Take a note of it, Constable, in case it's serious.' Whack, the man's head'd go on Smart's desk, sometimes losing a chunk of skin on the sharp edge. 'Dear me,' Smart'd say, 'the poor feller's dizzy. Stick something on that cut and see he gets to bed.'

"So we'd swab the cut with a drop of the stuff we used for the urinal and throw him in a dirty cell, the one the drunks spent the nights in.

"They were very bad men, Inspector, brutal men! Animals! Although I wouldn't say they were worse than Elphant."

142

"Okay, sir, which side of Elphant's face do I knock against the wall?" Hawker's face did not alter.

"You know, Mr. James, I've a certain kindness toward you and I've sometimes smoothed your way—when I could do it without inconveniencing myself." Hawker sniffed. "But I have my doubts as to whether you're hard enough inside. Oh, you can remain an inspector in some cushy job like directing crowds at sports meetings. I know that it's different nowadays. I know we work to strict rule. I know everybody's got civil rights, but you still have got to be hard. You see Elphant tomorrow and keep telling yourself you're tougher than he is. See what happens. Now, good night."

Chapter 5

The Inspector breakfasted at a grim little café near Victoria Station. His eyes smarted from lack of sleep and he had not felt like facing the Stanisgates.

At nine, he leafed dispiritedly through the routine requests that seemed to fill his in-basket as fast as he emptied it. He telephoned and was advised that Tosher had refused anything except a little bread and butter and a pint of white coffee. A doctor had examined the small man and merely shrugged his shoulders. Tosher would be duly escorted to Paddington Station by eleven o'clock.

He took a cab out to see Mr. Elphant and found himself in a bleak outer office where what he took in the dim morning light for an office boy turned out to be an old, wizened man with malicious black eyes peering through his spectacles.

"A police inspector, eh," said the old man, contemptuously emphasizing the rank. "Well, I don't think Mr. E. is in."

Harry lifted the flap of the counter and the old man started in astonishment and tried to bar the Inspector's path. A sharp push sent him to one side and Harry swung open the glass door at the end of the counter.

A little red-faced man sat behind a low desk on which his feet reposed and was flicking playing cards at a hat which stood in a corner. He merely paused in his game and stared at Harry with a pair of small, intelligent gray eyes. Harry heard the old man scuttle in behind him.

"Police Inspector James. You'd be Mr. Fuller?"

The old man said something incoherent, and the Inspector continued, "I'm afraid your father misunderstood what I said."

"My . . ." a gleam of amusement lit up Fuller's face. "I see. All right, Fred, and in future don't misunderstand police inspectors, it hurts their feelings."

As the door closed, Fuller resumed flicking his cards. "Every time I get in twenty straight, I go over the road for a beer. Happens about three times in a day."

"You must have a lot of practice."

"This job is just waiting for clients," said Fuller. "I read so many books that I started talking like an intellectual and alarmed the boss, so now I play this."

"By the way, is Mr. Elphant in?"

"That depends."

"It does, doesn't it," said the Inspector, smiling as nastily as he could.

The small gray eyes looked at him for a couple of seconds. Fuller swung his tan brogues to the floor.

"Wait here. Have a go at the cards if you want."

Fuller opened a door with heavily frosted glass and walked neatly through. Presently, Harry was conscious of feeling that he was being watched.

It was eight minutes before Fuller came back.

"The boss was on the phone, please come through."

Elphant was a big, superbly dressed, well-groomed man in his early fifties. His rather florid face was guileless and exuded cheerfulness.

"Well, Inspector James, so glad to meet you! Have a chair. Perhaps Fuller may stay, he's my confidential clerk, knows the business better than I."

"I'll come to the point," said Harry, "we think that sometime in the last three months somebody required space, perhaps only a small room with facilities for heating, but quite secure from being overlooked, etcetera."

"Well," said Elphant, "we specialize in big stuff, rooms aren't in our line."

"All the girls can't have gone out of business," snapped the Inspector feeling harsh, ugly lines beside his mouth.

Elphant's bland smile grew more solicitous. "I think . . ." he began.

"What you think doesn't matter," the Inspector

growled. "I think I've finished here. When I come back it will be with a warrant." He scuffed his chair back.

Elphant's neatly brushed eyebrows had been escalating toward his hairline, but his eyes flickered to one side and Harry from the corner of his eye saw Fuller's hand flick in a slight gesture

"Well, Inspector, I'm an officer of the court, although not in practice. You need not tell me my duty. Suppose you go out and talk it over with my man Fuller."

Harry kept his face impassive. "I hope you are not going to have any telephone conversations, Mr. Elphant." He turned abruptly and opened the frosted glass door.

"I say, I say," murmured Fuller in his faint cockney whine, "you *are* one of the tough ones!"

"Never mind what I am," said Harry, "in forty seconds I'm going out that outer door and, by Christ, you'll wish I hadn't! Ever heard of what accessories to the fact get if the police evidence is strong enough?"

Fuller blinked hard as though a torch had been shone in his face.

He said, "Two months ago, that was on October first, I received a telephone call. A male voice, strong baritone, said he had heard of us. He wanted a very secure room which could be kept at a constant temperature preferably. He said it need not be a very large room."

Fuller had shut his eyes and screwed up his red face in an agony of concentration, so that the knobs and valleys on his small face were accentuated. Harry wondered how the devil he shaved.

"I asked his name and he replied, 'Mr. John Post.' I consulted my files and told him that the best thing I had was a very secure room plus two lavatories and a small kitchen. It has a modern gas convection heater with thermostat, a large refrigerator, a big table and about thirty chairs. Its location is peculiar, inasmuch as it is at the top of a warehouse, situated on a gallery. Egress is not through the warehouse, but obtained via a flight of stairs at one side of the warehouse."

"You can only get up to this gallery flat from outside?"

"Let's see, as I remember it, there is an old hydraulic

lift inside the warehouse, but it's padlocked and I guess the key has been lost for years. God knows if the thing works—probably would come crashing down even if it did. It's four years since I saw it."

"Who operates the warehouse?"

"Dunno, we don't handle that, only the flat. When I was there, it was junk, old scaffolding, you know, long-term storage and maybe opened twice a month."

"Ownership?"

"Now, Inspector, I'm cooperating like a woolly lamb, but clients' names! No sir, get your warrant and the boss'll be getting injunctions like . . ."

"All right, what happened?"

"A messenger boy delivered a packet which contained pound notes. So much for three months' rent, so much for the inventory deposit. I sent a receipt, copy of the inventory and the keys to Mr. J. Post, post restante, Charing Cross Post Office. Everybody happy."

"How much?"

"We required a two-hundred-pound deposit against the inventory, but as for the rental, you'd have to subpoena me."

A fat chance of the two hundred ever being returned, thought Harry, wondering what else to ask. He glanced up and, to his surprise, saw a nervous twitch in Fuller's left cheek.

He kept silent.

"Look," said Fuller, "it's supply and demand, all real estate is. Nothing sinister about it. We do our best for the client and that's that."

"All right," said Harry, "let's have the address."

Like a conjuror, Fuller whipped out paper and carbon from the desk drawer and drew a small portable typewriter toward him. "Here," he said, taking up a pen, "I'll sign the original and you sign the carbon, just so that we've got proof we cooperated."

Harry thought for a moment, then waved aside the proffered pen and produced his own. He pocketed the original.

Very slowly the Inspector got to his feet and adjusted

the folds of his overcoat. In silence he reached for his hat and went to the door. As he went through, he turned and switched on a beaming smile.

"I see you flick those cards. Have you tried a slow underarm action?"

The old man at the front counter had his mouth buried in a meat pie. He scuttled aside so that the Inspector could pass, and ketchup oozed onto his chin.

At the Yard, the Inspector sought counsel and presently found it in the shape of a very knowledgeable inspector who specialized in Suspected Premises, whom he met in Hawker's office. Harry nodded and tried to remember his name.

"You'll note," he told the Superintendent, "that this address is within two miles of the Huntingtower Gallery."

"One of Jackie Parrott's places. He used to work through Elphant," said Suspected Premises.

"Haven't heard of Jackie in years. I heard he died of a broken heart when they legalized casinos and betting shops," said Hawker.

"No," said the omniscient man. "He retired to Clifton-ville. Had a drink with him last holiday at the Queens. Put on three stone—remember how skinny he was?—and grows fancy geraniums."

"Expand for benefit of young Mr. James," said Hawker.

"Parrott went for years, street bookie round Islington, plus gambling schools. He was the big one, specialized in visiting businessmen who wanted action—craps and baccarat. He was smart all right. Always had six premises and used each every ten days, never more. It was like this, you were told to be at a certain place, usually a small pub, at a certain time. A hire car would come and pick you—and your party—up. The games were straightish, no real mallarky, although Jack himself was a 'mechanic' with the cards if necessary, and very few complaints got to us. Not much in the way of trimmings except expensive snacks and masses of ice for the drinks. This place is typical. You're actually inside a warehouse. You went up a flight of outside stairs and into what used to be the offices in a gallery. Jack Parrott bought the best, reinforced, mortise locks. On a corner of the main room was a window so you could see straight concrete for a quarter of a mile."

"We never did catch that one," said Hawker.

"Tell you what," said Suspected Premises, whose name Harry remembered was Peters, "your only chance is at night. Fix it so that the street lights go off for half an hour. I did that once in '55. It was as near as we ever got to Parrott, about forty seconds after everybody got away. There were the cards on the table, six bottles of scotch, four of champagne, and one of brandy, three pounds of smoked salmon, some assorted French terrines and four plates of potted shrimp canapes. Well, it would have been a shame to let them go bad—don't know when I enjoyed a raid more. Me an' the boys played pontoon and ate and drank old Parrott's provender. The next week I saw Jackie in the street and he grinned and said, 'You're puttin' on weight, sergeant'—as I then was—'you must be living high on the hog.' "

"He took a thirty-year lease. It's got about seven to go. His other places he rented through Elphant on short leases."

"Do I take it that he owns the place?"

"I suppose I'll have to raid it," said Harry.

"Have we got enough for a warrant?" said Hawker.

"I'll sign a 'having good reason to believe,' " said Harry, "on the strength of my impressions at Elphant's."

"All right," said Hawker. "We'll get it through by the afternoon. What will you want?"

"Keep it light," advised Suspected Premises. "A big party stands out like a sore thumb in that locality."

"Well," said Harry, "I was thinking of the local station sergeant, Honeybody. He knows the manor like the back of his hand."

"Better take me," said Peters. "You, me, this fellow Honey-whatsisname, two constables. Do you think they might have a minder?"

"That's anybody's guess," said Harry.

"I tell you what went wrong before," said Peters. "In spite of the street lights being off, they probably spotted the party walking down that long stretch of pavement. It wasn't a very dark night. We think they got out via the warehouse."

"My man Fuller told me that there's only an ancient hydraulic lift that is locked."

"Well," drawled Peters, "the time I'm talking about there might have been a tip-off, there was a sergeant who was asked to resign a year later, but suppose we go through the warehouse first. I know how to approach the door from the loading bay so that you simply can't be seen from the flat upstairs. We synchronize so that the car with two constables draws up outside the stairs to the flat as we get inside.

"As far as getting up and down things," added Peters, "if the inside and outside of the buildings were Everest, I'd have been knighted long ago. As long as there is a fingerhold, I'm there."

Peters was a short chunky man and Harry looked at him with respect.

Hawker nodded. "We can thank our stars Mr. Peters came on to our side of the fence, Inspector. He can climb anything that's climbable and some things that aren't. Okay, you blokes go and arrange it, and, Mr. James, give me your affidavit for an entry warrant within the hour. Thank God we aren't in France."

Peters cocked a politely subordinate eye.

"You can't get a warrant to raid a house between sunset and dawn. Lord, man, that's how Landru and Petiot had such a long run, boiling down old ladies at night. Nobody could do a bloody thing. Take yer ma-in-law to Calais for a long weekend! Ta! Ta!"

"He's a rum old devil," said Peters as they descended in the lift

"My master is indeed rum to the point of being a proper old bastard. Between you and me and judge's rules."

Peters chuckled. "All those stories about him in the old days. He was a hard old devil. Lord, the men he's taken in his time."

"Amen," said Harry.

"I suggest," said Peters, slightly emphasizing his six or

seven years of seniority, "that you leave the car and the constables to me. I'll pick you and this Honey chap up at the local station.

"Let's see"—as they got out of the lift Peters took out a diary—"at ten it'll be as black as pitch, no moon. Suppose we hit the place at ten-thirty."

"You were saying about the street lamps."

Inspector Peters winked. "Leave it to me. From ten-twenty until ten-forty. All sweetness and cooperation and traffic diversions so we don't run the risk of trouble."

The Inspector saw his substitute about borrowing Sergeant Honeybody.

"Hm," said the sergeant himself, fiddling with one side of his mustache. "Corner of Wallace Street and Conklin Street. Let me think. Yes, a dirty old building, tall enough for three floors, but gutted inside. Conklin Street is a dead end. It's a commercial neighborhood, mostly small factories except for the big distillery, very quiet at night and not a great deal of traffic except for motorists taking a short cut."

"No rumors?" inquired the Inspector.

Honeybody shook his head regretfully. "Two years ago there was an epidemic of breaking and entering around there, but we got the chaps who were pulling it. Nothing since then. Tell you what, sir, I'm having a beer and sandwich at lunchtime with Mr. Lovers. There's not much doing in any warehouse that he doesn't know about. I'll ask him if he's heard anything about new people."

"What time?"

"I leave the station at twelve-thirty."

"Well, I might join you," said the Inspector and set off to pursue an entirely different matter involving the alleged theft of fifteen washing machines. After an unsatisfactory hour and a half, during which time he collected four statements, each of which contradicted the others in a quite remarkable fashion, he remembered in time to draw up in a taxi in front of the station just as Honeybody came out.

"Get in," called Harry, "we'll do it in style."

The sergeant had arranged to meet the burly Mr. Lovers at twelve forty-five and they were ten minutes

151

early. It was the sort of pub a connoisseur such as Lovers might choose, a medium-sized Victorian establishment in which the sense of the period had been discreetly preserved, so that the red plush was slightly faded and the gilding a trifle tarnished. The lights shone on wood for which a hundred years of polishing had achieved something that lamination could never emulate, once you compared the two, and the brass footrails gleamed in the indirect lighting.

The sergeant had led the way into a long, pleasant bar, marked "The Snuggery." A small but blazing fire at the far end made the central heating far more pleasant. It was well patronized but not crowded and they found a table.

"I can recommend the cold stuffed lamb sandwiches," said the sergeant, "likewise the lamb's tongue. They make little mutton pies, served hot; very tasty indeed. Meanwhile what can I get you to drink?"

"We might have a long evening," said Harry, regretfully, "so I think I'll nurse half of mild-and-bitter."

The sergeant came back and shook his head. Harry saw he was drinking a small rum and peppermint.

"When you get to my age," said Honeybody, "you stick to short ones if there is to be any hanging about. I remember last year this time. I'd been in the darts tournament at my club, six or seven pints of bitter during the evening, and then the station telephoned through." The sergeant gave a gusty sigh that swayed the waxen points of his mustache. "Emergency, half the station were down with flu, and a surveillance job has come up. It ends up with me accompanied by a woman constable standing for four hours in a freezing cold shop doorway. Cor' love us, it was agony! They had a tip that Joe Trotter, the forger, and his girl friend were making for a flat opposite. Of course, it was a red herring, but, Lord, since then it's short ones for me when there's work about!"

"Well, well, good to see you, Inspector," boomed Mr. Lovers heartily over Honeybody's shoulder. Harry was slightly amused to see that the stout man was accompanied by Miss Spotting. There was an answering gleam of amusement in Lovers' eye as he said, "I'm taking a course in art appreciation. Never knew what I missed."

152

"What I seem to be taking," said Miss Spotting, "is a course in pub and beer appreciation."

The sergeant returned from the bar with Miss Spotting's gin and Lovers' stout.

"Do you know the old warehouse on the corner of Wallace and Conklin?" asked Honeybody, diving into business. Lovers frowned and fixed his eyes on the opposite wall for a couple of seconds.

"Yes, I think so. At one time it was builders' supplies, scaffolding, concrete mixers, that sort of thing. Inconvenient old building. I believe now a firm of shop fitters use it for bulk storage. It's opened a few hours a week. Why, anything up?"

"We just got a rumor from an informer that there might be some stolen stuff around there," said Honeybody comfortably.

"I've heard nothing," said Lovers. "I suppose you'll raid it?"

"Well," said Harry, with the habitual caution he reserved for laymen. "It's not so easy as that. I wish it were. It would be nice, wouldn't it, Serge, if we could just stroll in where we like? But, no, Mr. Lovers, I might locate the leaseholders and ask their permission to take a look at the premises, but, of course, that has definite disadvantages. So if I did want to look see, I'd have to apply for a warrant and they are not lightly given, I assure you. Scarce as hens' teeth. I was hoping that you might have heard of something, so I could use it to support what is after all only a rumor.'

Lovers shook his head regretfully. "I wish I could help you. I suppose it takes time to get a warrant?"

"I've known it take a week, and then I got a note regretting that my evidence wasn't strong enough. Of course, if my boss really was in a hurry . . ." The Inspector shrugged.

"Tsk," said Lovers, almost petulantly, "I hate to see all this crime in our little neck of the woods. I see there has been no arrest in the Huntingtower case."

"I'm not on that," said the Inspector, "but as far as I know, we are pretty certain of the time but little else. Nobody will admit to seeing anything."

"I went and had a look at Merge's Alley," grunted Lovers. "I don't wonder why nobody saw anything late at night. However, for what it's worth, it occurred to me that Huntingtower must have known the murderer or murderers. The reason they were not seen is that they were all stealthy and watching, if you follow me. Noise would travel along that alley and unless you moved with stealth you'd get faces leering out of windows. All these semi-slum folk are nosy bastards, same as villagers. It's the middle class that mind their own business. Cheers!" Mr. Lovers plunged his R.A.F. mustache into the stout.

"That's very well thought out, sir," said Harry. "I don't know whether Mr. Porterman, who's in charge, has thought of it, probably has, I would say, with his experience, but I'll send him a note. Another round, and what about provender, the serge said something about mutton pies?"

Twenty minutes later the Inspector, comfortably greasy around his mouth, was thinking of having a word to Dora about putting Hildegard on a cram course in mutton-pie making. Rosemary, lot of onion, basil—he wished Elizabeth was here to consult—yes, perhaps a very little marjoram.

"By the way," he said to Lovers, "it's very remote, but have you heard anything about a bad man named Arthur Mace?"

"Let's see," said Lovers, stroking his solid chin, "Mace, unusual name. Oh, yes, that rings a little bell! One of my drivers; forgive the 'my' because I don't run to lorries, but he does steady contracting for me, mentioned the fellow. Some years back there was a gang who used to steal cargoes, and this fellow Mace was a strong-arm man who used to try to suborn the drivers. Well, this chap, Ted Riddle, said he saw Mace a couple of times round Clancochran Street with two of the foul Scobie clan. The old woman Scobie has got her house there, as you know."

"That is very interesting," said the Inspector. "I might like to meet this driver."

"He's taking a load of stuff for me to Liverpool," said Lovers, "then back-loading to Cardiff and then chancing his arm. But I'll telephone you when I see him."

He shifted his great bulk in the seat. "But all these Scobies—I suppose there'd be thirty of 'em counting the inlaws—are capable of anything."

"Hah," said the sergeant, "don't you know the honest one, him they call Red Hot Scobie?"

Lovers shook his head.

"He's Curzon Scobie, the last of the old man's brood. They call him Red Hot because he wouldn't, positively not, steal a red hot stove providing it was nailed down."

They all laughed, at least the Inspector did until he saw the dead whiteness of Dolores Spotting's face.

"I say," he began, but she shook her head.

"It's just," she said in a small voice, obviously wrestling her nerves under control, "that—I think it would be a fortnight before he died—but I was in his office, the one upstairs, when the phone rang. He listened and there was an odd expression on his face, and he said, 'Just a minute, Scobie,' and then asked me if I would wait in the library. It stuck in my mind because I was a little hurt. It sounded like a *business* call, Paul discouraged personal calls in business hours, and he never had any business secrets from me."

So you think, dear, thought the Inspector cynically.

Aloud, he asked, "No impression stuck in your mind?"

"I think he rather sounded as if he were addressing a younger man."

"Hey," said Lovers, and flicked out a hairy paw to steady her. Little beads of sweat lined her forehead. After a second, she brushed his hand away.

"No, it's just that I knew him. To you he's just a bloody statistic. Excuse me," and Miss Spotting began to cry gently into her handkerchief.

"That's all right, miss," said Honeybody, with unsuspected, stolid comfort in his voice. "It suddenly strikes you like lumbago. I've seen it a lot and there's no cure but a good cry, particularly for the ladies."

For some reason Miss Spotting's misty blue eyes peeped over her handkerchief without great affection.

"I should not have thought," she said icily, "that it was any different."

"Ah," said Honeybody, "the ladies have got soft hearts,

God bless 'em. When I was a constable, I was there when they pulled in Mrs. Wrench, four husbands, antimony after matrimony you might say. Cried like anything because she couldn't take her little pugdog along."

Fire entered Miss Spotting's eyes as they sought and held the sergeant's. "All right," she said, "fair shock treatment, but I wouldn't wonder if you had an occasional water jug broken over your head!"

"Occupational risk, ma'am," said Honeybody, getting up. "Well, sir, we must be getting along."

"I heard that your fellows had been asking round about a car, a big American job," said Lovers.

"Lord, sir," said Sergeant Honeybody, taking out an envelope, "my constables have worn out around six prints already. Take a look."

"You think it had some connection with the murder?"

"Perhaps with more than one murder," said the Inspector, and Lovers' mouth twisted in distaste.

"I'll have to think. I've got the idea I've seen this job sometime or another. Can I keep the picture?"

"Surely, sir," said the sergeant.

Miss Spotting had begun to dab her eyes again. "There, there, old girl," said Lovers, like an uneasy groom.

His black eyes flicked round the table. "Better talk of something else."

"How's the exhibition and old MacGlaishen?"

Miss Spotting dried her eyes, and coughed. "We open tomorrow, but the advance notices are good—even Blenkinsop wasn't too bad and he hates modern Spanish. MacGlaishen is purring and for one nasty moment he had thoughts of not selling. But he can't be in London and Edinburgh simultaneously and he'd never trust anybody with the till. Three buyers have turned up, now waiting on the accountancy report."

"You'll stay on?"

"It depends. Two of the potential buyers I like, and, yes, I'd stay if I was wanted. But the third, definitely not." She gave a faint smile. "MacGlaishen considers me an asset. I heard him say emphatically, 'And with an experienced manageress living a couple of blocks away!' immediately after he had mentioned the central heating system."

"I don't see how you can be taxed as a capital gain," said Harry.

"You would have to hold her for quite a few years," leered Lovers.

"On this pleasant note," said Harry, getting up and taking his coat from the adjacent rack, "the serge and I will say adieu. Thanks for the help, sir."

Harry and the sergeant decided to walk back. Snow had turned to a grayish mush which slopped above their shoes.

"A bit of a turn-up that, sir, about the Scobies."

"I'll get on to Chief Inspector Porterman. He'll take the Scobies apart, rather like interrogating the zoo, there's that many."

As they splashed along, Harry became lost in his thoughts until the sergeant nudged him.

"Cove following us, a hundred yards back. No mistaking it, ruddy amateur."

"All right," said Harry. "You lead, I'll follow."

Purposefully the sergeant made a left turn, Harry at his side, and ducked into a shop doorway.

A few depressed people passed without a side glance. Finally the Inspector heard the splash of hesitant steps. The long, anxious face of Leicestershire Stanisgate peered from side to side and focused within the doorway. The Stanisgates' eldest child jumped as he met the Inspector's glance, visibly jumped half an inch, slid on the icy slush and for a second poised uneasily on one leg, his arms waving at his sides.

"Afternoon, Leicestershire," said Harry, "lovely afternoon for a stroll."

"Yes, Harry," bleated Leicestershire. "I mean . . ." With a vague nod the youth walked rapidly on.

"Young friend of mine, gormless but harmless," said Harry in answer to the sergeant's raised eyebrows.

"See you at ten." Harry left the sergeant at the tube station.

There were only two things in his in-basket, the first a

letter signed "Joe Bliss, anarchist and proud of it." The writing was very small and the lines dead straight. The heading read, "for Inspector H. James, my recollections of Señor Castelano, deceased."

It was a recapitulation of what Harry had learned before, except for the penultimate paragraph. "Now I think of it, they both—not always but often enough for me to register the fact—registered apprehension at the sight of tall men, I have seen them freeze like a bairn in an orchard when the farmer passes. So I conclude they feared a tall man (men)."

He concluded, "You will be glad to know that I am still boarded at the expense of the cod-faced landlord. Your card, which I produced, brought on one of his dizzy spells. He sits in a chair in the kitchen and instructs me how to prepare the victuals."

The Inspector read it through twice.

The longer buff typescript bore a brief scribbled note in Porterman's big round handwriting. "For information, re Stanisgate."

As instructed, Constable Boreham and I took up positions near subject's residence at 10 P.M. At 3 A.M. subject was observed coming out of his house, wearing hat, gloves, a heavy overcoat and safari boots. He proceeded northwest in what appeared an aimless manner. After half an hour I was walking thirty yards behind the subject and in radio touch with Constable Boreham, who was driving the van. I became aware, in very bad light, that the subject had disappeared from view, and quickened my pace. I felt a hand on my shoulder and as I turned, I found it was the subject. He said, "I've had you little bastards creeping after me." I felt a blow—left eye—and found myself on the ground.

I made radio contact with Boreham, who located subject and followed him home, to which he went by the most direct route. Boreham thinks subject realized he was under surveillance because he kept stamping his foot and shaking his fist at the van. He went into his house at 4:25 A.M. and Boreham parked the van some distance while I took up position in an alley on the opposite side of the road.

There was no more activity until 7:30 A.M. when Constable Boreham and I went off duty after making this report. Signed, Graham Prout, Constable.

"A policeman's lot," hummed Harry as he reached for the telephone. He got on to Porterman's assistant.

"Mayhem at midnight, I understand, assault achemma!"

"That landlord of yours is an ugly devil," said the voice at the other end. "You should see Prout's shiner. It was the hour and the cold and the shock no doubt, but Prout's private narrative is 'In the Grip of the Faceless Fiend' class."

"Are we proceeding by summons?"

"No, Portyboy says we would look like b.f.s and besides we'd have to admit we had our eye on him, which might prejudice any other proceedings. No, poor Prout's eye is on the house, you might say."

On impulse the Inspector dialed Blood, Cupping and Fulsome. "Sorry," said the operator, "but Mr. Stanisgate is taking a few days off. He expects to be back next Wednesday."

"It's going to be an 'orrible bleedin' night," confided Sergeant Honeybody dispassionately later in the day, his face red as he bent down to pull on a pair of gumboots. "Drat these bloody things, they're always getting smaller."

Harry rather agreed as he wriggled his own toes in borrowed boots.

"I prefer these when there's the likelihood of climbing." Inspector Peters looked down at his gym shoes neatly covered with galoshes.

"Okay." Peters looked around, at Harry and the sergeant, and the two constables, Kelly and Drew.

"You'll do the driving, Kelly, which means you'll stay in the car until otherwise ordered. Now the sergeant, Inspector and me will start off by taking a look inside the warehouse. Conklin Street is a cul-de-sac with a distillery at the end. I have arranged to come through the distillery, which means it is impossible for any lookout to spot us. We get over the wall into the loading bay and then we'll see." Peters tapped the bulge in the breast of his overcoat.

"We'll be in the loading bay at ten-thirty. At ten thirty-two, two of you park the car dead in front of the ware-house and at the foot of the iron staircase which leads up to the flat. If anyone comes down that staircase, detain them."

Although a matter of fifty yards from the warehouse as the crow flies, the back entrance of the distillery, in a street running parallel to Wallace Street, was in practice three hundred yards or so by car or walking.

The three got out of the police car and Peters nodded to an elderly watchman who waited at a little door. "Take us through quick, Mr. Smith."

They followed the wavering blob of the man's torch.

"Smells of beer," said Honeybody.

"That's the mash," said the watchman. "I'm used to it. Here we are, I'll just open the door sufficient for you to nip out."

In the bitter air which plucked at Harry's nose and ears the blackness was almost tangible.

"I spent an hour on the distillery roof with a powerful glass." Peters' whisper barely reached their ears. "I'll take your hand, Inspector, you take the sergeant's." A small diamond of light hit the muddy snow ahead. Slowly, feet carefully placed, they moved along.

"This is the wall near the gate." The blob of light momentarily danced. "There's no glass left on top. I'll go first. After I get the ladder up."

There was the faintest of noises and for a moment the beam danced on the end of a nylon ladder dangling down. Harry took the torch.

"Okay," came Peters' voice, "now you, Sergeant."

Harry could hear Honeybody's heavy breathing before he in his turn went up and over.

"Release the ladder before you drop," whispered Peters. Harry handed it down.

"The main door is padlocked," whispered Peters. "Didn't look a very good one, but you never know. I don't want to force it, rather do a neat job."

For an instant the light flickered. "Right," whispered Peters. A faint wash of light suffused his cheek. He had fixed a cardboard box, open at both ends and containing a very small torch, over the padlock.

160

Harry watched, knowing that his fellow inspector had to work fast before the cold numbed his gloveless hand.

"Steady it please, Sergeant!" Honeybody's big hand went out and gripped.

The Inspector dropped a tool and gave a hiss as he bent and fumbled on the ground.

The luminous dial of Harry's wrist watch showed ten-forty before there was a slight grating sound.

"Okay," said Peters, flicking the torch, "those hinges don't look too bad. Both of you stand back."

There was a faint groaning noise and Harry cursed inwardly, but Peters worked with infinite patience and although it seemed much longer, Harry, counting seconds, made it two and a half minutes before one of the double doors had inched open enough to let them through.

Peters' voice drifted to them. "Harry, you take this low power torch, I'll use a medium, and you, Sergeant, keep that big 'un of yours for emergency. The gallery is above us on the left, and we'll go over and see that hydraulic hoist. You lead, Harry."

The floor space was stacked with articles the use of which Harry had no idea. Complicated erections of metal and wooden braces and struts. Eventually they came to the hoist, a platform from which rose several cables of varying thickness.

"I'll have to chance my torch." A narrow beam flickered briefly. "One of the cables looks bone dry," said Peters. "This hoist must have ended up at the old gallery, so I'll go up and take a look see."

"You'll be right?" whispered Harry.

"Piece of cake, son. Keep those torches out." Harry heard the Inspector's topcoat drop to the floor.

They waited perhaps a minute and a half in silence, then a great beam of light cut through and shattered the stifling darkness. For a moment Harry froze and then he reached and caught the sergeant's arm. The light was being shone down from the gallery and they were practically underneath it. The Inspector pulled the sergeant well into the side of the hoist. He stretched out his other hand and felt one of the cables rhythmically swaying. Evidently Peters had opted to continue to climb. Harry bent and felt on the floor and eventually encountered what felt like an old coach bolt. He threw it to the opposite wall, where it clattered dismally.

He felt the sergeant jump as there was a report from above and something momentarily ricocheted and whined. "Christ," said the sergeant gently.

"Use your torch." The sergeant flooded the big beam across the warehouse and froze.

"So help me," grunted Honeybody.

The broad beam rested on two enormous naked figures, seemingly suspended some feet up in the air. At each side were smaller equally nude figures and for one shocking moment the Inspector, his neck suddenly clammy, saw the brutish, inane smiles on their faces. Men, surely not?

"Dummies," said Honeybody quietly, "window dressing dummies, old fashioned ones. Look they've got them on trays suspended from the roof."

Like a ruddy orgy scene at Covent Garden opera, thought Harry, but his heart was beating a little faster than usual.

There was a further spang of sound and this time plaster clattered not far from them. Whoever was shooting must be leaning over the side of the gallery.

Honeybody methodically raked the place with his torch.

"A ladder!" he said.

The Inspector saw it was made of rope and light wooden slats and presumably descended from the gallery, but before he could properly digest its implications the sergeant, his torch held before him, was weaving rapidly between the piles of junk toward it. Cursing, the Inspector followed with his own small pinpoint of light making a miserable chorus.

Honeybody's own torch brushed his broad face, so that it gleamed on his mustache and eyes as he shone it up toward the roof. Next there was a fusillade of shots and, in slow motion, the beam of Honeybody's torch wavered and dropped and with a great crash and clatter his body crashed to the ground. Harry dropped to his knees beside him and fumbled in the near darkness. He sensed rather

162

than felt the presence of other people in the darkness around, and part of his mind, acting independently, registered that somebody had slid down the rope ladder fast. Almost simultaneously something caught him a blow on the side of the head and he dropped sideways half stunned onto Honeybody's chest. Twice he struggled to get up and fell back, feeling a wetness on his cheek and hearing the roar of a powerful motor revving, and the intermeshing of gears.

Somewhere Peters implored his Maker for the precise positioning of the very Freudian light switches.

As Peters eventually found them and the warehouse was filled with a washy economical glow, Harry got to his feet.

"Right?" yelled Peters.

"Get going," called Harry as the sound of the motor died away. He heard the sound of Peters' running steps.

The sergeant was breathing hard. A large plaster thigh reposed across one shoulder and great shards of plaster lay around him. His bowler hat was scarred and dented and crushed around his forehead.

A little to one side was a heavy T-joint, part of the matrix which supported the giant plaster model, thought Harry. This was what had poleaxed the sergeant.

He felt and found a pulse and as he did so, Honeybody opened his eyes. "What the hell . . . ?"

"A chunk of metal hit your skull. One of the shots brought one of those damned effigies down."

"Knocked out," said the sergeant, pushing the ground and sitting up. "First time, but I've seen it happen enough times. Well I'm damned, ruined my bowler!" His eyes focused. "All right in a minute. But what's the matter with you?"

Harry saw there was blood on his lapel and he touched the stickiness at the side of his head. "Probably swiped me with the gun."

He helped Honeybody to his feet. "I'm getting too old for this kind of lark," the sergeant muttered.

They walked slowly out and found that an ambulance was drawn up beside the police car.

163

"Constable Drew," grunted Peters, looking harassed. "He dashed round and the lorry swiped him, ribs and smashed legs I think. He said it was a two-tonner Leyland, and I've got the calls out. How're you?"

"Walking," said Harry.

The doors of the ambulance closed and it moved off.

"Up to coming to the Yard?" asked Peters.

"Right," said Honeybody. He peered into the car where Constable Kelly, a trifle white round the mouth, sat. "Oh, Constable, get somebody to get on the blower and tell my old woman I won't be home until all hours. Don't tell her I've been hurt."

"I was up that rope, three quarters way there," said Peters, "when the shots started. I felt like a target all right. So I went on up to chance my arm but very slowly. Then there was this great crash and down I went just as fast as I could."

"One or two came down the rope ladder, or slid," said Harry.

"I looked up and saw the bloke with the gun just before I blacked out," said Honeybody. "I'd say smallish, dark complexion, a couple of razor scars and a snappy brown soft hat."

Something clicked in Harry's mind. The smaller of the two men at the Whisky an', let's see, Gideon Lewis! He'd played worse hunches. He reached for the radio phone.

"Yes, sir," he told the impatient Hawker, "we're on our way. Meanwhile I want Gideon Lewis, he's on file, but I think Sergeant Crook might know him, it's worth a try."

Harry and the sergeant went straight up to Hawker's room. The Superintendent pushed over half a dozen photographs.

"Anybody you know, Sergeant?"

Without hesitation Honeybody selected one. "That's the little swine who had the gun."

Hawker nodded. "Your hunch paid off, Inspector. It's Lewis. You two better report to the doctor."

"The scalp is lacerated," the surgeon grunted as he dressed Harry's scalp. "Did you black out?"

"No, just felt dizzy."

164

"Come back if you get a headache."

He examined the sergeant at length. "Bit of concussion, I'm afraid. I'll have to get you into hospital for observation."

"I'm all right," protested Honeybody.

"I'm not thinking of you," said the surgeon adroitly. "If you turned your toes up, I'd be the one who got it in the neck."

"I'll call your wife," said Harry as he left.

He told Hawker.

"I thought he looked concussed," said the Superintendent. "Well, we got Lewis, or rather Sergeant Crook did. That fellow doesn't appear to sleep. We rang through at his home and he immediately dressed and raced round to where he knew Lewis' mistress lived. My bright boys had gone to his last known address. Anyway Crook got a constable off the beat to knock at the front door, and collared Lewis as he nicked out the back way with a small suitcase. Quite a struggle, I'm told, and Lewis got a broken wrist. No sign of the gun, but he had a passport in the name of Wright, two hundred in sterling and eight hundred dollars. He's at the local station and not talking, except to say that he's got an alibi for this evening—his girl friend and her brother.

"Crook is coming over, he should get a promotion out of this."

"Was the passport forged?"

"Genuine, lost or stolen, but some work done on the photo—Lewis' scar painted in. It was lost by a man named Wright in Greece last summer. They may have moved elsewhere, but there used to be a kind of clearing house in Tangiers for passports. A British one for eighty quid and up to a couple of hundred for some of the vaguer South American ones."

"Well," said Harry, "we've got that on him."

"Um." Hawker glowered. "Don't forget he'll have a slippery solicitor and two or three hundred quid's worth of counsel. Still the overnight case and the dollars should convince a jury. I hate to see a gunman get away with it."

165

When Crook came in he looked pleased in spite of the swelling and discoloration round his right eye.

"Butted me," he said. "Nasty little man is Gideon. I couldn't get the handcuffs on him, then he forced his way out of my wrist lock and I felt a bone go. That took the fight out of him."

"He's not talking?"

"They set his wrist temporarily and he told the D.D.I. that he'd been with his woman and her brother all evening. As per regulation he's in a nice comfortable hospital bed at this moment."

"What about his woman?"

"Daisy? As tough as he is, tougher maybe. She's lived with a string of tough boys. Eventually they go down and she shops for another. Been with Lewis about seven months. She says they stayed at home and watched teevee and drank."

"The brother?"

"Described as a salesman," said Crook contemptuously. "Actually he fiddles what he can with some pimping on the side. No convictions, just a louse with a pimply face. He's so scared of Daisy that you won't shake him."

"I suppose Arthur Mace comes into this somewhere?" The Superintendent kept his face expressionless.

Crook gave his thin smile which did not reach his eyes. "I am aware of my own obsession, thank you, sir. However, Mace has been putting in his days and nights in his cubbyhole at the back of his coffee bar. Unfortunately!"

"Any connection with Gideon Lewis?"

Crook shrugged. "I couldn't prove any, though he knows men who work for Mace. Since he was got out last time, we thought Lewis was working with one of the payroll snatching mobs."

The telephone rang and Hawker listened.

"Hell," he said, "the lorry got clean away, nobody can understand how. They thought they had it near Camden Town, but it was a load of stolen sugar. The flat was quite empty, of course, and free from prints. The gas heating system was turned on and there was an empty scotch bottle and three cheap, dirty glasses in the kitchen. Some signs that food had been consumed, crumbs of bread and

166

sausage. Two cigarette butts, and a yellowed piece of paper bearing a receipt in respect of Matisse. And so, as per usual, we are back to these ruddy paintings."

Harry did his best to soothe Mrs. Honeybody on the phone and went home.

Chapter 6

Breakfast at the Stanisgates' was a dull and depressing meal. Hildegard had put tinned sweet corn and cheese quite successfully into scrambled egg, but messed things up with cayenne. Leicestershire seemed unwilling to look anybody straight in the face, Dora wore what the Inspector privately thought of as her "bottomlike look" and Hubert himself was slightly twitchy.

Only Hildegard talked, a rather whiny mournful diatribe about having that morning to return the Skye terrier, who sat unhappily under the table, back to the kennels.

" 'Bye all!" said Hubert abruptly. "I may be working late."

The Inspector went to see Honeybody, who was sitting up drinking a cup of gray fluid.

"You're a detective," he said to Harry. "What's this stuff? I thought it was coffee."

Harry sniffed. "It's soup," he said. "You can always tell because it smells fattier than the coffee."

"Hm," said Honeybody, "the tea's horrible and I've got to stay on."

Harry raised his eyebrows and the sergeant gave a lugubrious grin. "They X-rayed and want me to stay for a couple of days."

He brought the sergeant up to date and promised him that any striking development should be relayed to him as soon as practicable.

At the Yard he was joined by Inspector Peters, who informed him that they were required at a conference at the office of the Director of Public Prosecutions, where they met a stringly old solicitor with a dyspeptic face and a fat middle-aged treasury junior whose name was Middle.

Middle fingered their reports without enthusiasm and addressed himself to Peters.

"Were these shots fired with intent to injure, Inspector?"

"I was hanging on to a cable thirty feet up in the air. The sound of any shooting in such circumstances is alarming.

"Quite." The pouched eyes turned toward Harry while the old solicitor apparently chewed something rapidly.

"No," said Harry, "he wasn't aiming at any person, just making a diversion. Gunplay does. We stop to size up the situation. He was spraying shots at the wall and the only risk was a ricochet."

"Then no intent to commit grievous bodily harm?"

"I couldn't support that charge," said Harry, "but assault with a deadly weapon, yes."

"I understand that he offers an alibi," said the junior, "a woman and her brother outside whose dwelling he was taken."

"No convictions, but known," said Harry.

"Mm," said Middle. "The defense would decline to examine on character of course."

The solicitor unexpectedly interposed in a rusty tap voice, "I, er, made inquiries. They are both unprepossessing, poor witnesses. She is brassy, very bold, and he looks a furtive, shifty type."

A pink tongue flickered out and refreshed Middle's large lips.

"This sergeant of yours, will he stand up?"

"Eh?"

"In the box, man, in the box."

"Yes, well, yes, sir, I guess."

"Don't guess," said the junior automatically, meaning nothing personal thought Harry.

Aloud he said, "Honeybody's an old-timer, given evidence hundreds of times."

"Precisely," said Mr. Middle. "A stolid old policeman saying 'in the execution of my duty.' Then, the circumstances. Knocked down by an oustize model of a nude woman. What I am referring to, Inspector, is yumor. If I were defending, I'd get in quite a lot of yumor—old-

169

fashioned policeman and bosomy wax figure on his helmet. Lighten it with *y*umor, leave the jury with a *y*umorous feeling."

"It wasn't funny," said Harry.

Colorless eyes flicked against him and the junior sniffed.

"Don't think me callous, Inspector. We respect the sergeant's gallantry, but the fact is that your only evidence is his recognition, recognition by a man who was shortly afterwards concussed. The more defense can lighten Honeybody's evidence, and the more they can edge him into the wings, the better chance they have."

"I understand," said Harry.

The junior looked past him at the solicitor, who slowly shook his head and chewed his jaws.

"Well, no," said Mr. Middle, "I'm afraid my advice is to proceed merely on the passport matter. I'm afraid a magistrate would hesitate to commit on the shooting. Evidence of flight would be difficult to bring in. Of course, if you establish anything else . . ."

"Obstructionist old ass," said Peters as he and Harry walked out into the cold.

"Oh, I dunno," said Harry, "does his duty according to his lights."

Peters frowned at him.

By public transport Harry pursued his investigations into the missing washing machines and had, so he thought, arrived at the concrete fact of who had actually had them in their charge at the time of their disappearance when the owner, a man with a nervous laugh, announced that they had turned up, mislaid, in another warehouse.

The Inspector, annoyed, wrote it off as an unsuccessful attempt at insurance fraud, impossible to prove, and returned to the Stanisgates' in search of lunch. Dora had pork chops and a harassed look.

"I'm worried," she said as they finished the meal. "I telephoned Hubert—I never do because he dosen't like it—and he isn't there."

Harry couldn't think of anything to say.

"Why I telephoned," said Dora with a faint tremor in

her voice, "is that a friend of Leicestershire's telephoned from his work to ask why he hadn't been in yesterday or today. And half an hour ago the lady who runs the kennels where Hildegard helps in the mornings rang and said that Hilde went out on an errand, hadn't come back." She put the dirty plates back on the table and sat down heavily.

"There's always some simple explanation," said Harry as soothingly as he could. "Let's see, Hilde was wearing gray pants and a yellow cardigan and she would have worn her black topcoat. Right?"

Dora nodded.

"I'll telephone in her description to the local station and they'll do what is necessary."

Dora brightened. Harry reflected that she had enormous faith in any kind of official machinery.

"Now, there's something for you to do. Do you know where Hubert keeps his bills and receipts, stuff like that?"

She nodded.

"Look back through them and see if there's anything you don't understand. Go back three months."

He got through to the station, with a premonition of disaster.

Presently Dora came back holding something. "He spikes receipts," she said, "on this. I've gone back and they are all usual things, except this."

It was a grimy, mean-looking piece of octavo paper, with a smeary letterhead. Jas. Martin acknowledged receipt of eight pounds from "Mr. Stanygate." The date was seven weeks ago.

"Mm," said Harry, "no more?"

"Just that."

By and large, thought the Inspector, Hubert was a man of precise patterns. He would tend to put every receipt, whatever for, on that file. Few people realized the extent to which their everyday existence became a pattern, he thought, and as a policeman thanked God for this frailty.

"The address isn't far from here, D. I'll take a look. Fifty to one old H. is having a drink somewhere, but I'll try it."

He got out his street map. As he had thought, it was familiar.

In a few minutes the Inspector leaned against the wall, looking at the recessed wall opposite. It had been less than a week since he first had seen the recessed space in the building opposite. Just now it existed as a piece of dingy gray landscape in a dull stage set devoid of highlights.

The morning crowd were memories, a very few shift workers debouched from the nearby tube station into the crossroads, sporadic groups of housewives, some wheeling pushers, walked unseeingly toward the high street and its shops, a man parked his six-horsepower car, removed a small cardboard carton, saw the Inspector and locked the doors.

Somewhere in time a sallow-skinned man had had a pitch where he showed paintings. Now nothing remained.

Jas. Martin occupied the grimier of the two tobacconists' shops opposite. The window was half occupied with advertising cards and the Inspector saw that there seemed to be a glut of secondhand prams.

The shop was gloomy and cold except for an eddy of heat from a tiny round electric fire behind the counter next to a youth in his late teens.

"Mr. Martin about?"

The youth gloomily shook his head and the Inspector noticed a certain sharpness about his face.

"I'm a police officer."

The youth looked amused. "You're in the wrong shop. Old Jas. wouldn't have the nerve to pinch his old woman."

"It's this receipt," said Harry, putting it on the counter.

"Can't help you. I only help out twice a week when he goes to have his rheumatic treatment. No, no, he hasn't got it, but it's warm at the clinic and they give him a free cupper and a bun."

"Close-mouthed is he?"

"Jas.? Frightened he's going to lose his choppers if he tells you the time. Hm. Let's have a look at that date! Of course, Jas. has let upstairs."

172

"A flat?"

"Well. I've been up there a couple of times when Jas. stored a few things there. Two floors, up rotten stairs. You could break your ankle easy. Hasn't been occupied for forty years, and doesn't it look like it! It'd cost hundreds to fix up so you could let it. The entrance is at the other side of the shopwindow. The key's here." He fumbled under the counter and produced an outsize rusty object.

"Well, a few weeks back I was passing one morning and there was a new padlock on the outside of the door. A good one, too. I had to buy a packet of fags so I asked old Jas. He just mumbled. When he doesn't want to tell you something, he just makes a mumbling noise. I just shrugged."

"Mind if I take a look see?"

"Far as I'm concerned you can," said the youth. "Matter of fact I'm locking up and clearing off for an hour for some food. I'm not going to catch pneumonia for old Jas. and there won't be anything doing until around six."

Harry stopped and watched the youth lock up the shop.

"If I thought you'd find anything, I'd come along. But knowing old Jas. you won't. So long."

The door had two steel rings screwed into the woodwork, but there was no padlock. He fitted the key into the lock, and tried to turn it. Instead the door creaked inward at the pressure. He pocketed the key and played his torch up a flight of decayed-looking stairs. The youth had not exaggerated, the risers were warped and often gaping.

"Police here," called Harry. "Anybody at home?"

There was a silence. Nevertheless the Inspector felt he was not alone. He hesitated. If there was to be any kind of roughhouse, he didn't want to have it on those stairs. However he supposed it would work both ways. Carefully he ascended the stairway, trying not to breathe too deeply of air which smelled of ancient drains. He paused on the shaky floorboards of the first landing. Three doors. One opened into the skeletal remains of what had been a combined kitchen and bathroom, judging from the vestiges of the plumbing. The second door was jammed tight.

173

He swung it inwards and followed the light beam in. Momentarily he was conscious that he was falling and then he blacked out.

Somebody was asking him if he could hear them. Over and over again. He was conscious of irritation. Presently he heard it was Hubert's voice.

"I can hear you," he said and realized his voice sounded queer.

"You've been out about three minutes. I suppose you're tied."

He found his hands and feet were tied behind him. A torch, probably his, was on the ground a few feet away and its rays shone on a part of a trouser leg. It looked familiar.

"Is that Hildegard?" said the Inspector incredulously.

"Oh, yes, indeed," said Hubert. "And to your left is Leicestershire. I dare say Dora's in one of the closets."

"I left her at home," said the Inspector.

"That's a comfort. I've been here since eleven. A big man came in that door and pointed a gun at me. He had some kind of nylon affair over his head. A smaller man was behind him. The big fellow went off at twelve and left the smaller man behind. At one there were steps and, lo and behold, there were the kids." Hubert laughed. "They talk of the viciousness of youth. Leicestershire assumed the classic upright posture of an English heavyweight and the little bastard right smartly kicked his feet from under him and clipped him behind the ear as he went down. He merely pushed Hildegard over and stuck his foot in her back while he tied the boy up."

"I'm going to take up judo," Hildegard said resentfully.

"Meantime how are you doing, Leicestershire?"

"I'm near it now. I'm feeling for the switch."

There was a slight click and light filled the room. Twisting his head the Inspector saw a powerful camping electric light, with Leicestershire sprawled on the floor beside it. Hubert lay on his side under the boarded up window with his daughter not far from his side.

"How long will we be?" There was a quiver in Hildegard's voice.

174

"I don't think the gentlemen are coming back. If the worst comes to the worst, I can probably wriggle to the door and kick it in. I don't much relish the stairs part," said Hubert.

Twice in forty-eight hours, thought the Inspector as his head began to ache. His eyes focused on a dirty-looking chair. On the floor beside it was a bottle and two small plastic containers.

"Whose bottle?"

"Them," said Hubert. "The smaller man mostly. It smelled like rum. The plastic things were loose enough so that they could get a cup underneath. No good expecting prints, they wore cotton gloves."

"You said one of them left?"

"The big one left at twelve. He came back at two for about half an hour. They were whispering together, couldn't hear what."

"What happened then?"

"Oh, we just laid around. He sat on that chair and had an occasional suck of rum. He was about to go just before you barged in, because he'd just tied Hildegard up, he hadn't troubled before."

"The swine," said the aggrieved Hildegard.

"And by the way!" said Stanisgate slowly, "I've been dreading this moment, but what did you put in his rum?"

"Put in his rum?" the Inspector heard himself echoing.

"Yes," said Hubert. "A couple of times he went and stood outside the door for ten minutes. I guess his nerves were twitching. The second time, shortly before you came on the scene, I saw my darling daughter put something in the bottle and shake it well. All right, Hildegard!"

"Tuppers Tapeworm Tablets," the girl said.

"I think," said Hubert carefully, "that I am going mad."

Hilde's garbled and slightly tearful explanation involved a description of a listless mastiff and the fame of Tuppers Tapeworm Tablets.

"Tell me, dear," said Hubert. "How many?"

"Thirty," sniffed Hildegard.

"And how many dogs does that dose, for God's sake?"

"One tablet does seven pounds of dog."

Hubert calculated. "Two hundred and ten pounds. I saw him finish the bottle after he cracked poor Harry. He'd weigh sixty pounds under that, all muscle but around five foot six. I hope you haven't . . ." Hubert bit back the words.

"Is anybody there?" Dora's soprano came from the stairs

"Come on up," bawled Hubert, his eyes wide. "Bring your auntie."

Dora's mild face froze as she opened the door. She was however competent in crises.

"My right-hand trouser pocket," said Hubert. "Cut Harry free first."

Without ado Dora found the penknife and rolled Harry on to his stomach. As she worked, she said simply, "I was sick with worry so I had to come."

Harry lost sense of time, but presently he found himself with the Stanisgates on the chilly pavement.

"You'd better come with me to the Yard, Hubert, and the children if they feel well enough."

"I don't know about that," rumbled Hubert, "perhaps tomorrow. . . ."

"We will all go in a cab," said Dora and the big man said nothing.

Harry got the cabman to stop at a telephone booth, and called Hawker.

"Where have you been?" said the Superintendent.

"I'm bringing in my landlord and his family."

"Nice, nothing I enjoy more than an intimate family gathering.

"And would you put out a general call for a man five feet six, around one fifty pounds, who may be taken to hospital? He has taken thirty Tuppers Tapeworm Tablets."

"Mr. James, are you drunk?"

"I wish I were." Harry replaced the handset.

Superintendent Hawker evinced what perhaps only Harry, with his knowledge of the old man's moods, spotted as slight nervousness as the Stanisgates came into the spacious office, and he remembered that the Superintendent was reputed to be frightened of women. All of which had not prevented him, when an Inspector, from cracking the skull of Mrs. Boardford, the Worthing baby farmer, with a skillfully flung truncheon as she climed out of her drawing-room window. Now he walked round the table and was introduced quite affably. Stanisgate, Harry observed, seemed quite at home.

"You know," he said, "I've a queer feeling that the big fellow was the same one who bashed into me when I had my wallet stolen. Great flabby blotched face."

"Excuse me, sir." Harry turned to the constable seated at the little desk in the corner. "Percy Foot, alias the Long 'un. Ask Records to send an identity selection, please."

"Now," said Hawker, reseating himself leisurely. "First I want to ask some questions. I will tell you that you may have your solicitor here, you may refuse to answer, but that I have at the moment no belief that any of you are guilty of a criminal offense. And of course it is the duty of every citizen to assist the police, not the right, but the duty."

In the pause that followed, Harry could see that Dora was vastly impressed.

"Some police questions are embarrassing," said Hawker. "For instance I want to know your surname, sir."

"I'm Hubert Stanisgate."

"I am aware of that. What were you christened and please don't attempt the feeble old one about N. or M."

"I've committed no offense," said Hubert, gloweringly erect in his chair.

"Mr. Stanisgate, now that it is come to this I shall get my answers one way or another, and perchance less pleasantly or more pleasantly. Believe me, if it would help us in a case, we would rouse the Prime Minister at three in the morning. Very reluctantly, but if it were considered necessary—and more than once it has been—he would be roused."

"All right, all right," said Hubert, "sell your reminiscences to Cecil King. I was christened Hubert Beer. You imagine all those heavy hopsy quips and the chops I had to smack. I believe in names. Nobody wanted artwork with Beer on it, so I changed. To the best of my belief I could call myself Donald Duck as long as I had no criminal intent." Hubert and the old Superintendent stared at each other for a long second.

"You know," said Hawker, "there is no need for you to be so defensive! As you say, you might be known as Minnie Mouse for all I care. It might be difficult for your children . . ."

"We don't care," said Leicestershire. "We are Stanis-gates."

"A chip off the old block, I see. Frankly, sir, we are looking for a bad man named Hubert Harcourt. He served in the army. So did you, but your wife says she got no allowance."

For an instant Hubert's black eyes switched to Harry. Then he gave his sudden, charming smile like the sun coming out. "Okay, old chap, I realize your difficulties."

Hubert switched back to Hawker. "I am the son of a Falmouth skipper who got killed mine-sweeping in forty-three. He married a Breton girl. She never spoke much English. Dad used to take she and I to see her relatives—hundreds of 'em—but generally she lived for Dad. She lived five weeks after she got the telegram. The point is that I talk French like a Breton peasant."

"I didn't know that," said Harry.

"Why the hell should I go around talking like a Breton peasant, for Christ's sake? Anyway I got put in this thing, which I imagine I still can't talk about. We were supposed to be single, but most of us had benefits of clergy or de factos. I thought it best not to claim D.'s subsidy just in case they put me back on to lat cleaning. I was a gallant capting, by the way, and they gave me a small gong or so."

"I congratulate you, sir." Hawker exuded amiability. "Constable, get me the War Office, Colonel Verteil if he's there, if not his deputy."

"You might remind them," said Hubert, "that they owe me two pounds twelve."

"Indeed, sir?" Hawker was solicitous.

"I had this coat with a French tailor's label, six inches of straw in each shoulder and soup grease on the lapels. I left it one morning when I jumped out a window. They docked two pounds twelve from my pay book. If I could only have returned a button, it would have been okay."

Hawker's number came through, and he spoke briefly and replaced the handset.

"Now, Inspector, suppose you tell me of your afternoon's tribulations. I see you have another lump over your lug. Punch-drunk inspectors end up guarding the Crown Jewels, remember."

Harry complied. Hawker's eyes were puzzled as they flickered around the room. As the Inspector finished, the telephone rang and Hawker listened quietly. "By the way," he said eventually, "do you owe him two pounds twelve?"

Hawker had on his reptilian smirk as he replaced the handset.

"Most of us would think a D.S.O. quite something, Mr. Stanisgate. The old W.O. sends you its love. The two pounds twelve would have been refunded any time you signed a simple form instead of scrawling vile words on it. I am informed that connoisseurs considered you among the top two hundred writers of venomous military memoranda. As an old hand at such things allow me to congratulate you."

Hubert looked baffled, but his wife said, "I do wish you wouldn't dramatize so, Hubert, particularly in front of the children."

"Remember this, Leicestershire," said Hubert, "if you have an adventurous life, if you retrace the Silk Road on foot, it will end in a middle-aged woman telling a middle-aged you not to dramatize."

"You're wonderful, Dad," said Hildegard, all banners flying. Leicestershire wore rather a hunted look.

A messenger had brought in a slip of paper.

Hawker read it and snorted. He stared at Hildegard and said, "You were capable, my dear young lady, although I would be careful, particularly as the Inspector once told me that you, ah, handle food. A man named Jockey Sperring—once a stableboy—collapsed on Charing Cross tube station clutching his belly. L.T.B., ever solicitous, sent him to the hospital, where, thanks to the Inspector, they were watching for tapewormed crooks. The Jockey, whom we can't interrogate tonight, is pumped and purged but physically prognosticated prime."

"I think I arrested him in Reading once," said Harry, "carrying some stolen stuff in a van."

"Indeed the Jockey is competent as a strong-arm man, but not intelligent. Frankly," said Hawker, "he drinks more than the heads like. On the credit side, the man will do anything and is sufficiently stunned not to notice details. He had a hundred and fifty pounds in his money belt."

There was an awkward silence, during which Hawker stared at Hubert. "Well," said the Super, "as my clients, say, this is the time you come to bat."

"I think," said Harry, neatly on cue, "that Hubert might like to talk to me."

"Oh, certainly," said Hawker.

"I think it concerns some paintings," the Inspector said.

"A fair cop, guv," said Hubert, the mocking little smile switching on.

"How many?" said Harry.

"Two Pissarros, a Renoir, and a Degas and twelve others. Finding's keepings, isn't it?"

"If you can find who the hell owns *them*, you're a better man etcetera."

"That's what I've been working back at. I've identified the Pissarros, last heard of in 1879. 'Course," added Stanisgate, "you do get canvases disappearing into the collections of people who don't believe in sharing the joy."

"Begin at the beginning and let's see if you're in any kind of a mess."

"I'm not in any mess," said Hubert sourly.

"In early September I went into that tobacco shop. The man there was having one of these interminable phone rows. It went on and on. Ordinarily I would have walked out, but"—he shrugged—"summer was dying outside and I thought, God, another day at the office! I was late already and there wasn't the usual crowd of sheep going past. I was starin' without knowing it at the pavement artist and his muck, and suddenly I thought, Great God, a

180

Renoir. No, of course, I knew it must have been a copy. It interested me. I thought maybe there might be some kind of picture story. I got the cigarettes from Scroggo, the tobacconist, and went and did my stuff, ten shots, walking up and down. Then, well on the tenth run I saw the old chap was standing against the wall just lookin' at me very oddly. When I came back on the eleventh time he'd gone."

"Leaving his gear?"

"Yup. Everything there, including the cigar box. I had a good look at the Renoir. A bloody good copy, I thought. Of course, some of the pro copyists are bloody good, they lay the paint on just as the original fellow did. But they work in galleries and I couldn't trace this Renoir in the reference books. However, I'm ahead of myself. He'd obviously crept off, so I went to the office. That evening he wasn't there, neither was he for the next week. One night I came home about ten, still a bit of light. I went over to his pitch and smoked a cigarette. I'd developed the film, otherwise I'd guess I was dreaming about the Renoir. Now where the edge of the building comes out there's a kind of cavity."

"I've seen it," said Harry, "quite a big hidey-hole."

"Well, in there was a suitcase, a cheap cardboard and cloth affair, dirty yellow. I went home and subsequently checked, just a quick glance, for two days. Apart from the grime getting thicker on it, it was untouched, I'd swear that. So one afternoon I sent it off. Just picked it up and strolled off. Just like that. Lost, stolen, strayed, abandoned, civic duty to help." Hubert stared around him.

"Ar, well. I couldn't take it home, not with all the little beady's I've got around. Once or twice I've talked to that loathsome little tobacco merchant, Scroggins, about his upstairs."

"His name is Jas. Martin."

"I always thought it was Scroggins," said Hubert regally.

"I've had a thought about some place where I could muck about a bit, thinking, with a bit of paint to slop around, you know. All I wanted was light and quiet. Now this verminous top of Scroggo's emporium has one room

181

—I guess it was some kind of servant's torture chamber—with a lot of glass that isn't broken. Needs a clean. I always told Scroggo I'd give him ten bob a week and pay, say, thirty quid on a bit of doing up. He always whined he couldn't do it under four pounds. I had to put the suitcases somewhere; it just didn't go with my dapper mien at all. I thought of the office, but the Littlest Bleeder would stumble on it, cut 'em about with a razor and use it for his paint campaign. The upshot was that I dangled eight nicker in front of Scroggo and said I'd have two months on appro. He said okay and gave me a receipt. Oh"—Hubert paused—"of course you found it. Force of habit, I stuck it on my spike automatically. Well, I dumped the bag upstairs and flew round to an ironmonger and got staples and a lock. I got back just in time to catch Scroggo creepin' up the stairs." He mimicked a cockney whine, " 'Just goin' to see things were all right, I'm sure.' Well, that's it."

"You have spent seven weeks examining the paintings."

"Yes," said Hubert. "Bastard of a job. I've been haunting libraries and borrowing books. Of course, I'm no chemist, but I know something about it and I took three into a fancy darkroom owned by a friend and did a few tests. The pigments were over fifty years old, that's as near as I could get. Hell!" Hubert shrugged his wide shoulders. "Nobody owned them. I was thinking of a reward, I've got two kids and a mind below money."

"I think," said Harry, who wasn't feeling well, "that you were spotted. You didn't fit in and there was some consternation, sufficient for your pocket to be picked to find out who you were. Then it was easy. They tailed you and when they were ready, wham."

"At least one man followed me last night," growled Hubert. "I punched his face."

"We had better not talk of that," said the Inspector, and Stanisgate gave an evil smile.

"Frankly, Mr. Stanisgate," said Hawker, "there is an offense known as stealing by finding. Roughly the law says that anybody who finds anything and takes it into custody

182

has a duty to make some attempt to find the rightful owner."

"Which is precisely what I was doing," said Hubert. "I thirsted for the rightful owner and his rewarding check like a hart."

Hawker gave his rare and surprising smile. "And now you're eight quid and some indignity out. I don't decide who is or who is not to be prosecuted, but I doubt whether you'll be hearing any more concerning this."

Dora gave a gusty sigh of relief, but Stanisgate seemed unmoved.

"And you two youngsters?" asked Hawker.

They looked at each other. Leicestershire led in his half-aggressive, half-ingratiating voice.

"Well, Hilde and I saw that Dad wasn't himself and that Dee was worried. He was abstracted, talking with half his brain. Something was up."

"We thought it was a woman," said Hildegard. "He's psychologically susceptible."

"My dear Hildegard," said Stanisgate, reddening, "you have no ground whatsoever . . ."

"I read a book."

"You two half-baked young idiots . . ." began Hubert.

"Now, H.," said Dora. "This is a scientific, probing age. They can't help being born in it."

"I wish to go home," said Stanisgate, "preferably alone."

Hawker held up his hand. "Can we confine ourselves to facts and leave Jung to the Jung?"

"Well," said Leicestershire, "he was taking time out from work. Hilde and I started to trail him. It was difficult. He went to the London Library and the British Mum, and the Tate a lot. We couldn't understand it."

"We thought it was assignations," said Hildegard.

"My dear young lady," said Hawker, "I have no doubt you will never need a place of assignation, but do remember, just in case, that the London Library is impossible."

Hubert guffawed and Dora looked disapproving. Harry thought that she disapproved of levity in a high official.

"Well," said Leicestershire, "that's about all. We stood opposite and watched him go into that place and shortly afterwards two men walked along. They were swaddled up because of the cold and we couldn't see their faces, but one was taller than Dad. He came out after half an hour and eventually Hilde and I went in. The front door wasn't locked.

"Lack of reasoning on my part," said Stanisgate. "I did not put the hasps for the padlock on the inside and the door lock didn't work that side."

"One more thing," said Harry, as the constable gave him a sheaf of photographs, "do you recognize anybody?"

Stanisgate riffled through them. "This," he said, "was the man who barged me when my wallet went. It could be that he was the tall man this afternoon. I think so, but that's not evidence."

"Well," said Hawker, looking at the clock, which registered nine. "I'll send you home in a car. If you will, please remain, Inspector."

"Whee," said Hawker, "I rather like that landlord of yours. War Office said he was a frightful tough and should be preserved in case of another outbreak."

"You'll check, sir?"

"Oh, yes, he'll be checked out six ways by nine tomorrow, but I don't much doubt the result. But you, looking groggy, can you stand another hour?"

"Sure."

"Porterman is due within a few minutes. Also your bearded art friend Blenkinsop and A. N. Other."

Harry found his face sour.

"One of those," said the Superintendent. "High Commissioner level. Nothing at all in law, but we guarantee anonymity."

Porterman entered first and Harry thought he looked ten years older, flesh sagging round his neck. Next Blenkinsop, writhing with inward spiritual pride which waggled his beard, plus a squat, fat man with a square uncompromising face.

"This gentleman," said Hawker, "is a Canadian citizen, produced by our good friend Mr. Blenkinsop. I want you to hear his story."

184

"Well," said the Canadian. "I was staying in Paris in August. I'm known as a collector. I was approached by an Englishman, a fat type of man. Was I in the market for a Renoir? My reply was that at present prices I could not afford one. He told me that this one had been smuggled out of Russia, that it was called *A Study in Green* and that it had been bought by a Vladimir Witte in 1896 and taken to Russia. I asked him to come back in a couple of days' time. He did not impress me."

"One moment," said Hawker, "is this the man?" He handed over a photograph.

"That's the guy."

"Polly Packer," said Hawker, "well known to us."

"I thought it was the usual con trick. I checked and there had been a painting of that name bought by a Vladimir Witte and subsequently lost to sight.

"This man, who called himself Price, came back and said that the painting was on offer for sixty thousand dollars American. Of course, it was cheap. That was all very well, I said, but what about the Vladimir Witte family?

"Price had all the answers. He named a town captured on some date in August 1919 by troops under Trotsky's direction. He showed me a photostat of some kind of printed bulletin which listed sixty people shot as counter-revolutionaries and general beasts. It included eight people named Witte. Price said that additionally they had shot the kids and a couple of women cousins and that the only survivor had eked out a living as a waiter in Moscow until he died in 1943. I don't speak Russian, but he left me the stat, and I got an expert. It did list these eight Wittes, including Vladimir, and the files showed that Trotsky's men did take this town on the date mentioned by Price.

"Anyway, Price came back again and by that time I'd got it sorted out in my mind that if it were true, why then the thing belonged to nobody, unless you said the Bolsheviks, whose seizure of property had never been recognized my side of the Atlantic. But I still had the stink of a con trick up my nose. When you got money, gentlemen, you've got the weasels working on you day and night. I expected to be asked for a ten thousand dollar deposit and was prepared to tell him to get to hell. But he was kind of coy and said that I should have my own expert look at it. I asked where and he said could I be in London the first week of September. I hummed and ha'd a bit, just to keep him on the hook, and finally said I could. He asked me what hotel and I told him. He said that the expert and I should be in the foyer at ten—on September the second.

"He took us out in a plain ordinary cab, and, for God's sake, I nearly keeled over. I don't know London and my expert was from Berlin. Mr. Blenkinsop agreed we would keep him out of it."

"Surely," said Hawker.

"We stopped outside some Italianate-looking old building. There was a recess in the wall and—this was when I could have fallen over—in there sat an old pavement artist with a dozen daubs and one Renoir. For God's sake, just propped there against the wall in a dollar frame with no glass."

The Canadian ran his fingers round the neck of his shirt. "Just lying there," he said in tones of wonder.

"Now, sir," said Hawker. "Will you take particular care from now on. Just go slowly."

"What happened was that the old artist just kept crouching there on a little chair. He didn't turn his head, just kept staring down at an old cigar box with a few coins in it. My expert picked up the Renoir and took it to the ledge of the side wall. He removed the frame. There was a receipt in French glued on and also a paper in Russian. The paper said that the painting had been on loan at the Raimir Gallery, St. Petersburg, in July 1912. I took a photo with the camera I carried and paid somebody to check. There was a Raimir Gallery in St. Petersburg run by a Frenchman named Carolos Kock which featured modern art shows.

"I tell you it looked like Renoir to me. My expert spent around ninety minutes. There had been a photograph taken of it and he had a blowup of it and he finally did some checking with calipers. Finally he turned to me and just nodded. Oh, one thing more, there was a man strolling up and down past us, like he was waiting for his wife, but he was a tough all right. I've seen enough pro toughs to know their cut. A big fellow."

"Can you describe him?"

"No, Superintendent, you don't look directly at those fellows. I was all right, I'd told Price I was carrying the camera and three sterling pounds and he kind of grinned.

"Finally we went back to the hotel in a cab, Price, or as you say Packer, with us. I said I'd buy and wanted to know what the terms were. He said a banker's check payable anywhere in the U.S.A. He'd hand the picture over to me and my expert and I would give him the check a day later. I said it would take me six days—I have money on short call in Detroit. He said he would ring, but he never has."

"Thank you, sir," said Hawker. "The man you know as Price is in Egypt. It is unlikely you will hear again in this matter."

The Canadian said goodbye.

"How did you unearth him?" Harry asked Blenkinsop, who was grinning amiably through his whiskers.

"Detective work, m' dear Watson. Around a hundred quid's worth of telephoning as far afield as Berlin and Rome. I asked one question 'Have you had any inquiries about lost paintings?' I got six responses. The Canadian was the only inquirer in London. Q.E.D."

"Who were the others?" said Porterman wearily.

"Two Americans, now back home. I managed to phone one of them. The story is practically identical, but a different painting, a Sisley, and he had no idea of the part of London he saw it in. There was one man who is a leading Venezuelan collector and another a Swiss. It's all written down for you."

"We'll have to follow them up," said Porterman, "but I'd just like some concrete link with Huntingtower."

"The note on his scratchpad," said Harry. "Eleven-ten plus twenty m. I think that Huntingtower was asking for twenty thousand pounds more than his agreed share and it was to be discussed at his eleven-ten appointment. Whoever was running it decided that Huntingtower had to be put out of the way."

"Let's hear more," said Hawker.

187

"It seems obvious that Huntingtower's job was to find the potential customers, then he and Polly Packer made the actual approach. There is some evidence that Polly held out for more money and was scared off. For some reason it was death for Huntingtower." Harry ran his hand through his hair. "This was a case where the protagonists distrusted each other. Brun and Castelano invented this method of keeping the paintings safely by juggling them between street pitches. I suggest that they gradually lost control of their own operation. Hubert Harcourt, if that is the man, decided he was going to have most of the cake. Castelano, who was afraid of nobody, was killed and left as a hit-and-run victim. Brun, who was chicken-hearted, locked himself in his room and died of malnutrition and neglect. You recall the fiver that Brun had. On it was penciled 'Peril à court.' It makes sense if you realize that a Spaniard writing in French would inscribe 'Danger, Harcourt' in that way—I would say that the fiver was the only paper Castelano possessed, so he scribbled on it with a greasy piece of crayon and dropped it into Brun's collecting box. They got Castelano, but Brun went to ground."

"It's full of damned holes," snapped Porterman without grace.

"And if you can find a better one . . ." said Hawker. "Now listen to me! This stinks of what the yanks call hijacking. Don't forget that these paintings are being vended by a Russian named Obermann. Having eliminated Brun, Castelano and Huntingtower, Harcourt may settle it with Obermann, or not, according to the danger in it. Now we stick close to the painting angle. I'll have to bring Interpol into it. And perhaps you, Mr. Blenkinsop, will get me out lists—I'll give you a couple of secretaries —of all likely dealers and collectors. We want ones we can approach very discreetly and who can be trusted to notify the police if they have the bait dangled in front of them."

Blenkinsop gave the unhappy nod of a man who sees a lot of work ahead of dubious utility.

Harry believed he had a few more ideas, but his head

had begun to hurt and he found himself slumped down in his chair.

"Hey," said Hawker and came round his desk with surprising speed. The Superintendent on one side and Porterman on the other supported him to the medical room, the equivalent, thought Harry, who felt lightheaded, of a state funeral with a Union Jack on the catafalque.

"Into bed with you, I think," said the sandy-haired little surgeon, and in the process of time Harry found himself in a bed opposite Sergeant Honeybody, the latter looking cheerful and interested.

The Inspector remembered that Hawker had promised to make necessary phone calls, and with a feeling of luxury took his bath, had his X-rays and consumed three pills. It was eight-thirty in the morning when he awoke, and his young woman, Elizabeth Holland, sat on the chair by his bed with a large thermos of kidney soup, six brown eggs which had veritably not seen an Egg Board, and a bottle of calves-foot jelly; all the delicacies which could be obtained by that hour. Honeybody, quaffing tea, was telling her about the evil lot of a policeman.

"Really, Harry," she said as she kissed him, "you'll have to go back to the accountancy. The sergeant was telling me that all higher ranks get ulcers."

"And flat feet and piles all round," said Honeybody helpfully.

"Don't talk," she said, "I'll find somebody to cook you a couple of these eggs."

"You shouldn't alarm her," Harry told the sergeant.

"Bless you, sir"—Honeybody waggled his big head—"she's a born copper's wife. I know all about them. You won't scare her."

A houseman casually floated through the door.

"Ah, the hardheaded cop," he said. "No alarm, sir, no fractures or detached retinas, but Sir Bradbury says at least two days in bed with nourishing food."

"Your coffee-cum-soup!"

"I only drink rum myself," said the young man withdrawing.

"I'm going to get on to your Hawker," said Elizabeth

189

when she came back. "You two should have a special diet; he should be able to arrange that."

"How long are you in this clink for, Honeybody?" asked Harry.

"Well, Mr. James, I think I could get out tomorrow. No damage done, but when I think of my feet and the weather outside, not to mention getting away from the family for a few nights, well I won't hurry in spite of the soup."

"I thought you said, Sergeant, that the worst drawback was being away from your wife for all hours?" said Elizabeth.

"Well, miss," said Honeybody, in no way perturbed, "you see, after twenty-four years of marriage you get a bit of a different perspective like. Mind you, I said the truth. Many's the time yours truly has been lurkin', up to his arse in mud and slush, if you'll pardon my French, and wishing I was back in bed with Dodo."

"Your missus is named Dodo?" asked the Inspector.

"Ah, yes," said Honeybody and the Inspector watched Elizabeth, seated for once at a loss for words.

"Well, I'll accept the ulcers, but I'm damned if I see why you all get piles," she said finally.

"All the paperwork on damp chairs."

"And why, Sergeant, should you sit on damp chairs?"

"Some of those station roofs leak chronic, miss."

"I think you are pulling my leg." With dignity Elizabeth took up her handbag and string carrier. "I shall see you both at one."

"A very nice young woman, if I may say so," said the sergeant. "And a good policeman's wife."

The Inspector loathed hospitals and the vast wakeful nights when he was ill, but in circumstances such as these he sneakingly enjoyed its odd resemblance to a large hygienic hotel, with the cheerful black faces about his room and even a sun-dried ex-Army nursing sister named Miss Phipps, who plainly regarded him and Honeybody as malingerers. The sergeant always asked if she was a sister to Jim Phipps, a white-slaver he had arrested in 1934.

On the Thursday night, Sir Bradbury having given permission for discharge, and both the sergeant's Dodo, a large sandy-haired woman with a capable, resigned face, and his attractive daughter, having gone—Elizabeth had tearfully departed to a conference in Manchester—there entered with red-faced jollity and a clinking noise that made Sister Phipps glare, the vast rotundity of Samuel Lovers.

"I heard you gentlemen were favored guests re visiting hours, police ward and all that." He glanced cunningly around. "I thought Guinness, gents, if we've got tooth glasses. Six bottles concealed around my person and a packet of ham sandwiches."

"Mr. Lovers," said Honeybody huskily, "stand at the next election. Me and mine are your voters."

"There is, I imagine, outside the door, a capable acidulated lady who gave you a certain look," said the Inspector. "She frightens me."

"Ex-Army nurse," said Lovers, going silently to the door.

They heard his orotund voice. "Now, me dear, this is Secret Service and the Official Secrets Act. See none of your people come near us unless I ring. You understand!"

"Salt of the earth," said Lovers, divesting himself of his overcoat and slipping two bottles out of his twin hip-pockets. "They're always the dicey ones, the rumpers. Sat down heavily once in a train and, God 'strewth, rum as it happened and four stitches in Wimbledon Station waiting room."

Lovers had the sort of personality that warmed a hospital room. "I tried to get my tailor to put in special bottle pockets, but he had a fit. I told him about the old ladies hobbling over the Gibraltar frontier clanking like engines, but he said I wasn't an old lady. Should have come before, but, truth to tell, I've got to know old MacGlaishen. Afraid I collect characters."

"How is the haggis-bashing old rascal?" said Harry as he savored the tang of ham and stout.

"Peace on earth tonight," said Lovers. "Confidentially, I had a word with him and if there's a good price on the gallery, he'll treat Dol Spotting fairly. Fine girl! No, the reviews were good, even that hairy man who I understand is your friend wrote it up favorably. Quite a few of the sellable things sold—my word, it's a nice business. I told Dol that I'd sell out and back her any day. The loan exhibition part of it goes to the United States, Los Angeles, on Tuesday, but it's crashed the show on—escalated, old MacGlaishen intones. Dol would have come round but they open until ten."

Harry's handset rang. He reluctantly put down his sandwich.

It was Sergeant Crook. "Sorry about your head, sir," he said perfunctorily.

"I shouldn't butt against walls."

"When are you out?"

"Tomorrow."

"I've got the itch. Something's going to happen in this manor. I can't get anybody enthused."

"Arthur Mace?"

"Suppose you say twenty years of experience."

"I'll have to clear with Hawker."

"Please do that and phone me tomorrow."

"Work?" said Lovers sympathetically.

"Yes."

"Well, since we are on that subject, I heard that the male brood of Scobies have gone to earth, leaving only the women and a couple of spotty youths."

"Any idea where?"

"A barman I know who knows the clan very well—his father was in jail with the original Scobie but he's straight himself—says that Bal Scobie, that's short for Balfour, for Lord's sake, has some warren of a broken-down house somewhere in Deptford where they sometimes secrete themselves."

"That's right," said Honeybody, "Bal's the brains among that lot, shrewd as six monkeys. He looks just like one, by the way. I think they call it a baboon. He's got no forehead, but you must be able to have a brain and no forehead because he's got plenty."

The sergeant drank half his stout at one swallow. By this time the Inspector was rather used to Honeybody's disquisitions.

"Yes, I will have another sandwich. Well, sir, Bal's got this broken-down house, like something out of Charles

Dickens it is, all cellars and doors and an old warehouse on the side that abuts clean onto the Thames. Bal used to bring Indian hemp in before the river police detailed a launch specially to watch him. Once you get the Scobies in there, it's hell's own job to winkle them out. I remember when Lucky Jack Turner and his two brothers said they'd shoot any Scobie on sight, all the Scobie men just vanished. Bossy Turner, he was the youngest and silliest, went down to Deptford and tried to force his way in. Somebody emptied a carboy of sulphuric acid from an upstairs window. It missed, but Bossy took a cab clear back to Turnham Green. Yes!" The sergeant drained his stout and looked thirsty.

"Give him another," said Harry, "and he'll get to the point."

Honeybody grinned. "My old schoolmaster—you met him, sir, the night his dog threw up on the carpet—always said I was slow. Well, what happened was we put the Turners away on a bank robbery that was two years old. Twelve, eight and seven, they got. And the info received came from the Scobies."

"Nice people!" said Lovers.

"They are all scum," said Honeybody. "That's what a copper learns. Robin Hood! My kids used to watch him on the teevee and I used to tell the wife that in real life he had his old mother and sister walking a beat in High Street, Nottingham."

"The historical speculations apart," said Harry, "you forecast that we'll get some sort of a squealing noise from the Scobies? Here, give me another glass before that monster downs it all!"

"We'll get a squeal," said Honeybody, wiping froth off the waxed points of his mustache.

"It certainly is a dirty business," said Lovers solemnly over his stout.

"The cliché is that somebody's got to do it," said Harry.

Chapter 7

Harry and Sergeant Honeybody strained Sir Bradbury's ukase to the extent of departing by taxi at seven the following morning, the sergeant roundly declaring to Sister Phipps that the breakfast sausages gave him wind round the heart and if he had too much lip he would summons her.

To his relief the Stanisgates were genuinely pleased to see him. Hildegard prepared to open a cherished tin of snails, but was manifestly relieved when Harry insisted on haddock.

"Nothing at all wrong?" asked Hubert for the fourth time.

"No, except the hospital food. You are not, by chance, Hildegard, planning a quasi-medical career?"

Hildegard stuck out her tongue, but amiably.

"One thing, Hubert, that I did think of. Who saw you when you were swiping that suitcase from the pavement pitch?"

"Not swiping, old lad, taking into protective custody. But it's a thought. If nobody saw me, nobody would have picked my pocket, etcetera. Wait a minute!"

Hubert combined poached egg with haddock and ate.

"No," he said finally, "I took precautions. In that wartime lurk you got a lecture. Lean against a wall, light a cigarette and as you do it look to the left. Throw the match away and glance right. As I recall it, there were one or two bods, heads down, plodding to the tube, a couple of errand boys. Didn't see anybody looking."

"The shops opposite?" said Harry.

"Yeah," said Hubert. "That would be it. The man who gave the lecture called it the imponderables. He told us

194

about two men talking in the country, miles from any big town. They were leaning against one of those peculiar French haystacks. Suddenly a Wehrmacht officer, sans pants, shoots out and points a gun at 'em. Both shot eventually. The German had been having a sylvan idyl when he and the girl heard people coming along, so they burrowed into the hay. It shook me. I asked, 'What the hell do you do?' The lecturer laughed and said, 'Avoid haystacks.' "

"I'll have those shopkeepers—about six from memory —shaken down," said Harry, "with the threat of Hilde's tapeworming."

"That nice old gentleman, Mr. Hawker, phoned," said Hildegard, "and said he thought I'd worry, but the man recovered and left hospital. He denied all knowledge of it, but the Superintendent said they could analyze his spew and stuff and maybe we could connect up . . ."

"Not when I'm having my breakfast," said Harry.

"I think it's interesting," said Hildegard. "Mr. Hawker said you need a strong stomach to be a policeman."

"You need a strong stomach to deal with Mr. Hawker," said Harry and remembered the words as he went into the Superintendent's office.

"What the devil are you doing here, Mr. James? Sir Bradbury—he's very careful about head injuries these days—said you and this Honeybody, should have extended leave."

"Fit, willing and compos, Honeybody ditto and not anxious to see Mrs. H. all day."

"Well, if you feel you are going dippy, do tell Sir Bradbury. Last evening Sergeant Honeybody's wife got a phone call. Dutifully she called me rather than worry you and him. The voice said, 'I heard the serge is in hospital, is 'e bad?' She said, 'No, coming home tomorrow.' The caller said, 'Tell him it's Scobie and I told him Arthur Mace was around the manor. We don't want a bar of him, so we're keeping out of it.' "

"They've got a hidey-hole in Deptford."

"So Records said. I'll have to send men in. From all reports you need about twenty men, like terriers flushing rats."

"You might let it go and try to get a line to the Scobies for clarification."

Hawker wrinkled his upper lip. "I'll try that, not but that a good shaking down of that particular rats' nest would do any harm."

"What I wanted to ask you, sir, was whether I could go along today with Sergeant Crook. He's got premonitions and his D.D.I. hasn't."

"Hm," said Hawker, "you start interfering in routine and you get a bash from the boss you don't forget and maybe loss of seniority. Hell, I *am* senior, aren't I? Sir Jack Hawker, M.B.E. I'll never be!"

The Superintendent leered. "I'll ring the D.D.I. and say you will be operating in his manor and can you borrow Crook, all amours propred, so to speak.

"On the night," said Hawker, "Mace was warranted playing chemmy and roulette within sight of a dozen people who knew him or recognized him afterwards.

"You know how Porterman works. He and his men have interviewed nineteen hundred persons, by Christ! He's come up with two identifications. A Miss Selma Smith, of dubious morals, identified from a photo lineup Arthur Mace walking slowly a hundred yards from Merge's Alley at one o'clock on the morning of the twenty-third. She's jumpy and on the dope, but she's certain! Second, a British Railways detective, going home, saw a man he thought was Mace, getting into a cab half a mile away from Merge's Alley at around one-thirty. He knew Mace from way back in connection with lifting goods. Third, the junior at the Huntingtower Gallery, a spinster named Robinson, says she was coming home from a political meeting one night, three months back, through some back streets near Kingsway. She's got pebble specs and worry about bombs. Good witness. She says that on August fourth and at approximately midnight she saw Huntingtower walking very slowly down this side street with somebody she identifies as Arthur Mace. Huntingtower saw her and he looked very embarrassed. More than that, kind of savage was her description."

An hour later the Inspector was having coffee with Crook.

"I've got three years before pension," said Crook, "and maybe I'll get one step up. Sometimes you get to wondering whether you are neurotic. I know *them* so well, and you get what the trick cyclists called transference. Everybody's got nerves, down to the little bloke who sells fake reconditioned alarm clocks. It's like a summer's day before an electric storm."

"I wish to Christ it was!" said Harry huddling in his coat over the marble table.

"Now, sir"—Crook was hurt—"you'll forgive me if I say that after all these years . . ."

"I was just saying that when I am reincarnated, I'll get a job in the Hong Kong police where the weather's okay."

"Just to be sure to be born yellow," said Crook, with an angled grin. "But I just want both of us to take a look at Arthur Mace. He sits all day in his coffee bar. At night he goes to the casino. I swear he's up to something big, maybe a big job. I want a second opinion, sir."

"Mace would know your face like the reflection of his own," said Harry. "Now, there was a station sergeant in the hospital with me, Honeybody by name, who is in the same position as I am, except he's got a family. He'd like to come along."

In an hour's time the sergeant, in a blue overcoat and bowler hat, loomed at them a hundred yards from Arthur Mace's coffee bar.

Harry introduced them, the gray, hard-faced sergeant, and the broad, oddly countrified, Honeybody, and felt a certain mutual respect between them, as of equals.

"Something to do rather than listen to the wife," Honeybody grunted.

"We'll drift along and take a look at this Mace," said Harry. "Suppose you wait in the car, Mr. Crook."

Honeybody and Harry walked past the coffeeshop. It had a disproportionately large plate glass window. It was not especially prepossessing, one of similar places which exist for no apparent reason. At the extreme back of the shop was what might be described as a largish cupboard with a door with a piece of glass set halfway up it. Harry could see Arthur Mace's massive head with its golden hair bowed over a small table.

197

"Let's try their delicacies," suggested Harry.

There were six tables, each with four chairs, and barely room to move between them. Behind a counter on which stood an urn of hot water was a thin wispy-haired woman who managed to give the impression of griminess and grimness. At one of the laminated-topped tables a man sat with an empty cup and saucer and a paper open at the racing page. The air was warm and stale as if no air managed to get in the door.

There was evidently only counter service and while Sergeant Honeybody seated himself, Harry approached the woman and ordered two coffees. She dripped black fluid out of a bottle into two thick mugs and dexterously filled them with boiling water to the point where they could not be moved without slopping.

"Anything else?"

"Just biscuits."

For a moment she seemed inclined to refuse, but then her dirty hand delved into some recess under the counter top and produced four biscuits, two of which she placed on each saucer.

"God forgive me," muttered Honeybody some minutes later, "for moaning about hospital coffee. Do you think the old bitch is trying to poison me?"

"It isn't intentional," said the Inspector and began to talk about a teevee program. From the corner of his eye he could see the back of Mace's head. The man with the racing page shuffled dismally out and two young lads came in. Regulars, for heaven's sake, thought the Inspector as they chorused, "How are you today, ma?" and the woman automatically passed over two mugs of tea.

There was a very faint ringing sound which he would hardly have caught had not everyone been silent. He saw Mace raise a handset to his ear. The Inspector thought that the cubicle must be insulated, for he could not hear the sound of Mace's voice. He pushed his three-quarter-full cup away from him and was about to suggest that they go, when a tall wiry man came in.

"Is Arfer in, missus?" he said in sharp cockney tones.

"You can bleedin' see he's in," said the beldame, "but

he ain't seein' no one until after five. You'll have to come back. 'E's too busy to muck around with you."

The man glared and walked out. Presently the sergeant and the Inspector followed. "I've seen that man's face in the files," grunted Harry. "Burglar, I am thinking."

They got into the warmth of the car beside Crook.

"I hope you didn't eat anything," he said.

"The serge bit into a coconut biscuit—at least it might have been one once—before I kicked his ankle."

"He'll probably live," said Crook. "It's the cheese-and-tomato sandwiches which are lethal, so they say, with the salmon-and-shrimp paste the runner-up."

"Only one entrance?"

"There's a lavatory, big kitchen which is hardly used and a tradesman's entrance out the back. That's all right. Artie doesn't keep anything there. I knock it over twice a year under warrant, but I never really expect him to be that careless. Did you see the guy who came out?"

"Burglar, I think. The old woman said Mace wouldn't see him before five."

"Yes, Sid Rowbottom. It's a funny thing, old Sid'll tell a man once that it's pronounced 'Row-bartharm' and the next time he's called Rowbottom he'll come out fighting. Three convictions for assault and once he got off up north. The magistrate was named Bottomley and had a fellow feeling." Crook gave his grating chuckle.

"Any info?"

"You remember the Aldingham burglary, out Wembley way eighteen months ago? Sid Rowbottom did that. Furs, eight hundred quid in cash, and a ruby and diamond ring valued at four thou. Sid fenced the lot except the ruby. Apparently it's an easily recognizable stone and the best offer he got was one-fifty from Arthur Mace. He's been whining and haggling for a year, but he'll end up taking Arthur's offer. Mace will have it taken to Egypt or Algiers, where the patriots are currently putting their lot into jewels. That's the diffreence, Sid's an honest burglar who doesn't know where Algiers is or that he could flog the stone for two thousand there."

"They'd rob him of his pants if he did go," grunted Harry.

"Sure," said Crook. "Mace gets rid of stuff like that in Paris as the staging post. He'll take around twelve hundred for his cut."

"Does he go abroad much?"

"Yes, not so much as he used to when he was in the hashish trade. He was clever—four university students with an old car. Three of them stayed on the Costa Brava, but the fourth went to Tangiers and brought back a couple of suitcases of pot. The girl who went to Tangiers returned separately. The other three—with no Moroccan passport endorsement—drove the old car back with the pot nicely packed around the petrol tank. He made a lot out of that until it blew up."

"Does he speak French?"

Crook looked injured. "I told you he was smart. He can speak French argot enough to make an agreement with a French thief. German, too."

Crook knew some good stories which whiled away the day until the police station that he had been looking after came on the phone. "P.C. Higgins would like a word with you, sir," said Honeybody's deputy.

"Higgins?" Harry remembered the elderly constable on the night of Huntingtower's murder. "All right, I'll drop by the station at two."

P. C. Higgins wore the air of quizzical simplicity that the Inspector well remembered.

"I don't expect you remember Merv Perkins, sir?"

The Inspector shook his head.

"On the night Mr. 'untingtower got done over, red-faced man giving lip from one of the houses."

"Oh, that bastard!"

P. C. Higgins wagged his head. "Merv is a gas fitter and works steady, but he likes his drink and when he's in drink 'e thinks about his rights. Then he gets on the toey side and a word is a blow. I got to thinking. Merv always gets out of the boozer at around ten, gets a bit of fish and goes home. The kids 'ave left home, so there's his wife and her old dad. He takes his quart and the fish up to the bedroom, where there's a nice gas fire and he eats it on the window ledge. Likes staring out the winder, does Merv. All that went through my head, sir."

"Ah," said the Inspector from experience.

"Now my old woman went to school with Edie Perkins and they worked in the same branch of Woolies. Not that I know Perkins, but the old lady sees Edie around the Co-op and such like and they 'ave a natter about what's the day's bargain. Merv drinks so 'eavy, Edie watches her pennies. Lately, my old girl sees that Edie's looking peaky like. She told me that it was like when she remembered Edie swearing she was under ten to get in at the pictures half price. So she said, what about a nice port and leming, Edie? She 'asn't 'ad a drink with her in fifteen years. They go to the Rose and Crown and after 'umming and 'ahing, Edie says that Merv was looking out of his window that night, or rather he'd gone to pee and was standing at the window doing himself up and staring out. 'Come and look, Ede,' he said, and she looked over his shoulder and saw two men come out of that old door at the beginning of the alley."

"Well, well," said the Inspector, "and he didn't tell that to Inspector Porterman?"

"You know how it is, sir," said P. C. Higgins. "He told her not to get mixed up with nothing. 'E'd already broken her upper set over something to do with the teevee on the Monday. Anyway, she told the wife that there were two great big men. One she couldn't see, but the second didn't wear a 'at and he had a great mane of blond hair, dyed Edie said, and she should know, my wife says."

Harry spoke to Porterman on the telephone. The burly Chief Inspector exploded with rage.

"Now, sir," said Harry. "It's a bit of bunce and a credit to the P.C. If we press this, you'll antagonize Perkins beyond redress. I suggest you authorize the P.C.'s wife—if she will do it—ten quid for entertainment."

Porterman rumbled grudging assent.

Arthur Mace did not emerge. Periodically Harry, Honeybody or the driver walked by the café.

"Like this every day," said Crook. "At seven he goes to the casino and leaves at one-thirty."

It was decided that Harry and Honeybody should go to the casino at six-thirty, with Crook stationed in a nearby café.

"Funny to see it legal, sir," said Honeybody. "I seem to have spent half my days chasing gamblers. I remember that I'd just joined up when three other chaps and I were sent along to a gambling school—pontoon it was. The sergeant was a terror named Jones and he told us to turn our pockets out and gave us three quid each. Well, the other boys lost but I couldn't go wrong. I was nineteen pounds up after an hour. I knew that they'd start to stack the cards against me, but the raiding party turned up at that point. At the station old Jones said, 'Turn your pockets out.' The other chaps had a few shillings each, but I had this wad of notes. I peeled three quid off and gave them to him. 'And the rest!' he said. 'It goes into station funds.' I've often wondered whether it did get paid in, but I was raw then and didn't know how to go about inquiring."

"I'm losing now," said Harry. "How much money have you got?"

"Six quid."

"I've got around five. He's just come in. To your right."

The man was playing roulette, desultorily backing five, nine, fourteen and twenty-three. He used ten-shilling counters and neither increased nor diminished his stake. After half an hour he had lost thirteen pounds. Four times he went to the room which had a Dutchman in clogs, performing an involved dance, on the door.

The second time Honeybody followed. "There's a public telephone in the place," he said. "He wasn't using it that time. No other exit."

After the third time, Harry looked at his watch. The golden head still drooped tiredly over the thin lapels of the tan suit. Something bored away inside Harry's mind. Hardly knowing why, he pushed back his chair and walked round the table, conscious of eyes looking at him and Honeybody's puzzled stare.

It was not Mace. As he peered, caution forgotten, the head raised and a pair of protuberant eyes looked at him in apprehension. There wasn't any great resemblance, apart from a general one of height and build. It was the

202

hair, of course, the old trick of the deceiver in keeping people's eyes focused on one flashy focal point.

He beckoned Honeybody, who scooped up his counters. Harry saw that the sergeant had won.

"Scarpered!"

"What's that?" Honeybody sounded amazed.

"It's another man, same hairdo and suit. The first time he went Mace telephoned. This substitute just came into the club, into the la and shut himself in a booth. When Mace was ready he went in, saw he wasn't followed and changed places. We saw a blond man come back. It was easy for Mace to slip out—maybe he wore a hat. Somebody tipped him he was wanted."

"If any of that crowd is conscious even . . ." said the sergeant looking back at the table of devotees and the endless repetition of the rites.

"The cigarette girl. Something wasn't quite right. She shoved matches at him and he gave a bit of a start."

The manager was suave and wore an old regimental tie and looked as if he would have worn several other ties if given half a chance.

"Dear me, what's all this? I hope there's been no trouble."

"We were watching a man. We think your cigarette girl tipped him."

"The staff are very carefully chosen, that's ninety-eight per cent of our battle."

"We might as well see her here as elsewhere," said Harry. "We'll treat it as a harmless girlish frolic. You might let me see your personnel record, if you would."

"Glad to," said the manager, wriggling his mustache momentarily.

The file showed she was married, living apart from her husband, with her parents, in an odor of staggering rectitude, thought Harry, reading the reports.

"Do you screen all your people as thoroughly as this?"

"More"—the manager gave his bright smile—"if they handle money. It's much harder to get a job here than elsewhere."

"I'll remember come pension day."

203

"As a matter of fact, we've got quite a few fellows who served their time in the force, and, in fact, I did a stint with the Palestine Police."

At close quarters Ethel was older than she had looked in the salon. Born 1928. But she had a kind look about her.

"Miss," the Inspector said, "I'm a policeman. Did you give a message to a big blond man at the roulette?"

She colored.

"Now," said Harry, "I'm not hauling you off to Dartmoor. You might be able to help me."

"I saw no harm in it. I . . ."

"Okay, just tell me, miss."

"Well, I do all the rooms, you know. I was in number one, that's the entrance, when this chap came up. I don't remember him before, but he was dark-haired and very gentlemanly, say about twenty-seven. He said he had a friend upstairs and described him, a big chap with a lot of fair wavy hair, seated at the roulette. He said would I be a sport and give him a box of matches. I asked him what he was getting at, and he showed me a box of new Vestas. Inside there was a bit of paper with some pencil writing on it."

"He was a nice young chap, was he?" Honeybody sounded fatherly.

"Oh, yes, sir, very nice. He said his friend's girl friend was coming in to look for him and that she didn't like him gambling, so would I give him this note."

She glanced nervously at the manager, whose bright smile had grown brittle.

"I thought there was no harm so I said I would. He tried to give me a pound, but I said no."

"Can you tell us what he looked like?"

She proved one of the surprisingly accurate witnesses who stand out like small gems in a hatful of dull marbles.

"About twenty-seven, five feet ten and slim, straight brown hair brushed back, gray eyes, regular features. Good-looking." She stopped and looked at Harry.

"You're doing fine, miss."

"He had on this gray suit, the material looked all right

204

but it didn't fit him too well. Oh, one thing. He didn't say his r's very well. Friend came out a bit like *fwend*.

"I put the matches on the tray. I recognized his friend straightaway by the blond hair and tan suit. I pushed the matches in front of him and said, 'Your matches, sir.' He looked startled for a minute and put them in his pocket. That's all."

"What did you think of the blond man?" said Harry.

She managed a slight blush. "I didn't like the look of him."

When she'd gone, the manager offered them a drink. They both asked for a scotch.

Before they had time to drink it, there was a tap at the door, and the cigarette girl entered. The manager registered annoyance. Probably he never liked being seen drinking.

"He's there," the girl said.

The sergeant glanced at Harry. "The man has come back, eh, miss?"

She nodded.

"In the casino." Honeybody's voice was fruity.

"He's playing," she said, "just like he was the other time."

"Just a minute," said Harry, "which man was it?"

"The man with the fair hair. The man I gave the matchbox to."

"At the same chair?"

"Near enough, sir. It's him."

"That'll do, miss," the manager said, after a brief, inquiring look at Harry. "Just go back to your work and forget it."

"Just follow me, gentlemen." He pressed a button beneath an oblong aquatint, *Cubbing with the Quorn*, and a section of the paneling rolled back to show the interior of a lift. The cage was barely large enough to contain the three men. The manager jabbed a button and the lift slid upwards.

They got out into a small room, six feet square. Before a square window sat a man with a pair of opera glasses and two telephone handsets on a small table. He pushed the glasses up momentarily and then returned to his scrutiny.

"One way window," said the manager, producing a set of glasses from his pocket and passing them to Harry.

The gambling room looked foreshortened and like a brilliantly lit stage. Even the people seemed theatrical.

"You get the feeling they can see you," grunted Harry.

"Don't worry, they can't."

It was Mace. The glasses held him in half profile. His face showed nothing beyond a slight, persistent fixed smirk.

"That's okay." He passed the glasses to Honeybody.

They went back down.

"Thanks," said Harry. "Don't blame the girl. They'd have got the message to him somehow; maybe brought in some of the boys to stage a diversion."

The manager gave a small sigh of relief.

"I'll have to call up reinforcements," said Harry. "Meantime, I'll be in the foyer. If that fellow moves, get word to me very quick."

"So damn simple!" said Harry, as they went down the rubber-cushioned stairs, "Nobody does it so we don't look for it. Even Crook saw goldilocks and a thick neck and thought, There's Arthur, safe and sound. I'll phone from the box in the foyer."

"All right," said Hawker, his voice crisp. "I'll have the place surrounded. Porterman will take charge. As for you and, what's his name, Honeybody, as soon as you get the okay, locate Sergeant Crook. Your job is to locate and bring in the ring-in. Take him to the local station. I'll be there."

In a quarter of an hour Porterman's assistant hurried in. "We've got the place completely covered. The Chief says we'll follow when he leaves, see where he goes."

"He's slippery!"

"The boss doesn't miss catches!"

When Harry told him in the police car, Sergeant Crook gave his rare smile. "In one way I'm pleased. Of course, I could kick myself, but, honestly, how the hell?"

"We're after the substitute."

Crook nodded and thought aloud. "Within, say, three minutes of the casino. There are six small cafés and a private club which Mace is interested in. He might reason that the club might come under normal spot inspection. The cafés first."

They drew a blank.

The club was a better-class drinking place, where Crook said the grills were quite famous locally. The headwaiter was smooth and tough, but Crook's shoulder hit his chin and jarred his head back. They walked rapidly through the tables and to a door in the side of the room.

Crook felt the doorknob and turned to the headwaiter who had followed them, a trickle of blood down one side of his mouth.

"I'll have your uniform!" the man said venomously and then flinched as Crook brought up a clenched fist.

"If you haven't unlocked this door by the time I count three, you'll go to hospital."

"You can't *do* this," said the man, nevertheless producing a key and turning the lock.

"Get back to your job," snarled Crook, opening the door. It was a very small room.

"You went too far, Sergeant!" Harry felt bound to say.

"Self-defense," said Crook coolly. "I thought he had a knife. Well, well." In the chair which was the only piece of furniture except for a small table sat a big, frightened-looking man with wide-spaced dark eyes and yellow hair, wearing a tan suit and black overcoat.

"Police here," said Crook. "We'd like the pleasure of your company, lover-boy."

"Where's your warrant?" The man had a very similar baritone voice to Arthur Mace, but now it was quavery with fright.

He seemed relieved when Crook produced his warrant. The Inspector noted that although the room was unheated, there were beads of sweat on the man's forehead.

"Afraid that Mace was going to dump you in the Thames?" he said.

"I don't know anything," the man whined.

"What's your name?" said Crook in the police car.

"Peter Byers."

"Well, Peter, you're going to see a very tough old gentleman, one of the old school. He hasn't got any kid

207

gloves. My advice to you is to keep talking and not hold anything back."

"What have we got here?" said Hawker who was seated behind two telephones in a chilly room that stank of disinfectant battling unsuccessfully against faulty drains.

"Peter Byers," said Harry.

"Now, Byers, we always check, so don't waste time lying, because if there is one thing we don't like it is having our time wasted. Are you known to the police?"

"No, sir. I've been straight, sir. Oh, one time, sir, drunk in Liverpool, sir, but I'd just got an honorable discharge from the Navy, sir, after six years, sir, and it was only five bob."

"All right," said Hawker. "What are your dealings with Arthur Mace?"

Byers had been discharged from the Navy with a microscopic disability pension. He was, he said with slightly pompous pride, a professional backer of horses.

"You hang around race meetings in the silver ring with your cuffs frayed," said Hawker brutally, watching the man flush. "What else do you do?"

"Barman," said the man, "I'm a union member."

When Byers' luck was out, and as Hawker probed into dates it seemed his luck was usually out, he tended bar, on racecourses themselves, or as a relieving barman in the towns where the meetings were held.

He had known Mace by sight as one of the men who had dealings with the "heads." Over the past two years he had developed a liver complaint which made it difficult for him to stand for long hours behind a bar. One day nine months ago a man, who seemed by description to be the Long 'un, met him at Newmarket, and told him Mace wanted to see him.

"Where?"

"In the back room of the coffeeshop."

Mace offered him fifteen pounds a week to work for Polly Packer, checking and supervising in Polly's dispatch room. He was told there would be an occasional bonus. It was sit-down work and he jumped at the chance. Mace gave him some lengths of cloth to take to a tailor to be

208

made into two suits and an overcoat. He also gave him two pairs of shoes, four shirts and some ties.

"Mace is fussy about his hair," said Byers dismally. "He has it tinted and waved like a woman. My hair is darker than the tint he wears and it is naturally wavy. Mace told me to go to a certain barber twice a week and specified the tint number."

"Now, about the occasions you stood in for Mace!"

"I had no guilty knowledge," said Byers. "It might have been a joke."

"Do you consider Mr. Mace a humorist?" There was a smile of mock benevolence on the Superintendent's face and he showed his yellowed teeth.

Byers flushed again. "Every so often, about twice a week, he'd phone me at Packer's or else send one of his boys to my lodging—I had a room just round the corner from Polly's office. I was told what to wear, suit, shirt, shoes. Mace never wears a hat. Then I'd go to a certain place and meet Mace. I would be wearing this black overcoat, see, and he'd have on one of those great flashy camel-hair ones that are his trademark. We'd swap coats, and I'd usually be told to go and sit in that office of his at the back of the coffeeshop. Once it was a theater and twice the dogs. Recently it's been the casino."

"Do you remember the night of the twenty-second and twenty-third of November?"

"Yes, sir."

"What happened?"

"Well, I'd given up working for Packer. I thought he and Mace had quarreled. Polly was decent about it. He said I could stay on at less money, but I was frightened of Mace. He phoned me and said I was working for him full time, but I had to stay in my room and out of sight most of the time. I went out at nights and laid in honey, cheese and milk and eggs—that's the diet I'm mostly on for my trouble. But a lot of days Mace would come by to my room and I'd go to the coffee bar. The old bag who runs it would tip me off when the time came and I'd go through the back door, into the old kitchen, and there would be Mace.

209

"On the night of the twenty-second Mace comes and tells me that he'll be at the casino until eleven. On this casino stunt I used to wait at the club where you took me tonight. Mace would ring and I'd put a hat on and meet him in the casino head. It was all right at the club, the dining room is full of people stuffing at the trough, wouldn't have noticed me naked."

For a moment Byers' backbone seemed to stiffen. It was odd, thought Harry, how dyspeptic and liver cases hated people enjoying a good rich paté.

"Well," said Byers, "he came through at five after eleven and I did my stuff. I can't stand the place. A horse now and seeing the colors. . . . But this wheel and the gray-faced man running it, it fair got on my tits, but, being frank with you, sir, Mace used to slip me a fiver when I done this."

"When did Mace return?" Hawker was all business and his face seemed carved from wood.

"It was two, sir. A late night, being Saturday. But they were thinning out, only the addicts"—Byers was contemptuous—"remaining. I was scared I'd be noticed."

"And why?" rasped Hawker.

"Because then Mace would be mad like a hornet."

"All right, get on with it."

"Well, the arrangement was that I should phone Mace's club every half hour. The one-thirty call was negative. That made me more jumpy, because the club closes at two-thirty and by that time it's empty except for maybe three or four people. But the two A.M. call, I get Mace. He says he'll come round to the casino. I guess both ways were risky. I took his overcoat and walked out."

"How was he?"

Byers knitted the skin on his forehead.

"Good lord," said Hawker, "we haven't given Mr. Byers a cup of tea. Or do you prefer coffee?"

"I can't drink either," said Byers. "Hot milk."

"Hot milk and a drop of Bovril, eh?"

"Yes, sir."

"Get two of 'em, Sergeant," said Hawker, looking at

Honeybody. "I like a drop of sherry wine in mine but I suppose it is beyond our resources."

"It happens, sir," said Honeybody, "that one of my daughters took advantage of an advertising offer last Christmas to give me a little flask of sherry, so tonight being cold . . ."

"Perfect, Sergeant," said Hawker, as Honeybody lumbered out. "Will you have a little wine, Mr. Byers, just a restorative tot?"

"Not a drop is allowed, sir, and it's hard when you work in a bar."

"Well, gents, we have a teetotal witness," said Hawker, looking in the direction of the shorthand writer. "What a change! Now, Mr. Byers, how did he look?"

Byers hesitated, "Kind of spent, sir, and happy, you know, like a guy who has been chasing this popsy and one night . . . but kind of vicious and nervy, too, sir. I didn't like the way he looked at me."

Hawker swigged his milk and after a minute Byers began to sip his.

"Take your time," said Hawker, largely, pouring a shot of sherry into his glass.

"Only this funny kind of het-up way of looking! And he had a bad cut on his hand. He'd staunched it with toilet paper, so it had congealed, like. He kept the hand, his left, in the pocket. He told me to start wearing a piece of flesh-colored bandage over my left hand."

Hawker watched Byers finish his milk and broadened his smile. "Now I wonder what you thought was the purpose of all this?"

"I was scared of Mace," said Byers sullenly.

"A lot of frightened men have been hanged," said Hawker.

Byers straightened and made an effort. "I'm a poor devil, sir, that's seen a lot of trouble. Mace scares me stiff. He's a killer, sir."

"But why did you think he employed you?" Hawker's voice was like a buzz saw.

"I look like him. Not if you see us in a mirror. But from a bit away if there's no real thinking, I look like him. But

211

no guilty knowledge, sir." Sweat was pouring down Byers' heavy face.

"How ill are you?" The Superintendent's face softened.

"The doctors say time and strict diet, sir."

"Now, Mr. Byers"—Hawker's voice was soft—"we look after people who look after us. You can walk out of here directly, but if you want—and only if you want—you can kip down in here. A man with your intelligence might come to certain conclusions about Arthur Mace. We'll have a statement for you to sign and we'll look after you. I'll see that the D.D.I. looks about for a job for you. How's that?"

"Thank you, sir."

A constable led Byers away.

"That should do it," said Hawker, sucking his lips. "The blood on that paper—your landlady's Christmas list—was a rare grouping."

"We can't take Mace's blood," said Harry.

"And then counsel asks him why he refuses to co-operate." Hawker's smile reflected Crook's face.

"Enough to hang Mace!" said Crook.

Hawker reached for the telephone. "Had to keep it off," he grunted. "Yes, yes." He listened.

Finally he replaced the handset. "That was Constable Higgins, or rather your deputy, plus Higgins. Mrs. Higgins was doing a spirited rendition of 'Knees up, Mother Brown' in the charge room after spending nine pounds ten and tuppence of the Queen's money on entertaining Merv and Edie Perkins, and the pa-in-law."

"Jesus!" said Honeybody.

"Precisely," said Hawker, "including four fillet steaks with chips, and ice cream to follow. Mrs. Perkins brought her old dad along. They joined Merv Perkins in his favorite pub and Mrs. Higgins said she'd touched a bit in the pools. By judicious spiking of drinks she got a positive identification of Mace, from a photo, as coming out of the door in Merge's Alley at eleven-ten. All three of them said they'd swear."

"That must have been judicious toping."

"Not for the record, of course," said Hawker, "but Mrs. H. had a tape recorder working in her bag. Mr. Porterman will take it round first thing tomorrow when they're having breakfast."

Porterman came in with a flurry of energy. "We'll take him in, of course."

Hawker suddenly crumpled his face into lines of worry. "I smell violence and all kinds of things, Mr. Porterman. Where is Mace now?"

"He remained at the casino until twenty minutes ago. I had a man in the managerial observation office with a walkie-talkie. He reported that Mace was getting upset, as if he was waiting for a date that didn't turn up. Finally he stamped out in a rage. Nothing to it. He has the bottom half of a maisonette fifteen minutes from the casino. He went in and slammed the door."

"What have you got?"

"Eight men and two cars, there is no back entrance."

"Better take him on suspicion," said Hawker wearily.

"Sir!" said Crook.

"Oh, yes, let the sergeant be in at the death. You might go along, too, Inspector."

They drove up to the neat blue façade of Mace's home at a sedate twenty miles per hour. They were fifty yards off when a taxi passed them and drew up abruptly. A big man emerged from the door, lamplight glinting on his hair, got swiftly in and the taxi pulled away. Porterman spoke quietly into the hand microphone. Two hundred yards ahead a big police car, sign flashing, eased into the path of the taxi. Routine, thought the Inspector as brakes squealed, but as he did so, the taxi door flew open and a figure in a camel coat threw himself out, hit the ground, staggered and ran. Porterman opened the door and slid out feet first as the police car jarred to a stop. Harry found himself following Crook and Porterman.

There was a side street twenty yards away and toward this Mace raced. Porterman was amazingly fast for his build and years and Harry, head down and outstripping Crook, remembered that he had been a Rugby cap in his day. At the corner Mace whirled and his hand dived into his pocket and came out with the glint of metal. Behind, Harry could hear running steps.

"Back," said Mace, his voice hard and clear. He raised

the pistol in front of his face, squinting along the barrel. "Get back." His voice had almost a whine.

Harry saw Porterman bunch and go forward in a sliding tackle and heard the belching snarl of the gun. Then the Chief Inspector hit Mace and both lay still.

Harry and a constable lugged Porterman to his feet.

"Careful, now," said the Inspector as he saw the mess on the Chief's face.

"No, no," said Porterman through clenched teeth. "It's not my blood. Hold me up, I've slipped a cartilage!"

Crook and two constables were kneeling beside Mace. The sergeant called, "The pistol exploded. He's gone! There's a great hole through his head."

Porterman was groaning with pain. "I'll have to have this knee strapped. Get a surgeon and an ambulance, and contact Mr. Hawker to take over."

Crook stood up and looked at Harry. "By the book, I should put my coat over his face. As it is, he can stare at the sky."

Presently Harry, Crook and a subdued Honeybody ate fish and chips at a night owl café.

"Enough to curdle your stomach," said Honeybody, "when they start using guns. And his head"—he wagged his own—"haven't seen anything like it since I was on traffic accidents."

"He was an amateur on guns," said Harry. "Did you see how he held it? I think he was trying to fire over our heads, lost his nerve a bit, and didn't know what the hell he was doing."

"A knife or a bit of cord was more down his street," grunted Crook. "He liked the bodily contact, as they say."

"Porterman came out well," said Honeybody, sucking tea through a slice of bread and butter.

"We always do," said Crook, his smile mocking. "In the force I've known grafters, moral cowards, slackers and one madman, but I've not yet known a physical coward when the chips were down."

"Amen!" said Harry. "Any case, this ties it up. There's the second man—any of the lot around Mace could be it. We'll find the paintings in one of Mace's places."

214

"Amazing the way the news travels," he grunted. "All Mace's lot have gone to ground. We'll winkle them out in time, of course. Meanwhile we can get the Coroner to bring in a verdict against Mace. Another one for the solved file. I'm glad for Porterman, he worked like a dog."

Hawker thought so when they retired to the station. The old Superintendent was drinking tomato soup.

"If that pistol hadn't exploded, he would probably be a dead dog," said Harry.

"The forensic men say it was an old Belgian job, made around 1911 when there was a flood of cheap Belgian firearms. It completely shattered, like a small grenade." The old Superintendent glanced unexpectedly at Crook. "You'll miss him."

"Yes," said Crook slowly, "in a way I shall."

Chapter 8

"So you solved it." Mr. Samuel Lovers leered across his glass appreciatively, while Sergeant Honeybody smirked gallantly at Miss Dolores Spotting.

They were having a lunchtime drink at the Dun Cow, one of the hostelries that Mr. Lovers favored.

"Death isn't much of a solution," said Harry, who had been closeted all morning, first with Hawker, who had groaned and summoned a limping, bad-tempered Porterman, then with a small solicitor, who had ha'd humph'd and finally talked, with the British Museum, and lastly with Honeybody.

"What a fortunate irony," said Miss Spotting, her face expressing well-bred distaste, "that he should, so to speak, have been hoist with his own petard."

"As a matter of fact, not," said Harry. "You find a man who knows all about guns, in fact did well in his Army armorer's course, and gets an old gun, doctors it, fills in the breech, puts a hopped-up charge in the cartridge and gives it to Mace, who doesn't know much about guns except what our friend told him and regards them simply as a useful sort of diversion."

A roar of laughter came from a group of young men near them at the bar.

"Some of these young chaps can't hold their drink," commented Lovers sourly. "But what a filthy thing!"

"I suppose bang goes MacGlaishen's chance of getting his Seurat back," said Miss Spotting with the air of one probing an old wound.

"You see that young barman, the one with the mop of black hair."

"Yes."

"He's a plainclothes constable. And you remember when I got the last round?"

Miss Spotting nodded without speech.

"Well," said Harry slowly, "he told me that the Seurat and other stuff had been recovered from Mr. Lovers' warehouse."

A split second later he was on the floor with a wave of agony consuming him from a knee in the groin. Somehow he was aware of Honeybody retching beside him on the floor. There was a lot of noise. The Inspector lay still and practiced deep breathing.

"Give you a hand up, sir." It was the young sergeant whom Honeybody had said had once been a reserve hooker for Swansea and was the toughest man in the division. His mouth was bloody.

"Got me in the throat," wheezed Honeybody, now at the counter. "Give us a double whisky, constable, and make a note of it for expenses."

Harry looked down at the writhing bulk on the floor, hands handcuffed, broad leather strap round the ankles.

"Jesus," said one of the plainclothesmen, "it looks like fat, but, man that's solid muscle. Took us four to hold him."

"Hubert Harcourt," intoned Harry, "alias Samuel Lovers, I have a warrant for your arrest in that on November twenty-second you did willfully murder Charles Huntingtower and I must caution you that anything you say may be used as evidence and must tell you that you may obtain legal advice."

He wiped his forehead. "Carry him out to the car."

Harry turned away, Harcourt's face as it writhed round was not pleasant to see.

Miss Spotting sat in her chair with a curiously boneless impression. Her face was scarlet.

"I told him it was too big!" she said and retched.

"We'll disregard that," said Harry. "Miss Spotting I have reason to regard you as accessory to felony and I must warn you that anything you say . . ."

"May be used as evidence," said Miss Spotting, like a tape recording.

"As long as you understand," said Harry. "Now, Constable Greening is taking you in for questioning."

"What was this all about, sir?" said Honeybody when they had gone.

"Well," said Harry, accepting a stout from the proprietor, who seemed to be planning to sell his reminiscences to *The People*.

"Thanks, guv," said the Inspector. "Just don't describe me as handsome, just hard-working."

"You see, Serge," said Harry, "I had been thinking about Lovers. The first time he came into the Huntingtower Gallery—so *he* said—he knew the way upstairs was through the little private office. And I watched him drinking. He always had a glass in his hand, but though he looked the part, he wasn't a hard drinker if you checked it."

"But the Lovers," muttered Honeybody.

"He *wasn't* a Lovers," said Harry. "Old family pretty well played out. One old man of eighty, Darcy Lovers, had a clapped-out shipping agency, last of an old line. He owned a thirty-year office lease in a building the family once built plus ditto on a small warehouse. I inquired by phone this morning. The business used to be slow transport to South America, but by the end of the war there was nothing left except one old man with the name, these two leases, and twelve hundred pounds."

Harry swallowed another mouthful of stout.

"Old pride stirring, memories that one time they owned the district lock, stock and barrel. There was a deceased distant cousin named Elderson who had at one time put a Miss Harcourt in the family way. It hadn't meant anything to old Lovers at the time—he'd had two sons who died in the war—but then he made a will leaving the business and his money to the Elderson-Harcourt if he took the name of Samuel Lovers."

The Inspector looked at the sergeant. "Kind of feudal. Everybody knows about the Lovers being a very old family. You see, the old family solicitor stuck a note in the *News of the World*—Elderson-Harcourt. I got wondering how the hell a man wanted for murder with fourteen pounds in his pocket could disappear! And it came to me,

218

if he fell into an inheritence! He must have been sweating it out in some little room knowing he'd have to come out battling, and then he saw the paper."

"Me and the wife always read it of a Sunday," agreed the sergeant.

"The solicitor was an old man on his last legs," said Harry. "Harcourt had the necessary personal papers and said he would change his name. He took no legal steps, but the old lawyer was sick and didn't care, just did the small probate job. So Harcourt became Mr. Samuel Lovers and kept well out of sight for a couple of years until he developed that mustache and membership of the local businessmen's group. The money just scraped him by; but then he realized what a wonderful front it was."

"I was a mug, sir," said Honeybody, keening over his gin.

"We were mugs," said Harry. "I just thought he was a lecher after Dol Spotting's virtue. He got the front and used it as an international fencing apparatus. These paintings were his big coup."

Harry ordered more stout. "Harcourt-Lovers had sacked his staff and had booked on a flight to Tetuan in three days' time. Dolores Spotting was personally flying to San Francisco with the Spanish loan collection. The other paintings would have been concealed in the frames. Obviously Harcourt would have eventually joined her there."

"She was well and truly in it?"

"There was originally Castelano and Brun. They approached Harcourt, which they bitterly regretted at a later stage. He had an association with Spotting and she told him that Huntingtower was unscrupulous and would accept a proposition. Mace and Polly Packer had been used by Harcourt before. Packer got greedy, but he was frightened away."

"And those paintings worth a king's ransom?"

"About twelve hundred quid," said the Inspector.

"But you said . . ."

"Amazingly good fakes," sighed Harry. "That was what Huntingtower spotted and demanded twenty thousand pounds in hard cash to keep his mouth buttoned. You see he was a man who never forgot anything he read. It killed him, because you don't put the black on a man like Harcourt. Huntingtower had got this Seurat—probably he had a client for it. Then a bell rang. There was a book missing from his library. I got a copy from the British Museum. It was by a dull English painter who worked in France. The point was that he was accurate to the point of boredom. Well he recorded that on August first, 1879, he met Paul Pont, the art dealer from the Rue de Chevalier. They had both quarreled with their mistresses, so on impulse they took a train to Juan les Pins and spent three weeks there.

"But," said Harry, "there was a receipt attached to the Seurat from Pont dated Paris on August twelve. That settled it."

"As simple as that," marveled Honeybody, massaging his neck.

"They tried to be too clever," said Harry. "These papers, the provenance, were bound to contain a flaw somewhere."

"If anybody had delved that far," said Honeybody shrewdly.

"Yes," said Harry. "The paintings themselves were so good no expert liked to say no. Since ten this morning, they've been back-pedaling. We got three art historians working at the Museum and they've turned up several little flaws in the papers and one case where a Russian address is badly out. So my bearded friend Blenkinsop and his cohorts are turning their thumbs down like so many Neros." He laughed, remembering the chapfallen looks and an old expert on Matisse who had had tears in his faded eyes.

"Anyway, Mace and Harcourt fixed Huntingtower. And it was Spotting, of course, who took the Seurat. Harcourt had tampered with the bars in the basement just in case. In many ways a shrewd fellow. You see, Mace didn't trust Harcourt and Spotting. Why should he? Mace's man had used a gun to stop us at that warehouse. At that we nearly got them plus the paintings. Harcourt heard us discussing the warehouse and saw the red light, but he didn't know we were acting so quickly."

"Probably the same gun," said the sergeant.

"I don't think so, but I guess it was Harcourt who kept the armory. Afterwards Mace stuck close to Harcourt. I'd guess that he spent a lot of time in the warehouse or even the office. There were a few unused rooms there as legitimate business was so little. It got a nuisance. The Scobies knew he was around and they didn't know what it meant. But they didn't like it.

"You see, Mace had no way of knowing we had any suspicions of him. He had this successful arrangement with the double. But Harcourt did. He knew that Mace was on our minds."

"I could kick myself," said Honeybody for the umpteenth time.

Harry looked at the used glasses. "Serge, we'd both fall flat on our faces if we tried. A drop of hard stuff for a binder, then off, eh?"

"I shall be full tonight," said Honeybody sipping his double scotch. "Only hope I don't trip over the teevee. I did last time and you should have heard Dodo. I didn't know whether the blue sparks were comin' from her or the set."

"I've got to pick up my girl," said the Inspector. "Anyway, Harcourt had this knowledge, so he got an old gun and made what was virtually a bomb. 'Take it, Arthur, just in case you have to scarper. Hold it close to your face and fire over their heads.' Brr, a cold-blooded swine! He knew sooner or later we would pick Mace up."

"Call for you." The landlord approached stealthily, with winks and nods. "My private office, eh?"

It was Hawker. "Harcourt is saying nothing except a request for Old Specs."

The same Old Specs was the shrewdest criminal solicitor in the country.

"Spotting's got a solicitor, one of her boy friends, I think. We've got a short, voluntary"—Hawker sucked his teeth audibly—"statement to say she knew Huntingtower was meeting Mace and Harcourt at Merge's Alley and that Harcourt phoned her at four in the morning telling her to take the Seurat and shut her trap. Nothing more."

"Will it convict?"

"I think so. The connecting up will be difficult. I've had Mr. Middle, the treasury junior, driving me insane. But now Mace's dead we took a blood sample"—Hawker chuckled—"a corpse having no legal value, and it matches that on the paper. You'll give evidence of arrest and then take a fortnight off, Porterman being rather sore. He's getting the police medal and will perk up. And by the way . . ."

"Sir," said Harry.

"What did you think of that Russian story?"

"My young woman put me off it."

"They do. Don't let her get away, my boy. A good woman is a pearl of infinite price. I have"—Hawker coughed—"been a widower for thirty-one years."

"She mentioned the Iron Curtain Customs."

"For your ears alone, official secrets and all that, she was right, but there are two Curtains."

"You mean?"

"It seems," said Hawker, "that at this juncture Red China could do with some dollars sited in America. The stuff came into France via Albania, so a faceless gentleman told me this afternoon. And an added little gift: if the forgeries were established—and why not—it wouldn't do the Russians any good, or the art treasure financial hedging of the hated capitalists. Huh?"

"Good God!"

"Don't forget to take two weeks off. 'All artists are bastards,' I quote Marx."

"I don't remember," said the Inspector, but the line had gone dead. He rejoined Honeybody and assisted him over the front step.

The British made amends for injustice, Harry remembered reading somewhere, by means of food and drink. Certainly Hubert had waylaid him early that morning and hemmed and hawed about a special little dinner that night, a case of bubbly donated along the line by the Bleeders and doubtless foul in origin, and would he care to bring Elizabeth.

They arrived at eight-thirty. Hildegard had grown up, as they did overnight, thought the Inspector.

"Something special tonight," boomed Stanisgate, kissing Elizabeth.

Her parents were looking at Hilde with a kind of shy pride, and Harry suddenly realized that however much you commiserated with parents about their children, you could never get this shy pride business to rights.

"The truth is," said Hubert, "that Hilde met this Moroccan girl who gave her all sorts of tips and told her all about the herbs and we planned having a Moroccan meal." At least he had the grace to sound a trifle forced, thought Harry.

"You have almonds and pigeon flesh and honey and spices," intoned Hildegard, "and pastry, very thin and made by old women."

"Very nice I'm sure," said Harry dyspeptically.

"She asked me to make the pastry and I said no," said Dora

"It started to taste horrible," said Hildegard, "so I threw it away and got Mummy to show me her steak, kidney and mushroom pud." She grinned.

"Great is Allah and his works," intoned Mr. Stanisgate as he led the way toward the dining table.